SNOW

For her father's sake Lissa had contracted
a marriage of convenience with Jarret
Earle—and as Jarret was an exceptionally
attractive man it was not long before she
had fallen in love with him. But Jarret
had had reasons of his own for wanting
her as his wife—and alas love was the
very last of them.

SNOW BRIDE

BY

MARGERY HILTON

MILLS & BOON LIMITED
17-19 FOLEY STREET
LONDON W1A 1DR

First published 1979
Australian copyright 1980
Philippine copyright 1980
This edition 1980

© Margery Hilton 1979

ISBN 0 263 73202 9

Set in Linotype Plantin 10 pt.

Made and printed in Great Britain by
Richard Clay (The Chaucer Press), Ltd., Bungay, Suffolk

CHAPTER ONE

'WAKE up, Lissa! Breakfast in bed for the bride! And it's snowing!'

'Snowing ...' Alyssa Vayle opened sleep-dazed eyes, heavy from the effects of the unaccustomed sleeping tablet her mother had insisted she take the previous night. Brilliant light streamed into the bedroom as her fourteen-year-old sister Philippa excitedly flung back the curtains.

'Yes! You're going to have a real white wedding!'

Wedding! Lissa was suddenly wide awake, staring round the room with fright in her blue eyes. Awareness, reality, and then sheer mounting panic swam into her consciousness and made her recoil against the pillow that was only marginally whiter than her cheeks. It couldn't be true. But it was. The day had dawned. The day she had tried to close out of her mind for the past month. The facts and the fear churned feverishly in her brain. At eleven o'clock she was to be married, to a man she hardly knew. To a man she didn't love, a man who didn't love her ...

'Morning, darling! Finished your breakfast? We'll have to allow plenty of time with this ghastly snow ...' Mrs Vayle bustled into the room and stopped short as she saw the untouched breakfast tray. 'Come on, Lissa—it's nearly eight!'

Lissa scarcely heard her. Nearly eight. Three hours to go. But she couldn't! She must have been mad to agree. 'No!' she cried aloud. 'I can't! I can't go through with it!'

Mrs Vayle and Philippa gaped at her, and Aunt Helen appeared in the doorway, her bright smile suddenly wiped from her pleasant, middle-aged face. 'Lissa!' they all exclaimed, practically simultaneously, as she scrambled out of bed and ran to the window.

She gripped the edge of the sill and stared out with frightened eyes at the patterns of snow lace across the garden. The white traceries had transformed completely the view from her window, making it alien now, no longer the familiar scene whose subtle changes with the seasons she had watched since childhood. Even her own safe comfortable bedroom was different. The small chest of drawers and the red tapestry chair had been moved into the spare room because of the extra visitors, and the old favourite garments had gone from her wardrobe. After all, you won't need them now—they can go to the church jumble sale, her mother had said practically. Space had to be made for the luxurious new dresses and separates, the fine wools, the pure silks, the hand-made shoes from Raynes, the cashmere two-piece—and stiff and rustling beneath its plastic cover, the snow-white glory of her wedding dress.

The waves of panic enveloped Lissa, making her feel faint. It must be an appalling dream! She had to wake up, find reality and the blessed relief of knowing that it couldn't be true. That in three short hours she wasn't going to be committed to a loveless marriage of convenience with a man who was virtually a stranger.

'Lissa, for heaven's sake, pull yourself together!' Mrs Vayle reached her side. 'You don't know what you're saying. It's only wedding nerves. Oh, Helen ...' she turned worriedly to her sister-in-law, 'would you get her a drink, quickly? She looks as if she's going to pass out.'

'You shouldn't have given her that sleeping pill, Mum,' Philippa cried. 'She's not used to them. It might have——'

'Be quiet, Pippa. I only wanted her to have a good night's sleep. Sit down, Lissa.'

Lissa sank back into the chair and pressed trembling hands to her pale cheeks. The strange sense of unreality still gripped her and the faces of her mother and Aunt Helen and scared little Pippa loomed above her like those of strangers.

Somewhere outside a car klaxon blared, and downstairs the telephone began to shrill imperatively.

'Bother!' muttered Mrs Vayle. 'Go and see who it is, Pippa.'

Unwillingly Pippa followed her Aunt Helen from the room, leaving Lissa alone with her mother.

'Now, darling,' Mrs Vayle made her tone gentle yet persuasive, 'do try to be sensible. We don't want to start going over all this again—not a couple of hours before the wedding.'

Lissa made an almost imperceptible movement of her head. How could she ever make her mother understand the panic now gripping her? How to convey to anyone that the sheer enormity of what was to happen today had at last struck home? That she felt as though a net was tightening about her, inexorably trapping her till there was no escape? She trembled violently. If she had realised it was going to be like this she would never have agreed to go through with it, even for the sake of——

'Darling! You're not *ill*?'

The frantic note in Mrs Vayle's voice penetrated the numbness holding Lissa prisoner. She shook her head wearily. 'No, Mother, I'm not ill. Just—scared.'

'But what on earth for?' Mrs Vayle's question was sharp with relief. 'You've less cause than many a bride for wedding nerves. I don't know what you're worrying about, I'm sure. A lot of girls would be jolly glad to be in your shoes today. And another thing,' her mouth tightened, 'if nothing else, I'd have thought you'd jump at the chance to show that Martin Blakey what you think of him. Walking out on you the way he did and marrying that creature he picked up in a London night club! After everybody in the village expected to hear your engagement announced any day. I don't know what his parents were thinking of to allow it. Well, that's one thing I'm looking forward to today; seeing his mother's face. As if her precious Martin could ever compare with Jarret Earle! He's got everything a woman could desire for her daughter—looks, charm, wealth, and obviously a decent background. And he's generous as well. Lissa! Are you listening?'

'Yes, Mother,' she whispered.

'You know that he spelled everything out. This marriage is to both your advantage,' Mrs Vayle went on. 'It's all quite civilised. You'll be free again in five years. So why all this panic? What's five years at your age, for heaven's sake? It's nothing.'

Five years! Lissa closed her eyes. It seemed like all eternity.

'Now listen, darling.' Mrs Vayle put a firm arm round

her daughter's trembling shoulders and bent close to her.
'You surely haven't forgotten? If you back out of this
marriage now we're ruined. If you won't think of me—and
what people will say!—try to think of your father.'

Lissa gulped. This was the one thought that had carried
her through the past few weeks; the only thought that
could sustain her through the ordeal ahead of her. If only
her mother would stop reminding her.

But the silent plea did not reach Mrs Vayle. She straightened. 'Now pull yourself together. Here, put on your dressing gown and stop worrying. You've scarcely turned
eighteen, it's no age. You'll be twenty-three before you
know where you are, with your life before you and free to
marry whom you please.' She sighed. 'I wish I were eighteen
again! And marrying Jarret Earle!'

She picked up the nightdress Lissa had numbly let fall
and absentmindedly folded it before tucking it back into
the furry panda case that had lived on Lissa's bed ever since
her sixth birthday.

'I can't understand why he wanted me.' Lissa shivered
within the warm folds of her dressing gown. 'He'd only seen
me once.'

'You're a very attractive girl. You'll play the part of his
wife very well. Now for goodness' sake eat that breakfast—
Pippa did the tray so nicely for you.' Mrs Vayle remembered that the nightdress would not be required again
and hauled it out of the case, energetically sweeping up
the bedclothes into a big armful, which Pippa arrived back
at the doorway just in time to receive. 'Push those in the
bottom of the cupboard—I'll sort them out later—and
fetch the clean sheets. I want this bed made up for your
grandmother and there'll be no time later.'

'Mum, that was Cousin Julie. The snow's very heavy
at Marchfield and she's afraid they might be late but they'll
get here somehow.'

'Is she all right? I've brought her some brandy. I
thought ...' Aunt Helen manoeuvred past Pippa and her
burden and came anxiously into the room.

Lissa began to feel as though she were in a madhouse.
The toast was going round and round in her mouth, and she

recoiled when Aunt Helen thrust the potent brandy under her nose.

'Just a sip,' said Mrs Vayle. 'We can't have you going to the altar reeking of spirits. It doesn't quite go with virginal white.'

'I don't want it,' Lissa said desperately. She managed to eat another morsel of toast, then escaped to the bathroom, where at least she gained a short respite from the turmoil in which she was the centre. But not for long ...

In a trance of rigid self-control she allowed them to begin the business of helping her to get ready. Braiding her long, honey-silk hair into the classic coronet style she had decided on, setting out the gossamer nylons, the filmy wisps of undies, the opening of the cards and gifts that had come with the morning post, and then the inevitable cup of tea her mother insisted on before she put on her extra careful make-up for this special day. And all the time her mind persisted in going back, reminding her, as though she could ever forget that dark, disturbing day last November ...

She had spent the weekend with Julie, after going with her and a party of young people to the annual St Catherine's Hospital Ball on the Friday evening. The invitation had all been part of the determined efforts of family and friends to cheer her after the shock ending of her long-standing affair with Martin Blakey, and somewhat to her surprise she had thoroughly enjoyed the ball and the subsequent weekend. She arrived home late on the Sunday afternoon, ready to give the full account Pippa would be waiting eagerly for, and was surprised to see a strange car parked in their drive, a long, sleek silver affair, definitely belonging to the exotic continental breed. Feeling rather curious about the unknown visitors, she let herself in and heard the voices coming from her father's study.

There was no sign of her mother, but Pippa came rushing down the stairs and stopped at the foot, raising a warning finger to her lips. Puzzled now, and with the first faint stirring of an alarm she could not pinpoint, Lissa followed her young sister through to the kitchen. 'Who is it?' she asked urgently as Pippa swung the door shut behind them.

'It's Daddy's solicitor and another man—don't know who he is. They've been in there nearly half an hour and Daddy said I hadn't to interrupt them. Lissa, do you think something's wrong?'

'I don't know. Where's Mum?'

'She's gone to see Mrs Brennan—she'd just left when they came.' Pippa looked uneasy. 'It's a funny time for them to come. I mean, if it's business. Isn't it?'

This thought had already occurred to Lissa. Her father, locally a fairly prominent building contractor, did occasionally entertain business associates or clients at home, but never on a Sunday. And why was their solicitor here? She tried to subdue her own unease and forced a smile at Pippa. 'I expect something's cropped up. There'll be a perfectly ordinary explanation.'

'Oh, don't *you* start as well!' exclaimed Pippa, with an abruptness that startled her sister. 'You're as bad as Mum. Something *is* going on and everybody's trying to keep it from me. Do you think I haven't noticed that Daddy's been different lately and Mummy's been worried? I'm not blind and deaf just because you all think I'm still just a kid, you know.'

For a moment Lissa did not know what to say. For it was all so unnervingly true. Their father *had* been withdrawn and preoccupied of late and his features seemed suddenly to have aged far beyond his forty-five years. And their dainty little mother—who possessed a deceptively steely streak under the outward fluffiness—had been fretful and irritable for some time. It seemed that Pippa too had become aware of the undercurrents of strain in the Vayle domain, the low-voiced discussions that tended to tail off suddenly into silence or abrupt changes of subject the moment either of the girls came near.

'Well, I'm not keeping anything from you, inquisitive infant.' Lissa aimed a teasing swipe at her leggy young sister and then launched into her account of the ball. As she had hoped, Pippa was distracted from the subject of the mysterious visitors and the two girls made themselves some tea which they shared companionably in the homely kitchen. But some twenty minutes later they were silent, and Pippa went to the door, to hover there for a few moments and then report that the low murmur of voices still sounded from the study along the hall. Lissa decided it was time she did something about it. Briskly she set out an immaculately laid tea tray, watched by a somewhat tremulous Pippa, and carried it along the hall. She rested it on the hall table and tapped firmly on the study door.

The voices stilled instantly, then her father swung open the door.

For an instant Lissa felt shock. His features were etched sharply with worry, and he stared at her, as though he scarcely recognised his own daughter. His mouth tightened impatiently. 'I thought I told——'

'Yes, she told me.' Lissa's voice was calm as she interrupted him gently and picked up the tray. 'But I'm sure your guests would like some refreshment, and you can discuss your business at the same time, Daddy.'

She advanced into the room, her gaze on the heavy tray as she carried it carefully. She was vaguely aware of the plump, dapper figure of Mr Brentlink, their solicitor, half rising from his chair by the fireside, and then someone in a sveltely tailored silvery grey suit obliterated her view.

'Let me take that.'

Well-shaped but strong hands closed over the ends of the tray, seeking the ornate scrolled handles of it and making a warm contact with her own fingers, and removing it firmly from her grip. She looked up, into the cool grey eyes of the stranger, and a curious tremor passed through her as his gaze locked with hers. He did not smile, and then the link broke as he turned away and placed the tray on her father's desk.

She separated the stacked cups and saucers and poured out the three cups of tea, milking and sugaring her father's and Mr Brentlink's, then looking enquiringly at the stranger.

He shook his head when she indicated the sugar bowl and refused anything to eat. Then her father seemed to collect himself. 'This is Mr Earle, my dear,' and to the younger man, 'My daughter Alyssa.'

The stranger inclined his head formally, and took her hand briefly, murmuring a conventional greeting. But his glance was deceptively assessing and again Lissa experienced a sense of power emanating from him.

He was tall, over six feet she estimated, broad of shoulder and slim of hip in the elegantly waisted grey suit. She got the impression that his mouth did not laugh easily, and there was hidden sensuousness in the long curve of the lower lip. His skin was lightly tanned, hinting at a fairly recent sojourn in a sunnier clime, his hair thick and dark, and his eyes the colour of lakeland slate with fringes of black lashes to contradict the coolness they framed. He had a disturbing way of lowering those hooded, dark-lashed lids as he spoke, giving the impression that he wasn't really interested in that particular moment of time, but Lissa sensed it was a subtle ploy to screen acute perception and his true mood.

'Thank you, Miss Vayle,' he murmured as he accepted the cup she handed to him. 'But are you not joining us?'

She caught her father's warning glance and shook her head, smiling a little. 'No ... I think I'd better leave you in peace to your business.' She turned away, still conscious of something disturbing about the mysterious Mr Earle. 'If you want anything else, Daddy, give me a call.'

She returned to Pippa, unable to produce any hard or fast facts to satisfy that young lady's curiosity, and tried to suppress her own growing tension. It was nearing six when the visitors departed, and she restrained herself as well as Pippa from emerging forth to linger in the hall. But the echoes of the departing car had scarcely died away before Mr Vayle came hurrying into the living room in search of his daughters. He was smiling and looking happier than Lissa had seen him look for weeks.

'Well, my pets,' he made for the whisky decanter on the side table, 'we can all sleep tonight—thank God!'

'But we always sleep at night, Daddy,' said Pippa.

'I don't.' Mr Vayle sank into an armchair and gave a deep sigh. 'This will be a load off your mother's mind.' He looked reflectively into the amber spirit in his glass, then met the unsmiling glances of his two daughters. 'I think we ought to celebrate—what are we eating tonight, girls?'

'Same as we always do on Sunday night—cold meat and whatever's left over from lunch,' Pippa said dryly. 'What did they want, Daddy, to make you look so scared and then pleased?'

'We've just weathered the worst crisis I've had in fifteen years,' he responded, 'thanks to Jarret Earle and Sam.'

Lissa waited, not voicing the obvious question that clamoured in her mind as instinct told her that her father was now ready to take them into his confidence at last. But when he did Lissa felt aghast. She had never dreamed how near disaster they had all been.

It seemed that a series of setbacks had beset their father during the past year. A recession in the building trade, a promised council contract that was cancelled, a labour dispute and strike, and then the most damaging blow of all; insinuations of bribery in a corruption scandal involving two other building contractors and several members of the Borough Council. There had been a trial and two of them had received prison sentences, but although Mr Vayle had been cleared of any suspicion his tenders for a new block of flats and an extension to a school nearby had failed. As he observed wryly, mud thrown tends to besmirch the innocent as well as the guilty, and he had found himself trapped in a situation by no means new. His resources were being drained by heavy overheads and lack of new contracts to replenish his working capital, and this bad period unfortunately coincided with a clamp on lending. And then the final blow; the investment he called their fail-safe fund crashed, leaving him on the verge of bankruptcy.

No wonder their father had lost weight and become so drawn and haggard during the past months, Lissa thought, getting up impulsively to hug him warmly. She had always felt closer to him than to her mother, sensing the nature she herself had inherited from him, the tendency to battle and keep troubles to herself to try to spare worry to those she loved. Now the burden was lifted, for thanks to little Mr Brentlink, help had come just in time.

A musing light entered her eyes. She would never have thought to connect their friendly, old-fashioned small-town solicitor with a wealthy property developer from the big city, least of all one with the sophisticated, man-of-the-world appearance of Jarret Earle. How had he pulled *that* rabbit out of his hat? And persuaded him not only to promise to put lucrative work in her father's way but also advance a hefty bridging loan that would clear his debts and enable him to stock up with ample supplies to start business again. But oh, the interest rate! Lissa uttered a fervent prayer that no more calamities would come his way—at least until the loan was fully repaid.

For a few weeks it seemed the benign fates had heard her prayers. Mrs Vayle no longer had to struggle and juggle with the housekeeping budget, Pippa was able to have the new school raincoat to replace the one she'd grown out of, and best of all, the dreadful sense of strain had lifted from the whole household. Happy preparations were made for Christmas, Pippa fell in love for the first time, the family were adopted by a stray cat of extremely strong character, and suddenly, at the time of year when he least expected it, a rush of jobs came for Mr Vayle.

They toasted one another happily that New Year's Eve, looking into the dawn of another year with hope and confidence, with no premonition of the fresh tragedy to come.

The day after New Year Mr Vayle suffered a stroke.

It robbed him of his speech, paralysed him down one side, and brought a medical verdict that it could be months before he walked again and there could be no guarantee that he would ever be able to work again. He wanted desperately to come home, but Mrs Vayle knew she would not be able to cope with the intensive nursing, and Lissa, who loved her father dearly and would have nursed him devotedly, dared not give up her receptionist job at a new management training unit on the outskirts of Lingwood. They would need every penny she could earn before they were through. So Mr Vayle was transferred to a long-stay rehabilitation hospital nearly twenty-five miles distant. This made visiting a problem as Mrs Vayle could not drive, Lissa had just begun to have driving lessons and of course Pippa was not yet old enough. And there was the problem of the business.

Mr Vayle had always held the controlling reins firmly in his own hands, and consequently his prolonged absence spelled disaster. His foreman, a loyal and capable elderly man who knew the practical side through and through, was the first to admit that he was hopelessly out of his element in the office side. So Lissa spent long evenings and most of her weekends trying to sort out books and invoices, going over the store room with Bill Amey to list what stock replenishments were needed, write letters to clients and try to persuade builders' merchants to supply goods on yet further extended credit. And Mrs Vayle wrung her hands despairingly at each plop of another bill on the mat, Pippa bemoaned the misery of being poor again, while the stricken Mr Vayle tried desperately to communicate some deep-set worry each time the family went to see him. It made Lissa's heart ache with compassion as he looked imploringly at them and tried yet again to form words with his poor speechless lips and make her understand.

Then Lissa realised what she believed was worrying him; the end of the financial year was only a few weeks away, with all it entailed for book-keeping and fiscal purposes, and the quarterly V.A.T. return was long overdue. Her father had always seen to these matters himself, and to his quick brain they had presented no difficulties. Mrs Vayle could not help admitting that she was hopeless at figures, and suggested they engage an accountant, but Lissa knew they could not afford the fees; she was also conscious of the interest payments mounting up relentlessly on the loan from Jarret Earle.

Lissa was a determined girl, and fortunately she had inherited some of her father's head for business matters. She struggled on, gradually getting a grasp on it all, but the long hours each evening on top of her own working day began to take their toll. She grew paler, with shadows under her blue eyes that were now heavy with strain, and her slim figure looked too frail to support the burden that she carried. But it had to be done.

'Why don't you take that lot home and do it in comfort, like your dad did?' asked Bill Amey, one Friday night as he donned his cap and overcoat and prepared to leave the little office.

She managed a smile at his obvious concern for her. 'It's easier here—the post comes here, and it's quieter.'

Bill nodded, more shrewd than she realised, and knowing that at home Pippa and her mother would interrupt and probably fret, making her task more difficult. He said goodnight and went out, leaving Lissa to her lonely task, the only sounds the occasional soft hiss and sputter of the old-fashioned gas-fire that heated the draughty, comfortless place. Darkness had long since fallen, and only one outside lamp remained burning over the black stretches of the builder's yard, but Lissa was not of a particularly nervous disposition and she had too much on her mind to worry about possible intruders.

It was about eight o'clock when she straightened and flexed her cramped shoulders. Only one item to see to now—a receipt to make out and drop in the post on her way home; thank goodness somebody had paid their account promptly. She became conscious of the stuffiness of the office and got up to turn off the fire. In another month it should be possible to dispense with it, thus making a much-needed economy, but the weather was so bitterly cold and her feet froze as she sat there ...

She was typing out the address on the envelope when she heard the sounds outside. The footsteps that rang on the frozen ground, stopped, and then came on again, nearer to the office.

Lissa swallowed, impatient of the sudden quickening thump of her heartbeats. Who was prowling around? She looked at the telephone, then for something to defend herself with should she need it. But the office seemed devoid of anything suitable—except hefty ledgers and a couple of chairs. With a jerked exclamation under her breath she ran to the door and flung it open.

'Who's there?' she cried.

The darkness outside seemed to rush into the office, and then a tall shadow moved, a few feet away. It came towards her.

'Miss Vayle?'

She did not realise she was putting up her hands defensively as she strained to see the identity of the stranger. 'Yes—what do you want?' Her hand reached for the edge of the door, ready to slam it shut.

'I'm sorry—I didn't mean to scare you.' The voice was

deep and calm, and at last the light from the office window fell across his face. With a small gasp she recognised the face of Jarret Earle.

'They told me I'd find you here.' He stared down into her pale face, reading the strain and the darkness of alarm in her wide eyes. 'Are you working here alone?'

'Yes—I'm finished now. I—I never expected to see——' she broke off, searching his features with worried eyes. 'Is something wrong? I——'

'Nothing's wrong. Except that you shouldn't be here in a place like this on your own.' He looked out through the open door and his mouth tightened grimly. 'Don't you have a guard dog?'

'No. We've not been vandalised—yet.'

'There's a first time for everything—but I didn't have exactly that kind of vandalism in mind,' he said curtly. 'I thought you were at that management training place,' he added abruptly.

'I am. But I usually put in a couple of hours here to keep the paper work going while my father——'

'I know. I just found out yesterday,' he broke in. 'Why didn't you let me know?'

She stared at him. 'I—I didn't think it was necessary. Except in case of ...'

'In case you couldn't meet the interest. Is that what you're trying to say?' he demanded.

She bit her lip, and nodded, her eyes afraid again. 'We haven't been late so far. We've——'

'God! Do you think that's why I've come? To make sure my pound of flesh is on the scale? What do you——?' Abruptly he stopped, noticing the quiver of her mouth at his rough tone and the tremors betrayed in her slender shoulders. 'You're shivering. Cold? Or did you imagine the worst when you heard me trying to find my way in?'

'A bit of each, I think. I—I wasn't expecting anyone, least of all ...' Her voice trailed off, and she made a determined effort to break free of the disturbing reaction that had induced such a stupid attack of the shakes, obvious enough for him to notice. 'I—I must finish this.'

She bent her head, seeking the receipted account to push

into the envelope, and realised she had removed the envelope from the typewriter before finishing the address. Acutely aware of the tall man in the heavy suede coat with the thick brown fur collar outlining his lean, smooth-shaven jaw, she exclaimed under her breath and started to fumble the envelope back into the machine, only to remember the account inside and that she could not remember the rest of the address.

For some crazy reason her eyes started to mist and her fingers trembled more than ever. Then a hand reached out and took the envelope from her. It was tossed down on the desk.

'Forget it,' he said curtly. 'Put your coat on. We have to talk, and it might as well be over food.'

'But there's nothing fit to——' Instinctively she had jumped to the conclusion that he meant to take her home, and there would be little in the way of hospitality to offer a man like Jarret Earle. Something her mother would be keeping hot for her, or a snack of baked beans or something similar ...

'I have no intention of inconveniencing your mother. Here,' he had spotted her shabby leather coat, now into its fourth winter, and was insisting she turned her back and slid her arms into the garment, 'and let's go. There must be some place round here where we can eat.'

'But my mother ...'

'Won't expect you home just yet.' He was checking the gas fire was turned off at both base and main taps. 'I called there—otherwise how would I know you were here? Where are the keys?'

'There.' She indicated a hook on the wall and put on her scarf and gloves. It seemed too difficult to avoid going along with him, but deep inside she was worrying and fretting over the purpose behind his unexpected visit. Did he want to recall the loan?

The thought made her feel sick with fear. It was impossible to repay it at this stage; they were only surviving from day to day, this was the quiet building time in any case, things wouldn't start livening up for another month, then people would start thinking about the repairs of winter ravages and the alterations and additions they would have done as the weather began to improve. But it would be ages before the prospect of repaying the loan became hopeful ... She swallowed hard and swung to face him. 'If you want to call in the loan you don't have to take me to a meal to tell me,' she stammered desperately, 'you can tell me now.'

'I have not come to call in the loan. I thought I'd already made that quite clear,' he exclaimed impatiently. 'Now, are you ready?'

'Yes, but,' she licked dry lips, 'I'm not dressed to go out eating.'

'You look all right to me.' He took her arm and urged her to the door, flicking off the light. 'What's the other key for?'

'The padlock on the main gate.' The biting cold wind taking her breath away, she stood back and let him lock the office door. They picked their way across the yard, the ice in the frozen puddles and tyre ruts crunching underfoot. A long, dark car stood in the lonely lane that skirted the premises, and Jarret Earle unlocked the passenger door, thrusting her into the dim interior before he shut the small access door in the big timber gates and secured the padlock in its hasp. He hurried to the car and tossed the keys into her lap as he entered.

'Now suggest somewhere and direct me,' he said brusquely as the engine kicked into life.

'There's the Crew's Return, only a few minutes away, they do decent sandwiches,' Lissa ventured after a moment of thought.

'I don't care for the sound of it. Is that all?'

'Apart from a transport café and a snack bar, yes,' she said wearily, stung by the unconscious arrogance in his tone.

'Think within a radius of twenty miles—there must be somewhere.'

She sighed; it would have to be Tony's, where she and Martin had spent so many happy evenings before ... At least they knew her there. But if only she'd been wearing something a bit more dressy than her plain jersey two-piece in which she'd come straight from work and her serviceable coat which was weatherproof and warm if not exactly glamorous. Especially as her companion's apparel spoke quietly of taste, style and the Midas touch that made it possible. But what did it all matter? she thought tiredly after she gave him directions and settled back in the luxurious warmth of the car. Only one thing mattered now; that her beloved father should recover, and that his livelihood should be kept safe for him and his family, no matter what it cost Lissa . . .

She liked to believe that it was because they knew her at Tony's that a secluded table was found for them in the quiet intimacy of the snug, but Lissa had a suspicion that Jarret Earle's aura of worldliness and authority exerted the real influence in the matter.

Despite his previous statement that they must talk he kept the conversation on an impersonal and strictly conventional level until the meal was almost over. Only then, when she was a little more relaxed, and warmed by the decidedly gourmet food he insisted she choose, did he say quietly: 'Now tell me about it, Lissa.'

Perhaps it was the wine that loosened her tongue, or perhaps the sheer relief of being able to talk to someone she scarcely knew, who seemed prepared to listen and understand her problems. It was not until much later that she realised how skillfully he drew the tragic story from her, or how shrewdly angled were his questions. Suddenly she became aware of the intentness in his grey eyes, how steadily they remained on her face, as though they penetrated all the despair and worry within and the dogged determination with which she coped with her problems. Suddenly she felt colour rising in her cheeks and full awareness of him rushed over her.

She said awkwardly, 'I'm sorry—I've talked you stiff. I shouldn't have imposed all that on a total——' she bit her lip, hurriedly catching back the unspoken conclusion. But he gave a slight shake of the head.

'Stranger? It's quite true.'

'Yes, but . . .' She looked away, uncertain and embarrassed.

He said nothing, and held up his hand to summon the waiter for the bill. When the folded slip came on the little salver Jarret Earle settled it and said briefly: 'I'll take you home.'

In silence she went with him to the car. But inside he made no move to switch on the engine. For a moment he stared through the windscreen at the canopy of leafless trees and the cold bluish radiance of the moonlight on the roof of the building. The white neon sign that read 'Tony's' cast an upside-down reflection on the bonnet of the car in the next parking place, and Lissa stared at it unseeingly, wondering why Jarret Earle stayed so silent. What was the matter?

As though he divined the unspoken question he said slowly, 'I have a proposition to make to you. Will you hear me out before you answer yes or no?'

Wariness made her stomach contract in a tight knot. She said, 'Yes, I'm listening.'

'I don't know if you were aware that Sam Brentlink, your father's solicitor, was a close friend of my late father. He was one of my godparents, and has always kept in touch with me. This is how I came to hear of your father's financial difficulties—and why he approached me for help.'

'I see,' she acknowledged, when he paused.

'Before I go any further I must tell you that my wife was involved in a fatal accident three years ago, and I have a daughter who is now seven years old. At present she is in the care of my late wife's family in Kent, for obvious reasons. Much as I would have liked to have her with me I had no faith in my ability to cope with a four-year-old girl—my business entails a certain amount of travel, and at the time I had no intention of ever remarrying. Now my sister-in-law is about to marry, and because of this, and another reason I don't wish to discuss at the moment, I don't want Emma to remain with them.'

He paused, still immobile in that strange, carven stillness. 'Are you beginning to have an inkling of what I'm about to say?'

Lissa's hands clenched tightly in her gloves. 'I—I'm not sure,' she said faintly.

'There are certain other aspects which may become clear to you later on,' he continued in that same, flat, emotionless voice. 'At the moment lengthy explanations wouldn't make a very clear picture because you don't know the individuals concerned, and still less their motives. How old are you, Lissa?'

The sudden change of angle threw her for a moment, then she said, 'Nearly nineteen. But ... I'm sorry, Mr Earle, about your wife, and your little girl. It must have been a tragic——'

He raised his hand, and Lissa fell silent. It seemed he did not welcome her sympathy. Then abruptly he moved, turning his head to look directly at her through the dimness.

'I need a wife to settle my domestic problems,' he said coolly, 'and this is my proposition. If you're prepared to marry me I will wipe out your father's debt and ensure that your mother and sister are provided for until such time as he is able to do so himself. I will also make sure he has every possible medical care to assist his recovery. I assure you——' he stopped. 'What's the matter? Have I shocked you?' he exclaimed sharply.

Lissa had recoiled, wondering if she had heard or dreamed those startling suggestions. *Marry him!* After two brief meetings. In return for ... 'Are you *serious*?' she whispered unbelievingly.

'Do I sound as though I were joking?'

'No.' She closed her eyes weakly. 'But it's impossible! Surely you can't mean it. We——'

'I do mean it. And the fact that we don't know each other is matterless. Still less the question of love,' he said flatly. 'There are no strings attached to my proposition as far as that aspect is concerned. I simply want you to appear to the world as my wife, be hostess in my home in that capacity, and be prepared to care for my daughter. The contract is for five years, by which time Emma will be at boarding school and will be old enough to be left in my home, under the supervision of a housekeeper, during my absences abroad. At the end of that time you will have your freedom. A divorce will be arranged. I can promise there will be no difficulties in that respect, and you will be free to continue your life in whatever way you wish.'

There was a silence that seemed to press against Lissa's

ears in a hissing rush when he stopped speaking. She sat like one stunned, for the moment unable to articulate the turmoil of reaction to the shock of his proposal.

'In short,' he said clearly, 'I wish to buy five years of your time, and I'm prepared to be generous.'

Lissa's mouth worked. 'I—I don't know what to say. I—I can't believe——'

Abruptly he switched on the ignition. 'You need say nothing now. I'll give you two days to think it over, then I'll ring you, when I'll expect your decision. Now, I'll take you home.'

Five years ... *He wanted to buy her for five years!*

*   *   *

'Lissa! Get a move on! The cars are here and Jarret just rang to say that Daddy's at the church.'

Pippa's urgent voice dragged Lissa back to the present. She stood up on legs that felt as though they might buckle under her at any moment and waited like an automaton while her mother and Pippa reverently slid the white bridal gown over her head.

'Now the veil ... you still look terribly white,' fretted her mother. 'Now are you sure you packed everything? We don't want to have to come rushing back here because you've forgotten something.'

'No, I didn't forget anything,' Lissa said tonelessly.

'I must say it's marvellous having a man to look after things again, especially one who knows what he's doing.' Mrs Vayle surveyed her daughter critically, missing nothing, adjusting a gossamer fold there, tucking in a wisp of soft honey hair that had dared to displace itself under the coronet. 'I don't know how we'd have managed if Jarret hadn't taken over, and actually arranging to have your father brought by special car from the hospital so that he can give you away ... Now, Pippa, keep that dress clear of the stairs as she goes down, and then get Susan and Janet and Carol out to the first car. And don't let your dresses touch the ground, do you hear?' Mrs Vayle doled out the four bridesmaids' posies and chivvied them out to the first car. 'Now, Lissa, are you ready? I've got your shoes ... watch your dress as you get into the car ...'

Mrs Vayle pulled the front door shut and hurried out to the beribboned car. She put Lissa's white satin shoes on the seat and climbed in beside her daughter. The chauffeur closed the door, and a moment later the car slid through the drive gates.

Lissa was on her way to her loveless marriage.

CHAPTER TWO

THE hours of her wedding day passed in a haze of unreality to Lissa. It was as though she had ascended to some strange astral viewpoint and watched the shell of herself in that snow-white bridal array go through all the actions expected of a bride.

The heavy fall of crisp snow, an unseasonably late shock in the last week of March, transformed the old church into a Christmas-card scene and laid its own virginal bridal veil over the village where Lissa had lived all her eighteen years. It also lent an eerie silence and subtly changed the old familiar landscape into a scene recognised yet not known.

Although it was bitterly cold and the four young brides-maids' pinched, rosy little faces brought murmurs of concern about colds and pneumonia from nervous mothers Lissa felt nothing. The numbness of her body and spirit owed nothing to the climatic conditions. Only twice during the ceremony did her mind thaw into agonising life. The first occasion was when she entered the church porch and quickly changed into her white satin shoes. As she straightened she saw the wheelchair, and her father sitting there, a warm rug across his knees. He looked up at her and smiled his little one-sided smile, raising his good arm towards her.

'Oh, Daddy!' Painful tears smarted her eyes as she bent to embrace him and heard his whisper of her name.

His speech was slowly returning but words still eluded him as the damaged speech centre struggled to regain its mastery. 'Look beautiful ...' his hand tightened on hers, 'don't cry, darling ... spoil it all ...'

She blinked hard and fought to maintain control. Slowly, her head high and her hand tight within his clasp, she heard the pealing summons of the organ and began her walk towards the altar. An usher guided the wheelchair and Pippa took care that Lissa's billowing gown was kept free

25

of the wheel. As she walked, she looked directly ahead, seeing yet not seeing, and not daring to allow herself to glance once towards the backs of the two men who awaited her; one tall, unmoving, dark groomed head very erect, the other shorter, brown-haired, a young man called Giles Gordon who was best man. Then the organ notes died into silence.

'Dearly beloved, we are gathered together here ...'

The silences in the church seemed to absorb her responses, as though they were whispers she'd scarcely spoken, but her father's movement was firm and confident at the point where he gave her hand. The cool, papery-dry touch of the clergyman brushed her fingers as he made the union, and then strong fingers, full of warmth, closed over and imprisoned her hand.

'I, Jarret, take thee, Alyssa to my wedded wife ... for better, for worse ... to love and to cherish ... give my troth ... with my body I thee worship ... my worldly goods I thee endow ...' The ring slid on to her third finger, an unyielding, constraining band, and then the pressure of those warm firm fingers reminded her to kneel.

It was done. She was joined in holy matrimony to her husband. And it was all a mockery—a five-year contract. She heard the drone of the prayers and her heart raged. Why had she allowed them all to talk her into the full wedding rigmarole? She had wanted a civil ceremony, one that would in some way assuage the guilt in her heart, not this lovely, hallowed old rite that meant love and joy and humility and sanctity ... But she had yielded for her father's sake, because if he had had the remotest suspicion that it was all for his sake his heart as well as his body would have been broken.

'Those whom God hath joined together let no man put asunder.'

Lissa shivered. How was she going to go from here to the reception? To present a false picture of a radiant bride, to cut the great three-tier wedding cake and laugh joyously as the telegrams were read out? Hear all the wishes for happiness ringing about her, and throw her bouquet to the bridesmaids before she left for the honeymoon. The honeymoon that would merely be a holiday, taken for appearances' sake ... How could she ever pray again without guilt in her heart?

'It's customary to kiss the bride.'

She saw the dark and the white of Jarret's groom's suit swim in front of her eyes, felt his hands close lightly on her shoulders, and then for the first time the pressure of his lips. His mouth was firm and warm, and her own like pale ice, without sensation. He did not prolong the kiss, and only Lissa heard the whispered words, 'Snow bride ...' Was there a sardonic inflection in the deep tones?

The air of celebration began in the vestry, with the signing of the register and the best man and the witnesses claiming the traditional privilege of kissing the bride. Lissa lost count of the number of times she was kissed during the reception that followed in Lingwood's premier hotel, and she was painfully conscious of how many relations the Vayle family had. Far more than from Jarret's side.

He had not spoken much of his own family, and she knew only that his father was dead and his mother had remarried and was now living in New Zealand. She would not be able to be present for the wedding, but she had sent a charming greetings telegram and Jarret had said she and his stepfather would be coming to England for an extended holiday either later in the year or during the following spring. It was not until later that Lissa realised that when he spoke of his family he seemed automatically to include the family of his first wife, Claudine.

Yet none of them were present at the wedding, nor had he provided either instructions or addresses for them to be sent invitations. And what of Emma?

He had said it was better that Emma did not attend the wedding, and because of the circumstances Lissa could do little other than accept his dictate. To any who asked he said simply that Emma had a cold and it had been thought safer not to let her make the journey from Kent.

More and more there seemed so much Jarret was keeping secret, and the questions became more and more urgent. How was Emma going to take to the advent of a stranger? How was she going to accept being taken away from the aunt and grandmother she had lived with for so long? It could upset the small motherless girl more than Jarret had even contemplated and destroy the fragile security built up since the loss of her mother.

So many doubts, and Jarret had been brusque and dismissive of them on the occasion she had ventured to voice her misgivings. Looking at him now, she could only sigh and hope that somehow it was all going to work out. He was so urbane and unruffled, charming the more matronly Vayle relations, skilfully parrying inquisitive little remarks about the whirlwind courtship of their niece, but Lissa recognised the shuttered expression in those cool slate eyes. He was giving nothing away of his true feelings, and now she was secretly conscious of relief that none of his close family were present. It had been bad enough explaining this precipitate marriage to her own friends and family, even with the aid of her mother's loquacity. The strain of the wedding was enough for one day; the ordeal of meeting his family was a hurdle still in the distance.

She felt his touch on her arm. 'It's time to say goodbye to your father, Lissa.'

She put down her glass of champagne and hurried across the big reception room. Her father was beginning to look very tired, and not sorry to retreat from the noise and the strain of trying to communicate with such a large number of well-meaning friends and relations who all wanted to know how he felt. With her mother and Pippa and Jarret she went to the hotel entrance to see him esconced safely in the car that was to take him back to the hospital. For a moment she clung to his hand, knowing that to her he still represented all the love and security of her childhood and adolescence, and felt almost unbearably bereft when the car slid away along the snow-banked road.

And then it was time to go to the room set aside for her to change. For all the good wishes and the smiles and the kisses, and the knowing little grins of the men. Pippa unexpectedly burst into tears, having just realised that Lissa would not be coming home any more, but the bridesmaids' gifts, which Jarret had withheld until now, brought incredulous smiles of joy through the glisten of tears as Pippa opened the jeweller's case to reveal an exquisite gold watch on the slenderest of bracelets.

'Oh! It's fantastic!' she cried: 'Thank you, Jarret—I *can* call you Jarret now, can't I? Because you're my brother-in-law now, aren't you?'

'I shall be honoured,' he said gravely, then patted her shoulder as she suddenly remembered to thank him and embarrassment at the brief lapse turned her cheeks scarlet. 'Take care of your mother,' he added, 'and we'll come to see you as soon as we return.'

'Will you bring Emma?'

The darkening cloud across his eyes was so fleeting that only Lissa noticed it, then he was smiling again. 'Yes, we'll bring Emma.'

At last they were free, the farewells and the wavings far behind, and there was only Jarret's presence at her side in the car that was speeding them to the airport. The village passed, her own home, the loop in the road that bypassed Lingwood, and then the motorway, like a great grey river running through the snow-clad countryside. Lissa looked out of the window, conscious of the silence stretching taut as a bow-string between herself and the man who was now her husband and the total inability to speak that had gripped her. Under her glove the new gold band seemed to burn into her finger, a small yet potent power that transmitted the same message that reiterated in her brain. *It's done ... you're married ... you belong to Jarret Earle ... five years, five years, five ...*

'Well, I suppose you're glad *that's* over!'

His voice sounded cold, uninterested.

'In a way.' She turned her head and saw only his profile, sharply etched, unreadable.

'I expect it must be an ordeal, an exhausting one.'

'Yes.' Desperately she sought for some small comment that would break this impasse, but she was caught anew in the same spell that had held her enmeshed all day. The toils of uncertainty, wariness, and the haunting fear of the unknown that lay ahead. The silence descended again and she sensed his movement as he settled deeper into the opposite corner.

'If you don't feel inclined for conversation don't try to force it,' he said in the same even tones. 'The quality of silence is rapidly becoming an underrated blessing in today's world.'

'Yes,' she said wanly, after another small, uncertain glance at that profile. Perhaps he's tired as well, she thought. Why should a man be considered automatically immune to weariness simply because he appears tall and lean and strong and fit, with the kind of infallible dependability her mother had recognised instantly with unabashed thankfulness?

At least it was something to be grateful for, she reflected after they boarded the plane at Heathrow. Jarret Earle had the air of a man who knew what he wanted and had no intention of being intimidated by anyone in the process. Airport formalities held neither mystery nor hold-ups for him, and in a crowd his was the eye of authority that always commanded—and got—attention.

All the pertinent decisions had been made in the space of an evening, much in the way he might have checked through the details of a contract. The date and time and place of the wedding; the venue of the supposed honeymoon. From the plethora of exotic holiday spots he suggested Lissa had chosen Egypt without even considering any of the alternatives simply because she suddenly recalled a long ago childhood whim to see the pyramids. He had agreed without demur, seeming pleased with her choice and remarking that there would be so much to see that two weeks should pass without boredom. As though he couldn't be done quickly enough with the conventional trappings that appearances' sake demanded, she thought sadly.

And now she was bound for Cairo, all her new honeymoon clothes packed in the luxurious new Italian matching luggage, and her heart suddenly trembling with a fresh fear. Jarret had promised her no strings. *'I don't expect your love as part of the bargain . . .'*

Lissa shivered. She had accepted the flat statement without question, her imagination supplying a ready picture of the woman he had lost. For if love was deep enough and true enough a lifetime, let alone three years, was not long enough to forget. But she had not dared to ask, and until this moment it had not occurred to her that love and sex could be two separate things. It was quite possible to have the second without the first ... What if he decided to make demands and expect her to accede ...?

She stole a glance at him, wondering if he were really concentrating on the paperback in his hand. Or was he thinking ahead, to the dark hours of the night? But surely he would have betrayed any secret desire, in a sensual caress, a certain glance, all the ways a man made his intention unmistakable ... Lissa stared unseeingly at the pages of the magazine open on her lap, trying to subdue the quivers coursing through her body. Why should she distrust him? He had stated quite flatly that it was a matter of convenience. A part she would play ... A job for five years. *Experience of love not required,* she thought bitterly. But what would she say to him if all those assurances proved to be empty words?

She became more and more aware of a rather searching quality in Jarret's glances at her during the closing stages of that long journey that brought them at last into the star-studded Egyptian night and the imposing hotel in a desert garden where Jarret had reserved the principal suite. Although he made no comment on her strained efforts at normality there was tension now in his own manner as they were greeted by a portly, smiling man in formal suit and dark red fez and then swept along opulent corridors, followed by a small retinue of staff intent that nothing should be lacking in the welcome.

The portly man opened a heavily panelled white door and gestured dramatically for them to enter, and for a few minutes the place seemed to buzz like a beehive, then Jarret turned from tipping the boys who had carried in the luggage, and the tautness in his expression showed in the lines at the sides of his mouth. For a moment he stared at Lissa, unsmiling, as she stood uncertainly in the centre of the huge, luxuriously furnished sitting room.

'Well, having got rid of the reception committee ...' he said on a sigh, as though he had wearied of the long day of make-believe, 'are you ready to start on that?'

'That' was the magnum of champagne in a silver ice bucket that nestled on a table amid a positive tower of blossoms, only one of a mass of flower arrangements that filled the room with their scent. Lissa shook her head helplessly. She felt more lost and uncertain than ever in her life, and her first, inconsequent thought was a protest at what all this must be costing—or rather what it was going to cost by the time the two weeks were over.

She looked round her and took a step towards the minaret-shaped arch which led to a dining alcove and a balcony, then turned back. 'Is—is all this necessary ...?' Her gesture took in the room, the flowers, the champagne, the other doors opening off at the sides which obviously led to bedrooms and bathroom.

There was a pop of the champagne cork, then he shrugged. 'I loathe being stifled.'

'Yes, but ...' She shook her head again, guilt swamping her as she remembered how much of the expense of the wedding he had insisted on meeting.

'Does it worry you?' he exclaimed, the lift of his brows faintly cynical.

'Yes, it does.' She slipped off her light linen jacket and dropped it over a chair back, on top of the coat she'd carried since leaving England's chill. Suddenly she wished she had been firmer in exercising what, after all, was a bride's prerogative, instead of allowing Jarret to dictate and her mother to take advantage of his careless generosity. Then she would not be feeling so utterly beholden to him and bitterly conscious that every stitch of clothing she wore at the moment had been paid for by him as just another item of that cold, calculated marriage contract.

'Anything but the real thing would never have convinced your father today,' Jarret said flatly, as though he had read her thoughts.

But it isn't the real thing! the small inward voice taunted her, even as she knew he spoke only the truth. For what torment of dangerous worry might have possessed the sick man if the slightest suspicion regarding the sanctity of his beloved elder daughter's whirlwind marriage had entered his head.

'Because there's little doubt that your father is perfectly aware of everything happening about him,' Jarret went on in the same flat voice, 'and it doesn't take much imagination to picture oneself in the same appalling state; able to hear and understand but unable to speak properly or even write down all the fears clamouring in one's head, while friends and family murmur comforting baby talk around you as though you weren't quite right in the head.'

'I know.' She swallowed hard, wanting to thank him for his understanding, but the words that would tell him how fervently she appreciated all he had done to ease her father's situation refused to come while he was in this cold, unapproachable mood. 'It worried me so much. But I—I wish it hadn't had to happen this way.'

'It's too late now for regrets.' He stood in front of her, proffering the misty glass of sparkling pink bubbles. 'But surely you didn't imagine I'd expect you to forgo *all* the trimmings?'

'No—I appreciate that. But I didn't expect so many of them. I—I didn't——' Lissa bit her lip on impulsive words and took a hasty sip of champagne. But he caught her up quickly on the choked back indiscretion.

'You didn't what?'

She shook her head, suddenly aware of desperate tiredness and that she was dangerously near losing control. 'It doesn't matter. I—I'm just a bit tired.'

He looked at her levelly, his mouth hard. 'You were going to say you didn't want any trimmings, weren't you? You'd have preferred a hole-and-corner formality that would merely have convinced everybody it was a shotgun wedding.'

'Oh, no!' She recoiled, and set down her glass before the sparkling wine cascaded down her wrist. 'I never thought anything of the kind.'

'No?' He continued to stare at her with those quelling grey eyes. 'Lissa, this is one thing that must be understood. Everything about this marriage must convince my family that it's the real thing. No matter what your—or my—private feelings about the matter might be, no one must guess the truth. Is that understood?'

The intensity in his voice frightened her. Again she began to wonder why he had embarked on this baffling course. The reason he had given didn't quite ring true, somehow. It should be possible to engage a perfectly

trustworthy woman to care for Emma, if he did not wish
to leave her in his sister-in-law's care. Lots of men became
widowers and had to cope with being breadwinner and
taking on the role of both parents in one. And what if
Emma got fond of her? Had he considered the child's
feelings if she got attached to the stepmother about to be
thrust into her young life? How would the child feel in
five years' time?

'Lissa! Did you hear me?'

'Yes,' she whispered. 'I understood all that right from
the start. Do you really believe I'd go back on my word?
After ...'

'You'd better not,' he said grimly. 'You are now
Mrs Jarret Earle, and you will remain as such for the
next five years. So the sooner you can start at least a token
pretence of that the easier it'll be for both of us.'

'I thought the pretence had already started,' she said
bitterly.

'Not very convincingly, I'm afraid. Judging by your
performance today.'

Lissa recoiled. 'What do you mean? What did you
expect? A bride hanging round your neck among the
horde at the reception? A—a song and dance in church?
Just what did you expect of me?'

'Only a girl who looked like a warm, living human
being. Not one who looked as though she was carved out
of the wretched snow that covered everything.'

She stared at him with eyes like great pools of hurt. Was
that how she appeared to him? Her hand fluttered to her
throat and she looked round desperately, wanting only to
escape the knife thrusts of pain he seemed determined to
inflict on her. A nerve throbbed in his jaw, a tiny, unheeded
warning of the abrupt step he made forward.

'I think it's time to start breaking down the barriers,'
he exclaimed. Before she realised his intent he seized her
by the shoulders and pulled her roughly against him.

Her startled gasp was smothered by the descent of his
mouth, hard and bruising, possessing without tenderness
or passion in its determination. Lissa's heart began to thud,
and instinctively her hands went up against his chest, trying
to push him away. But her strength was puny against his,

and he chose to ignore the small, desperate thrusts while his mouth moved deliberately over her lips, forcing them apart as though he would mould them to his will in the same way as his arms were curving her body like a supple bow until it was taut against his own.

The room swam and time vanished. Lissa felt as though she were drowning, swamped by shock, desperation, and a sheer male power she had never experienced. A man who was still a total stranger to her emotions, yet whose body even now spoke its own message and stirred strange answering tremors deep within her own physical being.

'No!' she cried inwardly and against that invading mouth. She turned her head frantically, straining away, only to expose her throat to further invasion. Then abruptly she was free, so suddenly she almost lost her balance and would have fallen but for his hand gripping her arm.

Afterwards, she wondered what the outcome might have been had the interruption not come when it did. She had not heard the tap on the door, and she turned away, trying to hide her distraught face and spilling tears from the waiter who had arrived with a dinner trolley. Dimly she heard Jarret speak to the man, sensed the trolley being wheeled past her, towards the minaret arch that occupied part of one wall and opened to a dining alcove and balcony.

Lissa moved shaking hands over her hot cheeks, smoothed back disturbed hair and adjusted the gaping lapels of her blouse. She took several deep, unsteady breaths, fighting to regain control while her painfully acute senses told her of the curious glance cast towards her by the waiter as Jarret dismissed the man. Then she heard the firm footfalls crossing the thick carpet. Jarret's voice said: 'The food's ready.'

'I don't want anything.'

She could sense him close behind her.

'Don't be foolish. You've eaten virtually nothing all day.'

'I'm not hungry.'

'Lissa ...' his voice was dangerously quiet, 'if you don't make at least a token attempt to eat I shall be tempted to finish what I just started.'

Conviction like a small electric shock told her that the words held no empty threat. Like an automaton she turned and moved towards the alcove. Suddenly the food she had not wanted seemed to beckon like sanity; at least during the eating of it he could not make demands she was neither prepared for nor ready to grant. Love was not in the agreement . . .

The table had been set with snowy linen, and an appetising smell rose from the dishes temptingly arrayed on the trolley. Jarret drew out a chair for her and moved round the table to seat himself and shake out the folded napkin. He looked cool and unflustered, and infuriatingly handsome, in complete opposition to the way Lissa felt. Obviously he expected her to serve the portions, and anger spurted in her; why had he sent the waiter away instead of letting him do the job he had been sent to do? With hands still disposed to unsteadiness Lissa carefully disentangled the kebabs and offered Jarret the accompanying tehina salad.

'Do you want some of this dressing?' she asked stiffly.

'Of course,' he said smoothly, 'it'll be sesame seed, and very good.'

She passed the sauce boat to him and in silence began her own meal. The food was superb, and for the first time that day she felt hungry, but her senses were so acutely aware of the man opposite and his enigmatic mien she did not dare relax her guard and give herself to unallayed enjoyment of the meal. Reality had taken over at last, superseding the endless shadow-play the day had seemed, and she realised she was actually married, actually here, in a luxury suite in a luxury hotel set against the fabled panorama of the east. The river they had crossed was the Nile, blue artery of Egypt, the legendary Pyramids were but a short drive distant, and the age-old magic of the desert waited to make its claim. A childhood dream had come true at last, but through undreamed-of circumstances. And she had never felt so forlorn and unhappy in her life.

'Fruit?' His invitation broke the silence, and soberly she looked at the platter of enticing fruit—oranges like great golden globes, rich dark dates, tender figs, pears cloaked with thorns, and luscious grapes veiled in bloom.

She bit into a grape, her tongue hurriedly chasing the spurt of sweet juice on her lip, and again felt his gaze on her face. Jarret stood up, and instantly her stomach knotted with tension. But he merely reached for the coffee pot and proceeded to fill the tiny fluted silver cups. The ornate, chased lines of the tall Eastern coffee pot appeared to fascinate him. He studied it at length, remarked on its attractiveness, and Lissa found herself caught by a strange compulsion. But it was his hands she was noticing, the lean, well-shaped strength of them, cared-for nails, and the hint of sensuousness in the long fingers that almost caressed the swelling curve of the coffee pot handle.

Lissa dragged her gaze away. A surreptitious glance at her watch showed that midnight was not far distant. The meal could not be prolonged much longer, and she had not even seen her bedroom, let alone begun to unpack, yet she could not summon the courage to make the first move. Then the movement of Jarret brought her head up sharply. He was pushing his chair back, looking at her.

'Like to go out?'

Her mouth parted. 'Go out?'

'Yes.' He stood up and moved towards the balcony, standing with his back to her and looking out into the hidden night. One hand rested negligently on the edge of the partly open balcony door, the other hung loosely at his side. A wild, unreasoning anger rose in Lissa. How could he be so casual, as though—as though that onslaught of cruel kisses had never taken place? After those brutal remarks he had flung at her, and the way he had held her ...

With an effort she controlled the threatening tumult of emotion; the night and whatever it might bring had to be faced, as had all the nights and days of the future. There was no escape.

She said tonelessly: 'Do you want to go out?'

'Not especially. But I was asking *you*,' he returned coolly. 'It occurred to me that you might find a brief stroll refreshing after all those hours cooped up on the plane. Who knows, you may even discover all the romance of the desert by moonlight,' he added cynically.

'Isn't the romance of the desert a figment of imagination?' she responded flatly.

'Like all romance it depends on the strength of the individual's imagination.'

'So you don't believe it exists,' she said softly.

'No. My youthful illusions were destroyed a long time ago.'

She sighed. 'At least you're honest.'

'Do you want me to pretend?'

'That's the last thing I want you to do.'

'So,' he turned to face her, 'I take it that the desert by moonlight doesn't tempt.'

Lissa's mouth hardened. 'The only thing that tempts me at the moment is my room and getting unpacked,' she said distinctly.

'Of course.' His tone was expressionless. 'I should have remembered that wedding days are traditionally exhausting for brides and tearful for their mothers.' He gestured. 'The choice is the lady's.'

She shrugged. 'They're probably both the same.'

'Probably.' Impatience betrayed itself in his abrupt strides to the nearest of the two doors leading from the sitting room. He flung it open, and wordlessly Lissa went to it and stood for a moment looking into the big white room. Like the sitting room it was sumptuously furnished. Fitted wardrobes ran the length of one wall, the king-size bed was draped with a rich turquoise satin spread, above it was a gilded frieze of ancient Egyptian motifs which were in complete contrast to the white telephone by the bed and the glimpse through a partly open further door of cool, sea-green tiles and the end of a sunken bath with glittering gold taps.

She turned back to collect her cases, but Jarret had forestalled her. He placed them on the slatted stand and stood watching her.

'Thank you,' she murmured with more outward than inward calm, then pointedly turned her back on him and unlocked the smaller of the two cases. It took only a moment to find her night things, then she took her robe and walked into the bathroom.

When she closed the door a great weakness overtook her limbs. She started to run her bath, then sat limply on the stool savouring the sheer relief of being at last able to shed the burden of pretence. An era seemed to separate her from the panic-stricken girl of that morning. If ever a bride had been stricken with stage-fright she had—still was, she amended ruefully, even though she had tried to prepare herself for the acceptance of the fact that this day would not prove to be the traditional day of bridal radiance. Sighing, she stripped off her clothes and surrendered to the soothing warmth of scented water.

It was no good giving way to self-pity; she had walked into this marriage with her eyes open; logically her motive had been quite as cold-blooded as Jarret's and she could not in all honesty blame him for any loss of her own sweet romantic illusions. So far he had kept his part of the bargain, more than generously; before dawn she would discover just how much or little she had understood the terms of the contract ...

She trembled as she stepped out of the bath, trying to close her mind to the possibility of how complete that contract might yet prove to be. But the fear refused to be ignored. What was it like to be possessed by a man without love?

Lissa stared unseeingly at herself in the great wall mirror, then turned away abruptly and shouldered into her wrap. Uncaring of her appearance she left her hair pinned in its bunch on top of her head and walked back into the bedroom.

Jarret was sitting on the bed.

His dark hair was tousled, he wore a white towelling robe, and his gaze fixed unblinkingly on her as she stopped in a frozen attitude and stared at him.

'You've been very quick for a woman,' he observed dryly.

She stayed mute, the beats of her heart starting their ball-race again. Dragging her transfixed gaze away from him she went slowly to the dressing table and began to take the clips out of her hair. As it fell about her shoulders she saw the other movement reflected in the mirror.

'We have to get used to seeing each other in various stages of dress—and undress,' he said in flat tones. 'So we may as well start now.'

'We?' She did not turn her head.

'All right; *you*. I'm used to seeing a woman about the house, minus the cloak of make-up and clothes she dons for outsiders,' he said crisply.

Lissa's mouth set. 'I didn't expect to find you here,' she said pointedly, 'or I'd have endeavoured to don some kind of a cloak.'

There was a brief pause, then he moved closer behind her, to look directly into her eyes through the mirror. 'How long do you intend to treat me as an outsider?' he asked quietly.

Lissa was the first to break that electric contact of glance. She looked down, bereft of words and totally without any idea of how to deal with this situation. Temper she could have responded to, brusqueness she might have countermanded but she was suddenly aghast to find herself experiencing a totally unexpected sense of guilt. But what did he expect? she asked herself hopelessly. Did he imagine she could throw herself into his arms as though he were a lover? Make the silent, sensuous invitations to passion he must want? Let him take her solely for the satisfaction of physical passion? *We're married; we might as well make the most of it!*

She took a deep, shuddering breath, tensing for the invasion of his touch, but it did not come. Instead, she heard him say in the same quiet words: 'I've just unpacked this—your wedding present.'

Slowly she looked up, seeing the blue leather jeweller's case in his hand, and then a sparkle of rainbow facets. Caught in a trance, she could only stand numbly while he carefully took out the pendant and delicate gold chain.

It was oval, with a filigree of gold lace around the setting, and in the heart a single diamond like a tear-drop in platinum. It slipped to its nadir on the chain, like a tear-drop of ice between her breasts as he passed the chain around her slender throat and fastened it. The touch of his fingers on the nape of her neck sent a tremor through her, then he ran his fingers through her hair, drawing the still damp tresses back from her face and letting them fall back on her shoulders.

'You're not exactly dressed for it—I should have given it to you earlier,' he said, stepping back slightly.

She looked down, her finger-tips going to touch the pendant, and a bewilderment of mingled emotions besieging her. His unerring taste had selected perfectly a piece of jewellery that was exactly right; a heavy, elaborate creation would have been too ostentatious and overpowering for her delicate colouring, slender neck and small, well-shaped head. But through the surprise came that rush of guilt again and a dreadful remorse. Now, too late, she realised her appalling oversight; she had no gift for her husband.

If only she had remembered! But the past few weeks had been so full of rush, the preparations for the wedding, worry about her father and the chill, secret fears of the future. All these and her acceptance of the true nature of her forthcoming marriage had driven away any thought of the traditional exchanging of gifts between bride and groom from her mind. Jarret had said nothing about such a gift, and his presents to the bridesmaids had come as a complete surprise only that morning. There had been no trace of sentiment in his attitude. He had not consulted her about the choice of the ring. He had simply taken her little Scottish silver ring as a guide to size because it fitted her third finger best. Oh, if only her mother had thought to remind her! But then she—the only one—knew the truth ...

'Don't you like it?' he said sharply.

Lissa was brought back to the tall strength of him waiting. She could not bear to look up directly into his face. Her gaze stayed unhappily at the vee of his throat between the white lapels of his robe.

'It—it's very beautiful. I—I don't know how to thank you,' she said brokenly, 'but you shouldn't ...'

'I shouldn't what?' he demanded.

She shook her head miserably. 'You—it makes me feel so guilty.'

'Why?'

'Because I didn't—I haven't anything to give you in return.'

'You think I'm expecting something in return?'

She heard the hardening note in his voice and despite the warmth of the room a chill began to pervade her body. Her hands strayed to the edges of her wrap, unconsciously closing it more tightly across her breast. 'Yes—no—well, it's the custom, isn't it?' she stammered.

The grey eyes had followed those betraying movements. He said coldly: 'I'm not looking for a return compliment, Lissa. This,' his hand went to the pendant, flicking it away from her skin with an almost contemptuous gesture, 'was never intended to be part of that contract, which will be kept to the letter!' he added scornfully.

'You mean ... ?'

His mouth twisted at the corners and he dropped the pendant against her breast as though it offended him. 'I mean that I haven't forgotten my side of the agreement. Or my promise—despite my recent lapse into stress.'

She looked up at him now, tears smarting her eyes and misting the cold hard expression that had set his features into a mask. For a long moment he held her tremulous gaze, then he dropped the blue leather case on the dressing table.

'I have never yet had to resort to buying the use of a woman's body. I don't intend to start now!'

Lissa recoiled from the cruel lash of words. Shock numbed her, and her eyes widened with horror as he strode to the door. With a flick of his hand Jarret withdrew the key from the lock and swung round.

'Perhaps this will reassure you!'

He threw the key on the bed and walked out.

The slam of the door reverberated in Lissa's ears, and she had no idea of how long she stood there before life crept back into her numbed limbs. At last, like a wounded creature, she crept into the huge bed, to lie there small, lost and forlorn. Nothing in her nebulous misgivings had prepared her for the misery of this, her wedding night.

So much for all her tender, secret little adolescent dreams of the time when she would surrender her heart and herself! Of the unknown man who would journey with her along the ways of love, through the vales of sweet camaraderie, and aloft to the peaks of physical ecstasy. Now the years stretched ahead, like an empty desert barren of the promise of either ...

The moon waned, and the desert slept, watched over by the age-old majesty of the Pyramids. Weeping brought its exhaustion and at last Lissa slept, unconscious of the pendant forgotten about her throat. Unseen, it pressed beneath her weight, imprinting its own small pyramid into her breast. The brand symbolic of Jarret Earle; the miniature tomb of her happiness.

CHAPTER THREE

LISSA was startled out of sleep shortly after eight the next morning. A slender dark-eyed maid in a rose silk *melaaya* that might have been designed by Yuki, so gracefully draped was it about her shapely form, stood by the bedside.

In charmingly accented English she bade Lissa good morning and placed a tray bearing continental breakfast on the table by the bed. The little maid smiled. 'Is right—as you ordered?'

Memory and awareness rushed back to envelope Lissa. Jarret must have ordered breakfast to be sent to the suite. Suddenly aware that she must look as wretched as she felt, she thanked the girl and reached gratefully for the tall glass of golden fruit juice. Ice chips danced in its refreshing depths and Lissa gulped it down thirstily, then went to the bathroom to splash her face with cold water before she sat on the edge of the bed and poured a cup of coffee.

There was no sound from outside the bedroom, the only movements those of the curtains wafting slightly from the window the maid had opened wide. Restlessly she stood up and went to the window, a still warm croissant half eaten in her hand. She looked out over the gardens that were spiked with palms and verdant with shrubs and blossoms under an incredibly blue sky. Beyond was the Nile itself, a sparkling expanse reflecting the sky. Along its nearside bank stretched a terrace and wide steps leading from the garden to a landing stage a short distance along to Lissa's right. Small craft were lined up alongside, waiting for hotel guests who might wish to hire them, and out in midstream wide-beamed feluccas with their tall, curving lateen sails skimmed the waters like flotillas of graceful swans.

Lissa sighed. The air felt dry and warm, unbelievably different from the damp biting atmosphere of a snowy

English March left behind less than twenty-four hours ago.
But the alien beauty of the scene could not melt the chill
core of unhappiness that lay like lead in her heart. She
drifted back into the room and her unfinished breakfast,
senses acutely honed for sounds of Jarret's presence.

How was she going to face him after last night?

But the disturbing silence still reigned almost an hour
later, by which time she had washed, dressed, applied a
light film of make-up that discreetly masked the blue
shadows of strain under her eyes and the wan hollows of
her cheeks, and completed her unpacking. She glanced
round the room then slowly opened the door and walked
into the sitting room. It was empty, and the door to the
other bedroom stood open, a certain stillness emanating
from it that told Lissa it too was deserted.

For a moment she experienced an attack of unreasoning
panic. *Had he checked out?* Then common sense reasser-
ted itself and she drew a shaky breath. Jarret would not do
that. He had not come this far to walk out on her. All the
same ... Lissa glanced at her watch; he might have decided
to leave her to her own devices.

She paced uncertainly about the room, then an idea
struck her and she returned to her own room. Possibly he
had left a message. She stood looking down at the phone,
her mouth soft with indecision. She couldn't ring the desk
and ask if her husband had left a message; she would feel
such an idiot ... Then her mouth tightened. Was she
going to stooge around in her room all morning? A moment
later she was asking if any message had been left for Mrs
Earle, biting her lip while they checked, then replacing
the receiver when the negative reply came in polite but
impersonal tones.

Very well. If he couldn't leave a message letting her
know what was happening she might as well go out herself, even if only into the gardens. But first she had better
make sure that he had indeed left the suite. She picked
up her bag and a lightweight jacket and once again crossed
the sitting room. On the threshold of Jarret's bedroom she
looked into a room identical in layout and furnishings to
her own. Its traces of his occupation were sparse, a leather
clothes brush and a comb on the dressing chest, a paper-

back on the bedside table, and the white towelling robe dropped across the back of a cane chair.

'Looking for something?'

With a gasp of shock she spun round and met Jarret's direct, enquiring stare.

'I—I didn't hear you come in,' she said unsteadily. 'I—I thought you'd—you'd gone.'

'I've been making some travel arrangements for the next few days.' He shouldered past her and dropped a handful of leaflets on the dressing chest. 'Did you sleep well?'

Just like that! As though his last words to her had not contained one of the cruellest insults a man could inflict on a woman.

'No,' she said flatly.

'Did you have breakfast?'

'Yes.'

'I trust it was sufficient.' He was riffling through garments in the wardrobe. 'I guessed you wouldn't want anything cooked.'

'No,' she said tonelessly, and added after a pause, 'Thank you for ordering it for me.'

'I thought it was better that way.' He selected a cream cotton casual, blouson-styled, and slipped it on over the dark brown sports shirt he was wearing. With his back to her, he said, 'I want to talk to you, Lissa, so sit down. We might as well get it done right now.'

She remained silent, unmoving, and he swung round. His darkly handsome features were cast into shadow by the movement, but his voice was crisp and unemotional.

'I must apologise for my behaviour last night. What I said was unforgivable, even though you left me in no doubt of your belief regarding my motive for giving you that bauble.'

Lissa's mouth parted, then she made a small, protesting gesture. 'No! That's wrong! I never imagined that you—that you—— It wasn't because of the necklace at all.'

'Wasn't it?' Disbelief was clear in his tone. 'You're a very poor liar, my dear. But you can't deny what was eating you last night. It didn't need much insight to realise that you spent most of last evening wondering how to keep me out of your bed. It's true, isn't it?'

A tremulous sigh escaped her; what was the point of lying? 'Yes,' she said in a small voice.

'But why?' he demanded. 'Did you think I'd refuse to keep my word?'

She looked away. 'What else was I to think? After ...'

'After what?'

'After your attempts to start breaking down what you called the barriers,' she admitted reluctantly, unable to look directly at him.

'What? Oh ...'

For an incredulous moment she thought he was laughing. Then he moved again, towards her, and light fell across his face, revealing only the traces of puzzlement and suddenly dawning comprehension. He'd forgotten! she thought unbelievingly He'd forgotten those hard, possessive yet strangely passionless kisses so soon after the arrival last night. It seemed he had also forgotten the curt accusations he had flung at her, apparently because she had failed to display the measured amount of warmth and animation he deemed suitable during the occasion of their wedding.

Her eyes clouded with hurt. Although she was a serious-natured girl in comparison to her more extrovert mother and sister she possessed a warm, deeply sensitive disposition that responded quickly to affection once her trust had been given. The moment Jarret had made his apology, somewhat qualified though it had been, she had begun to soften, prepared to understand that he too suffered from the strain and tension of the long day and ready to forgive the irritability that could be a natural reaction. But now she retreated defensively behind the barrier of caution as she saw him shrug carelessly.

'So I kissed you and spoke my mind. Under stress—as I said. What is there to say about that?'

'Yes. What?' she agreed sadly.

His mouth compressed and for a moment he was silent. Then he sighed. 'I've apologised. You're not being exactly helpful, are you?'

She shot him a guarded look, then seated herself in the nearest chair, composing her hands in her lap. She appeared a great deal more self-possessed than she felt, but she had suddenly made up her mind to try to end this verbal fencing once and for all. If they could not arrive at a more amicable understanding life threatened to become a very stressful business indeed.

She took a deep breath and said quietly: 'You're right, we do have to talk. But first, I want to say how much I appreciate all you've done for my father. Perhaps it's disloyal and I shouldn't say it, but I've always felt so much closer to him than to my mother, and these past few months I've been sick with worry about him, not about what might happen to us—I've never been afraid of work, and Mother and Pippa could have gone to Aunt Helen if the worst happened and we had to sell everything. But it was knowing how he would be worrying about us, worrying about the money. I was so desperate that I——'

'Lissa, I know all this,' he broke in. 'The set-up was quite clear to me, even without the clarification from Sam Brentlink.'

'Yes, but I wanted to say it.' She tried to look at him steadily. 'I'm very grateful. You've been more than generous to—to people who were virtually strangers to you, and that I'll never forget, even though I still don't understand why you did it, and in this particular way. And so I'll try to run your home and care for your little daughter to the best of my ability, if only you'll give me just a little time to—to find my way and get used to a new way of life. Because at this moment I feel so terribly uncertain of everything.'

She hesitated, her composure threatening to desert her under his cool, considering regard. 'That's why I think you'd better tell me exactly what you want me to be to you.'

'I thought I'd already spelled it out.'

'So did I. Until last night.'

'What are you trying to tell me, Lissa?' His voice was still cool, giving no indication of his inward feelings.

Her fingers tightened in their clasp, betraying her nervousness. But she said with equal coolness: 'Now you're being unhelpful. You know what I mean.'

'Do I? Does this mean you're now prepared to yield the great sacrifice of yourself?' His tone hardened.

'No, because it has never occurred to me to see this marriage in the light of a sacrifice. It means that I'm finding it very difficult to predict your reactions. Last night, when you gave me the pendant, I wasn't thinking of it as a kind of—of bribe. Believe me, that was the last thing to enter my head,' she added vehemently.

'What were you thinking of, then?'

Her gaze dropped to her hands. 'I felt terribly guilty. Because I'd never expected a—a personal gift from you, and I realised that I'd forgotten about this completely. Then, when you thought I didn't like your gift, I felt appalled and ashamed. That was all I could think of that moment, how stupid I'd been. And I began to wonder how you were feeling, if you felt as worried and uncertain and afraid as I did, if it was going to work out or if we'd made a dreadful mistake ... Then when you said ...'

Lissa's voice trailed away. She was lapsing into the danger she'd intended to avoid at all cost, that of allowing emotion to override expedience. How foolish could she get? Attributing to this worldly, autocratic man the foolish imaginings of a girl.

The ensuing silence seemed fraught with his scorn, then Jarret moved restlessly across the room. 'The one thing I forgot to take into consideration,' he said resignedly. 'A woman's emotional angle.'

'It can be quite as valid as logic in some circumstances,' she defended hotly.

'Not being a woman, I'm unable to follow emotional logic.' He swung round, a frown between his dark brows. 'What you are trying to say, Lissa, is simply that we don't know each other.'

'Yes,' she said flatly. 'And in two weeks' time I have to start caring for Emma. What's she going to think of me? A total stranger suddenly pitchforked into her young life. She's never seen me. I've never seen her. I don't even know what she looks like ...'

'That's easily remedied.' Jarret took out his pocket-book and drew out a photograph. He handed it to Lissa.

'She was six then. The man is her Great-uncle Daniel.'

Lissa held it to the light, her hand a little unsteady. A colour print taken on a bright summer day in some anonymous garden, it showed an elderly white-haired man with a genial smile and a dark-haired little girl in a blue print frock. The sun was in her eyes and the smile on the dazzled little face seemed slightly forced, but the small chin showed determination and the slim little body was very straight, even though there was a suggestion in her expression that she was not entirely happy at the time. She was holding very tightly to the white-headed man's hand. Lissa glanced up at Jarret, then back to the picture, looking for resemblance between father and daughter.

As though he picked up the casual thought Jarret said carelessly, 'It's not a very good one of her—she was a bit gap-toothed at the time. I must get a decent one of her done to send to my mother. Perhaps you could arrange that later on?'

'Yes, of course.' Lissa handed back the snap.

He studied it a moment, a brooding quality in his pursed mouth, then abruptly he pushed it back into his pocket-book. 'Most people think she's like her mother,' he added, as he slipped the leather case into his pocket.

Lissa nodded, instinct warning her that this was not the time to venture any interest, no matter how innocent or polite, in Jarret's late wife. But during those brief moments centred on Emma she had sensed the first faint suggestion of rapport between herself and the enigmatic stranger she had married. Although rapport was too optimistic a choice of meaning to describe the normality of those moments, she amended inwardly. But even though it might prove sadly transient it least it was a beginning. As he had observed in a flat concise statement that summed up all her cautious, fumbling attempts to establish a basis to begin their relationship: they didn't know each other.

'Now,' he broke in, with a brisk snatch at the leaflets he'd left on the dressing chest, 'this is the itinerary I've planned ...'

Afterwards, when Lissa looked back on the travel-packed interlude her honeymoon became, she wondered how Jarret had managed to fit in such an extensive programme of sightseeing in the two weeks at their disposal. By the end of the first week she was bemused by antiquities; the Marble Mosque, the treasures of Tutankhamun, the great Citadel built by Saladin, friezes, carvings, ancient Memphis and the towering Rameses staring sightlessly across his three-thousand-year-old realm. She had her first sail on the Nile, chose a lucky scarab brooch for Emma and received one herself from Jarret while exploring the bazaars, and remedied the omission that had troubled her by buying a gold cravat pin which she spotted Jarret examining with interest. Firmly she ignored his protests when he realised her intention, and later she added a new silk cravat to complete her gift.

At last she was daring to relax. Since that emotionally fraught night Jarret had chosen to show another facet of what Lissa was to discover was a complex personality—at least as far as she was concerned. He proceeded to escort her round Cairo and its environs with a disarming blend of attentiveness and care. He was courteous, urbane and protective, but with just a subtle enough hint of impersonality to give Lissa the breathing space she desperately needed.

He encouraged her to talk about herself and she responded instantly, too inexperienced to realise that while he skilfully drew her out to confide about her childhood, her family, her interests and her hopes and disappointments in life he volunteered very little information about himself.

As the crowded, sun-filled days began to slide past Lissa became conscious of an odd sense of dissatisfaction. Jarret seemed so impervious to her now, totally unmoved beneath that polished façade.

Oh, she was being hopelessly irrational, she told herself impatiently. What on earth was the matter with her? It was impossible to fault his behaviour, but there was that sense of a barrier between them, indefinable and unexplainable. He would be talking easily, he would smile, take her arm to guide her, place his arm around her shoulders to draw her protectively aside should the occasion demand it, and yet there was nothing behind it all, and in his eyes she would suddenly notice that strangely disturbing quality which had intrigued her at their very first meeting. From behind it he observed everything but allowed no one, even her, a glimpse of his true thoughts.

She began to worry. Was he hopelessly bored with her company? Putting up with it until the mock honeymoon was over and they returned to London, where he would lose himself in his work and his interests, whatever they might be, leaving her to make her own life within the outer frame they presented to the onlooker. She discovered that this possibility was as daunting as her first fear of demands for a sexual relationship without love. Certainly there seemed no likelihood of that fear ever being realised now! Not since that first night had he made the slightest attempt to kiss her, let alone anything else.

She found her curiosity about him becoming more demanding and almost like a child hoarding secrets she stored up the little she did learn of him through day to day observation.

He disliked untidiness. He was extremely fastidious about cleanliness and his clothes. He enjoyed football but not cricket, swimming but not tennis; he liked the theatre and orchestral music but not opera.

'It was spoiled for me for ever at my very first opera when I was about fifteen,' he told her one evening as they returned to the hotel after the awe-inspiring and memorable performance of Son et Lumière under the rich starry sky at Giza.

Lissa was still profoundly moved by the spectacular play of light and the dramatic intensity of the story of old Egypt. Jarret's mention of opera made her think of the first time she had seen Verdi's *Traviata* and how instantly the passion of the music could evoke sheer emotional spine tingles in someone as romantically receptive as herself.

'What happened?' she asked, sensing a wave of re-membered amusement in him. 'Did the scenery fall over, or something?'

'Not exactly. But the tenor was quite rotund and Mimi somewhat substantial. When they got to the death-throes duet he had to sink frantically down beside her on the bed and sing his heart out, but the bed gave a most alarm-ing creak and started to sag visibly. My friend started to giggle, all those ominous creaks that were never in Puccini's score, and at the finish we just fell about in our seats, I'm afraid. Since then I've never been able to suspend disbelief sufficiently to take opera seriously.'

'You should try just listening to it,' she suggested gently.

'Maybe I will some time.'

So he did possess a sense of humour, albeit a wicked one, she thought, and hoped that the intervening years of adulthood had not eradicated it altogether from his nature. Shared laughter could be a vital bridge between two people whose other bridges had yet to be forged.

'By the way, did you do those cards?' he asked.

'Yes. I posted them this morning.'

That was another of his dislikes. He hated letter writing, and while he was quite willing to help choose the inevitable picture postcards to send off to all the people who would be affronted if they were not remembered he would write only the one for Emma. Lissa had to do the rest. It was no use shutting one's eyes to one certain fact; he was arrogant in some ways. He expected service to be impeccable and was quite capable of summoning higher authority if some underling failed to match up to his standard. And when Lissa's heart was touched by the hordes of dark-eyed appealing children who importuned the tourists at every turn he was not taken in by their crafty young wiles. He would brush them aside, impervious to their heart-melting protests, and stride on, urging Lissa ahead.

But he could be kind.

There was another English guest on their floor, whose table was next to theirs. She was a gentle little woman, about sixty, with that sad, indefinable look of being alone in the world. One morning, while Jarret was having some difficulty in making a phone call to his London office, Lissa wandered out into the sunshine to wait for him and encountered Miss Chalmers in the palm garden.

It was the old, familiar story that was poured out into Lissa's sympathetic ear; the unmarried daughter left at home, to nurse first an ageing father and then a cantankerous mother, who at last departed this world at the age of eighty-nine with a grumble still on her lips. Miss Chalmers was alone, with a great rambling old house, unmodernised since its Edwardian bricks were first laid, filled with the sad ghosts of her lost youth. Bewildered by her new freedom, unable to believe that there was no one left to bully her, Henrietta Chalmers gave in to the urging of friends and took what was for her long-crushed spirit a tremendous plunge. She sold the great house, bought a neat little modern flat, and spent some of her legacy on new clothes, a hair-do, and the kind of holiday she'd never had in a lifetime.

'Mother would never go anywhere else but Eastbourne,' she told Lissa, touching her obviously unfamiliar new hair-style. 'Of course it's a nice place, but we always had the same rooms in the same guest-house. The wallpaper got as familiar as the one at home,' she added sadly.

Within a few hours of this conversation little Miss Chalmers suffered a heart attack. The excitement and the unaccustomed heat proved too much for her. Lissa and Jarret had arrived back at the hotel just as the commotion was at its full height, and Jarret promptly took over.

He organised everything—comforted the stricken woman, dealt with formalities, ensured that she would have the best possible treatment, and contacted her closest friend back home. He also visited poor frightened Miss Chalmers in hospital the following day and promised to keep in touch, assuring her that if it became necessary he would see to all the arrangements for her flight home.

'But I'm sure you'll be feeling much better by the time we get back next week,' he told her. 'The doctors says it's just a minor attack, but they want to make sure you rest. Now promise me you won't lie here and worry yourself sick.'

A faint touch of pink came into Miss Chalmers' wan cheeks as he patted her hand. 'You're too kind, all this trouble for someone you don't know,' she whispered.

'Nonsense!'

It was another memory for Lissa, another piece to add to the incomplete jigsaw of the man who stood tall and authoritative by the bedside. He exuded strength and reliability, and Lissa was beginning to realise how easy it would be simply to take advantage of this and lean on his strength. When one saw this side of his nature one could forgive that arrogance which irked her at times.

He did not forget his promise when he and Lissa departed at the weekend to fly to Aswan for the second stage of their supposed honeymoon. The magic of discovery and the fabled sights that awaited her fired Lissa with renewed wonder during the journey into Egypt's past. Slowly she was gaining confidence and losing the dreadful apprehension that had hung over her wedding day like a dark cloud. She was beginning to enjoy herself, and the realisation of her childhood dream was heightened by a tiny, secret flowering of tenderness for this other discovery, that this enigmatic man who had taken over her life was prepared to do so much for a stranger.

Yet why should his kindness to poor Miss Chalmers surprise her? she wondered. Wouldn't anyone have done the same? She would have done all in her power to help had he not been present—even if she wouldn't have organised the aid as quickly and efficiently as the masterful Jarret, who at this moment had gone to telephone the hospital.

And so the wonders encountered on the journey through Upper Egypt were pinpointed like flags on a map by the reports on Miss Chalmers' progress. The evening at Abu Simbel found her comfortable, at Edfu they heard she was improving, by enchanting Luxor and the Valley of the Kings she was feeling better, and on the evening after their explorations at Karnak they were told she would probably be well enough to be discharged from hospital by the weekend and resume her holiday provided she took things very quietly.

They found her looking pale but strangely tranquil when they flew back to Cairo that second weekend. Lissa felt surprise; she had expected a tremulous, scared woman, feverishly packing to get back home as quickly as possible, to friends and familiar neighbours before anything else happened to her. But no, Miss Chalmers had another two weeks booked and she was going to stay, heart attacks or not.

'If I go home I shall have to look after myself—cook

and wash dishes,' she said calmly. 'Here I can sit down at the dining table and be waited on—and then get up and leave it all afterwards.'

She held out thin, blue-veined hands that betrayed traces of many years of servitude. 'I can never thank you for being so very kind to me—I wish there were something I could do in return.'

'Please—don't.' Jarret held up his hand. 'It was nothing.'

'To me it was a great deal. But I mustn't keep you.' Miss Chalmers released Lissa's hand. 'You'll be wanting to go out on the town as this is your last night.'

Jarret glanced at his watch, and smiled faintly. 'I don't think so—I'm taking my wife to make her farewell to the Pyramids at dawn. That is, if I can persuade her to get up early enough.'

This husbandly quip, delivered with a suitably teasing sidelong glance at Lissa, drew a chuckle from Miss Chalmers, as doubtless Jarret intended it should. He thrust a friendly hand under Lissa's arm as they bade Miss Chalmers goodnight and turned away, and Lissa experienced a sudden rush of pleasure. The way he had said it, as though she truly belonged to him, was strangely warming.

The sense of pleasure lasted until they reached their suite, even though he had dropped his hand away from her almost immediately they left Miss Chalmers. Then as she walked into the sitting room Lissa looked at Jarret and saw that his expression had become remote.

She smiled tentatively at him, suddenly wanting to retain that fleeting sense of belonging, and said brightly, 'Miss Chalmers looked much better than I expected, didn't she?'

'Yes.' The withdrawn expression did not change. 'Do you want a drink or anything?'

'No, thanks.' Her smile ebbed and she felt empty.

'I should turn in then. We'll be having a very early call.'

The whole look of him as he turned away was impersonal, and for a moment she stared at the dark back of his head and the broad outline of his shoulders under the crisp beige cotton of his shirt. Then the door of his bedroom swung partly closed, cutting off the sight of him, and Lissa was alone, alone with a strange sensation of something very like rejection. Abruptly, and impatient with herself, she went into her own room to sort out her packing.

They'd been living out of suitcases for the past week of travel; she'd better decide on what she would wear for the morning's trip and leave out her travelling outfit and then do as much packing as she could now. There wouldn't be much time tomorrow ... She was foolish imagining that cold air of rejection ... Jarret was probably travel-weary. They'd covered a tremendous area this past week, so much that her own memories were becoming a little confused when she tried to remember each day clearly. And it had been incredibly hot. She hadn't imagined it could be so hot in early April, far hotter than any English midsummer heatwave she could recall. It was bound to affect a person's temperament. But he had turned away without saying goodnight.

Lissa settled down to sleep, trying to subdue renewed doubts and fears. She had to realise that two weeks was far too brief a space of time in which to build a stable and amicable relationship with a stranger, especially when one had married that stranger within the kind of circumstance that no normal marriage began with. And she had been just as much a stranger to him ...

How had he felt, deep within, under that cool, self-possessed façade of his? Had he been beset by any regrets on that coldly functional and strangely unreal day two weeks ago—and the debacle the night had become? Had he suddenly come to his senses and wondered what madness had possessed him to enter into such a marriage? And what were those 'domestic problems' he had mentioned that evening when he made his startling proposal of marriage? Problems which only a wife could solve?

Tomorrow they would be going back. Tomorrow she would have to begin facing those unknown problems ...

The thought brought her quivering back to full wakefulness. She caught at the timorous concern, trying to check it; she must not allow herself to become emotional again. Jarret had set an easy pace during these last two weeks, proving himself to be courteous, considerate and undemanding emotionally, almost as though he intended to smooth her new path as much as possible during the first few difficult weeks, and when she pondered on this it was difficult to believe that he had given way to that turbulent onslaught of contempt on their wedding night. She sighed; no one could ever predict and iron out all the ragged edges in the weave of human nature. All she could do was to resolve to play the part she had undertaken. And she could best do that by remaining calm and rational, remembering always the very real debt she had now to begin repaying.

She closed her eyes, aware of the knot of tension within her at last releasing its grip now that she was satisfied the answers logic had provided. Presently she slept, no breath of suspicion coming to disturb her—or warn that within a few hours something was to happen that would make this frail resolve almost impossible to keep.

At first it seemed as though it was going to be easier than she expected.

After their early start the next morning, and she noticed that Jarret still wore that air of restraint as they were driven to Giza through the cool mist of pre-dawn, Lissa simply stayed quiet. If he felt moody, or just uncommunicative, she would be patient until he emerged from it. After all, she told herself with this precious new-found calmness, when two people lived together there had to come a time for dropping the façade of polite pretence. Marriage, even a pretend marriage, must take on the quality of family life, with its give and take, its squabbles and its loyalties, and most of all, of being able to be oneself. But when the mist turned to gold, a beautiful veil that began to part like webs of gossamer, and then revealed the great conical shapes outlined against the sky and the mystical reaches of the desert, she could not stem an exclamation of sheer wonder.

'Isn't it beautiful? I—I can't think of words to describe it!' she exclaimed in wonder.

'Why try, then?' he said in prosaic tones.

The smile stopped curving her mouth. She turned to look at his profile. 'Jarret ...' she bit her lip and hesitated for a moment, 'is something worrying you?'

'No.' His head did not turn in acknowledgement. 'Why should I be worried?'

'I don't know. I—I just wondered.' She sighed inwardly; there didn't seem anything else to say to his unhelpful reply.

The car stopped, and soon she had something to take her mind, even if only temporarily, off Jarret's aloofness. Their guide and camels awaited to take them the rest of the way to the Great Pyramid of Cheops.

Lissa looked uncertainly at the camel allotted to her, and the camel stared surlily into the distance. Its handler made encouraging gestures, and aware of Jarret waiting somewhat impatiently to see her safely mounted she approached her kneeling steed cautiously. Climbing on to the big saddle with its ornamental fringe was comparatively easy, but how she managed to stay aboard as the great beast lumbered to its feet at the guide's command she never knew. She was pitched forward, sideways and back, hanging on frantically to the pommels, while her ship of the desert splayed out first one foot, then the second, then the third and then the fourth until his four great lanky legs were planted foursquare and the ground seemed a frighteningly long way below. Then the camel plodded forward, and Lissa did not dare look back to see how Jarret was faring.

She was just beginning to get into the rhythm of camel riding by the time they reached the base of the Pyramid and the performance of getting off had to be faced. It wasn't as bad this time, and when Chocko had stowed away his complement of legs and she slid to the ground she was helpless with laughter. Chocko returned to his disdainful survey of the horizon; he spent his days transporting stupid humans who were too lazy to walk the last hundred yards or so, and Lissa changed her English mind about venturing a friendly pat anywhere near those large teeth.

'Congratulations! You stayed on!' Jarret came to her side, and as he looked down into her mirthful face his own expression had lightened and she felt a sudden welling of relief.

'Of course I stayed on—I thoroughly enjoyed it. Now what?'

'We go up.'

'Up?'

'Yes. I thought we'd climb to the top—I gather it's one of the routine "musts", like doing the Tower in London.' Jarret paused enquiringly. 'If you've got the strength and the nerve, of course.'

Lissa craned her head back to stare up the vast edifice. Scramble up those great uneven blocks of time-worn stone that soared skywards to the apex! Some of those blocks were so massive they would dwarf her if she stood against one of them. But why not? Think of the view!

'Come on, then!' she cried recklessly. 'What makes you think I haven't the nerve?' She saw Jarret's left brow twitch slightly but expressively, and suddenly she was possessed by wild exhilaration, as though she could tackle the world. She began to run forward, eagerly looking for the first foothold of what would surely prove a most memorable ascent. But the guide checked her.

'This way. It is better to begin here,' he directed, and paused, waiting for Jarret to move to where Lissa waited impatiently.

'Go on.' Jarret gave her a nudge, adding dryly, 'Ladies first!'

They began what was to be over an hour's exhausting climb. Long before she was halfway up Lissa was perspiring and beginning to slow her impetuous initial onslaught. She paused once to push back an irritating strand of hair which had escaped its clasp at the nape of her neck and persisted in sticking across her eyes. Her hand felt hot and rough from the scramble up the uneven tiers of stone, and she was aware of sudden impatience with herself when she measured her progress against the tireless agility of their guide. He was not a young man. His brown-burnt skin was lined and his hair grizzled where it showed under his white headdress, but she had a strong suspicion that he could have reached the top long since without her hampering presence.

Patiently, as though he divined her thought, he bade her rest a while, but she shook her head and started off again determinedly, realising that Jarret had planned their early start so that they would accomplish the climb, or most of it, before the rising sun poured its full heat into the morning air.

At last that tantalising apex seemed to stop appearing as far away as ever and actually be within reach. Lissa hauled herself triumphantly over the last great step, scarcely conscious of a quick, shadowing movement overtaking her, and then Jarret was reaching down to grasp her hand and pull her on to the summit.

Too spent to speak, she collapsed breathlessly on the smooth, worn surface and gazed up at him.

'Don't look at me,' he said dryly. 'Look at that view.'

He took her hand to draw her up to his side as he spoke, and placed his arm round her shoulder. Instantly she was thankful for its steadying presence. Her head was spinning, and her body seemed to have lost its equilibrium, almost as though it no longer belonged to her. She rested back against Jarret, taking deep breaths and feeling the quickened rise and fall of his own breathing against her shoulder. A sudden impulse warned her not to look down—not yet!—and she resisted the instinctive temptation to take that enquiring glance down at the dwarfed scene so far below. Instead she looked straight into the distance, and it was as wonderful and awe-inspiring as she had imagined.

There seemed no words to express the sense of wonder and the atmosphere the very air possessed. There was the great sea of desert, stretching towards infinity, timeless as the three great sentinels of the Pharaohs, mysterious as the strange, watchful Sphinx, that inscrutable guardian of the gates of history itself, making man's time so transient and his being so puny against the might his own strength had raised as a monument to his passing.

'There's Cairo,' Jarret murmured, pointing.

She turned her head, seeing to the east the sprawl of the city, faintly misted by distance, unreal, like a tinted illustration from an Arabian Nights story book.

Jarret's arm fell away from her shoulder. 'Shall we sit down and rest for a while?'

Without speaking Lissa sat down on the smooth, warm stone, seeing the network of carved initials imprinted

there by travellers down the ages. Some were weather-
worn, some looking as fresh cut as though abraded only
yesterday, and she wondered how many down the ages had
sat here, wondering, awed, moved by the age-old magic
of Egypt and compelled to leave the small, innocent de-
facement as a subconsciously defiant gesture to prove that
they too had once, fleetingly, been part of that magic.

Jarret seemed disinclined to talk and she made no attempt
to break in on his mood. Silence was right at this moment,
and she folded her arms round her up-drawn knees and
allowed the sense of timelessness to steal over her, making
her forget her aching limbs and the thirst that was drying
her mouth. The real world, her world, had receded far
away and she had no wish to recall it. Their guide had
ceased his tourist piece and moved a couple of stone
blocks distant, to seat himself on the edge and stare
silently into infinity, at once merging into the scene that
was today and four thousand years old. Then Jarret moved
slightly, the now brilliant sun struck a glancing spark off the
glass of his wrist watch, and suddenly Lissa felt as though
she had received an electric shock. The strange disem-
bodied sensation left her, she forgot her surroundings,
past and present, and all the musing thoughts that had
flitted through her mind. Her whole being was awake,
totally sensitive and aware of only one thing; the man at
her side.

She swallowed through a dry throat and stared at the
watch on Jarret's wrist. It was like the hypnotist's talisman
swinging on a chain, the key to the threshold of trance. Or
the ordained code symbol that snapped one back into
reality!

She did not know how long the spell of fascination lasted.
She knew only that everything about Jarret was newly
and acutely defined, with the sharpness and clarity of
crystal, and it was as though she were seeing him for the
first time. And then looking was not enough.

Lissa began to tremble inside herself. She tightened her
fingers where they clasped round her knees, willing them
not to betray her disturbing impulses. She dared not
reach out to touch Jarret's tanned forearm, experience the
sensuous roughness of the dark hairs that glinted with

bronze lights where the sunlight touched them ... trace the pulsing cord of the vein that ridged under the skin and linger on the hard sweep of sinew that ran from wrist to elbow, warm and male and strong ... Lissa's heart was thumping, and she dragged her gaze away. But it proved a dangerously disturbing move.

Jarret was staring meditatively into the distance, seemingly unconscious even of her presence and unaware that her feverish eyes were drinking in his features as never before. His profile. A broad forehead with the beginning of a slightly crooked worry line running obliquely across it. Dark hair with a bronze glaze rippling over it. Shadowing brows and those thick black lashes fringing hooded lids that had affected her at the first moment of meeting— except that no omen had warned her of the devastating effect to come. Why did the lean cheek and jawline above a stubborn chin make one man into magic? And a special serious mouth with certain clear-cut lines make her fingertips ache to trace its contours?

A soft, tremulous sigh escaped Lissa. Still he did not move, and inexorably this new, overwhelming power of emotion drove her gaze to explore anew the shape of his head, the strong curve of his throat, and the way the front of his open-necked shirt fell away slightly at one side, forming an almost irresistible invitation to a soft, tentative hand to steal into that secret shadowy place and caressingly explore the hard male shape of shoulder and chest ...

He turned his head and looked straight into her eyes.

Lissa froze. Of its own volition her hand was in mid-air, as though seeking, and then her whole body was shaking all over, as though with an ague. Then the dangerous, erotic fantasy was broken and she felt waves of scarlet heat flood up into her face. She must be insane!

For what seemed like an eternity she withstood that long, considering gaze that must see right into the guilty depths of her soul. She tried to laugh, to say something normal as she thrust her trembling hands behind her back before they betrayed her any further, but her mouth felt paralysed and her mind empty of everything except shame and the appalling realisation of what had happened to her.

Jarret's brows went up, and the corners of his mouth

lifted a fraction in what might be the beginning of a smile—
or the derisive recognition of the cause of the agitation
surely written clearly all over her face.

But all he said was, 'If you're rested now, we'll move.'

Lissa felt faint with reaction. 'Yes—of course. If you
... yes, we'd better get back. The packing ... But isn't it
all wonderful ...?' Her voice trailed away. She knew she
was stammering hopelessly, but she was incapable of
stringing together lucid sentences at that moment. Fear
was sharp in her; *had he noticed?* If only he hadn't guessed.
She'd once read somewhere that a man could always tell
when a woman was physically aware of him. Oh, how could
she bear it if he knew?

Fighting for control, she scrambled to her feet, making
much of the actions of dusting down her pale green slacks
and straightening the set of her thin lemon cotton blouson,
praying as she did so that the warmth of shame would fade
from her cheeks. The tall Arab had seen them move and
was now waiting to guide them down the descent. It was
then that Lissa, desperate to escape those disturbing moments, made an unsteady step and stumbled. She had
not yet regained composure, and as she saw the great side
of the Pyramid falling away beneath her, down that tremendous distance to where the figures of people looked
like pygmies and a Land Rover on the blue-grey ribbon
of track seemed reduced to the dimensions of a child's
miniature toy, a wave of dizziness sent her off balance.
Then a hard, swift arm gripped round her waist and pulled
her against warm, firm security.

'Take your time!' Jarret exclaimed. 'The Pyramids are
definitely not for falling off!'

It sounded like a joke, but there was certainly no humour
in his voice. Lissa giggled on a note suspiciously like
hysteria. 'Perhaps it's the curse of the Kings!'

'I don't think so. I forgot to ask you if you've a good
head for heights!'

'But I have as a rule—*oh!* My shoe!'

In her stumble her heel had come partly out of her
light casual shoe, and as she straightened, drawing away
from Jarret's supporting arm, it slipped off her foot and
went bouncing down the uneven blocks below.

'Oh, God!' Jarret groaned. 'Look—sit down, Lissa, and try not to do anything else silly.' He moved away, beginning to clamber down towards where the errant shoe had, fortunately, come to rest on a ledge about fifteen feet below.

But the guide was almost there before Jarret got the words out of his mouth. His brown face smiling now, the Arab came swiftly back up again, holding out the shoe to Lissa. He murmured something which Lissa did not quite catch, except for the word eagle, and she shook her head slightly as she smiled and thanked him, then bent to put on her shoe. When she straightened Jarret was grinning.

'Queen Cinderella!' he said, sardonically. 'Let me make sure that flimsy bit of footwear really fits.'

To her surprise, he bent and put his hand round her instep, making sure the shoe was snugly in place.

'And what was all that about?' she asked, when he stood straight.

'There's an old legend about a queen of ancient Egypt,' he told her, 'the very first Cinderella. A beautiful young girl called Nitaquert, whose golden sandal was stolen by an eagle one day when she was bathing in the river. The legend has it that the eagle flew to the King's court and dropped the golden sandal right into the King's lap. And surely you can guess the rest,' he concluded with a cynical grin.

'Oh, yes, the King sent his servants out all over the land to find the girl who fitted the golden sandal and then married her.' The incident had given Lissa a chance to regain her normal manner and she met Jarret's teasing grin quite levelly. 'Now pull the other one!'

'Not until we're safely down.' The teasing tone had vanished and for a moment he studied her flushed face. 'Just try to keep your mind on that, Lissa,' he added somewhat grimly.

Her expression sobered, and she avoided his eyes as she turned obediently towards the guide. The descent proved to be a nerve-tautening experience, one that demanded full control over one's wits. But despite this Lissa found it extremely difficult to dispel every other consideration but the one most immediate. Not when she had made such a shattering discovery about the state of her heart! Or the loss of it!

For somehow, somewhere during these two brief weeks Jarret had taken possession, not only of the next five years of life, but of her love as well.

CHAPTER FOUR

THE flight home was not exactly uneventful. There was a storm over Europe, a middle-aged passenger was taken ill and was found to be a diabetic in need of glucose to counteract a threatening insulin coma, and a small boy travelling by air for the first time was fractious and temperamental for a good deal of the flight time, refusing to respond to all efforts made to divert his boredom.

'At least you won't have any nonsense like that from Emma,' Jarret remarked when the problem child was carried screaming and kicking back to his place for about the sixth time. 'She's a very well behaved little girl,' he added.

'Will she be meeting us?' Lissa asked.

'No. I thought we'd drive down tomorrow and collect her. With air travel as it is these days one has to be prepared for delays and there's no sense in having a young child hanging around waiting at the airport and getting strung up with excitement.' He glanced at his watch. 'Though we seem to be well on time so far.'

So they would be on their own tonight. Lissa felt mingled disappointment and relief. She was looking forward to meeting Emma with a certain amount of trepidation. Supposing Emma did not like her; there was always an element of unpredictability where a child was concerned. Emma might resent her, might secretly hate the thought of anyone coming to usurp her mother's place. Equally, Emma might be thankful that Lissa's advent meant the renewal of her home relationship with her father.

How close were father and daughter? Lissa wondered. Jarret had not been exactly forthcoming about his personal life and his little girl. Did the child still grieve desperately for her mother?

Lissa began to feel more and more uncertain as the flight neared its destination. She knew so little of what awaited her. A strange home, strange possessions, and strange faces, and only an enigmatic man to guide her through the maze of new relationships she would have to enter.

It was raining when they finally touched down, a thin drizzle that chilled the air and rapidly banished the lingering warmth of the Egyptian sun. When they were cleared and getting into the car Lissa was beginning to feel very much as she had felt exactly two weeks before. Then she was setting out with a man she hardly knew, now she was returning to almost as much bewildering uncertainty.

She lapsed into silence, for once thankful that Jarret was not the kind of man who indulged in much small-talk, still less when he was driving, and allowed her imagination to travel ahead to his home. All she knew was that it was a penthouse in a luxury block overlooking Hyde Park. An address with prestige, Lissa's mother had observed with satisfaction, but Jarret had not taken Lissa to see the place which was to be her future home. A disturbing thought occurred as she remembered this; surely he did not intend to cut her off from her family? But she dismissed the fear as quickly as it came; there would be a reason behind Jarret's reticence.

The reason was disclosed sooner than Lissa expected.

She had been prepared for luxury, but Jarret's home rendered her almost speechless when the lift decanted them out at the top floor and Jarret opened the white door.

Lissa walked into the largest sitting room she had ever entered. It was split level, with the lower section in the shape of a vast piano lid, and the big curve formed a lushly cushioned seating area. Walls, carpet and upholstery were in ivory, with only the muted colours of smoke glassware dotted about and scattered cushions of an unusual terra-cotta silk material. There was a wall-to-wall window curtained with heavy flax, again of the same toning ivory tint, and centre of the lower level was a great square fireplace with a beaten copper hood. Lissa walked round it, with the interest of someone conditioned by the centuries of convention that placed a fireplace firmly against a wall. Closer inspection showed the fire to be electric, giving little heat when Jarret flipped a switch; as the room was perfectly warm the glowing logs were purely psychological comfort.

Jarret crossed the room and touched another switch, and Lissa forgot the fire. Three square columns marched the width of the far end of the room, whether for support or ornamentation she did not know, but the concealed lighting that had sprung to life was sheer theatrical embellishment. Pink, blue, amber, green ... the spectrum of soft colours played and changed and reached up the columns. Jarret touched her arm.

'I'll show you the rest of the place.'

The 'rest of the place' was equally luxurious and effectively designed. The first bedroom was large, done in varying shades of lilac with white furnishing and hangings. There was a modern four-poster bed of delicately scrolled satin brass and white lace curtains looped back with violet velvet ties. The carpet of deep purple provided a rich contrast.

The same colour theme was contained in the adjoining bathroom, where an ankle-deep white carpet framed a sunken bath of a luscious dark plum colour and a positive conservatory of tropical plants draped their exotic leaves and tendrils over serried glass shelves.

'Most of it was done to Claudine's design,' Jarret said as he led the way to another room, 'except this one and Emma's.'

Lissa felt a sharp little contraction in the pit of her stomach. This was the first time he had referred to his late wife in the course of casual conversation. But Lissa made no comment beyond a conventional response, knowing already that Jarret would impart personal details of his life prior to marrying herself only when he was ready. Then an involuntary murmur not exactly of disappointment but something little short of it escaped her as she walked through the doorway of the second bedroom.

It was so plain, in total contrast to the luxury she had just left. Cream walls, curtains of an uninspired abstract design of brown and cream, with the same pattern repeated in the duvet flung over the divan bed, and fitted furniture of the simplest, severest lines. There was a third bedroom, this time stunningly aglow with crimsons and the palest of pinks; plainly this one owed its style to Claudine, as did the kitchen, a huge, farmhouse pine affair with every fitting the kitchen slave could wish.

A slight smile touched Jarret's mouth while Lissa went eagerly from gleaming double-bowled sink to split-level cooker and the broad preparation area with the big food mixer and the row of copper pans above that shone as though they were never used. She opened unit doors, peeped into the fitted cutlery drawer, and eyed the hostess trolley with its flambé gadget. It would take her a week to discover everything!

Emma's room proved to be a small girl's dream domain—a miniature suite, tailored within the reach of a little girl, sunshine yellow and white decor, and Emma's own special touches. A big panda poster on the wall near the bed—and Paddington. Paddington on the pillows, Paddington on the walls, and Paddington on the bed. Only the famous bear himself was missing, doubtless keeping Emma company wherever she happened to be at that moment.

They returned to the living room and Lissa said slowly, 'It's a beautiful home. Your wife—Claudine,' she hesitated a little awkwardly, 'she had a tremendous flair for colour.'

'Yes.' Jarret's response sounded non-committal.

Lissa saw the closed expression forming its shutter over his features. She said hastily. 'Shall I make some coffee? I've got to start finding my way round the kitchen before the next meal-time comes round.'

'Yes, do that.' His voice wasn't quite so clipped this time. 'I'll see to those cases. Which room would you like?'

Lissa had not yet thought of this and she hesitated. Jarret waited in the doorway, then gave an impatient gesture of dismissal. 'You'd better have the main one—you won't be there for long, anyway.'

'I won't be . . . ?' Lissa stared at him, not comprehending.

'For God's sake!' he exclaimed roughly. 'Don't start reading *that* into a remark that means something totally different. I'm not suggesting that you'll be moving in with me! I——'

'But I didn't think that!' she broke in wildly. 'It was just that I hadn't thought ... I——'

'You were wondering where exactly I intended sleeping.' He cut her stammering protests short. 'Don't worry—I haven't forgotten the rules of the contract,' he added curtly.

'Please—hear me out,' she begged. 'I was wondering which room *you* would want. And I certainly won't take the principal room—either of the others—the little one will do me fine. We may have guests ... No, you stay in the——'

'Amid all that purple? Like a funeral parlour? No, thanks.' He stepped out into the hall and picked up one of the cases. 'It's a woman's room, pure and simple.'

Sudden hysteria overcame Lissa for a moment. 'Not for the murder in the purple penthouse?'

He shot her a quelling look; plainly his sense of humour had not yet made it back from Cairo. 'Why don't you get on with the coffee and stop arguing?' he suggested in a bored voice.

Biting her lip, Lissa went to obey. The brief flash of hysterical mirth had gone, leaving a hurt look in her eyes as she began to search for the necessary things. It seemed the honeymoon was well and truly over, but then it wasn't a honeymoon, she reminded herself bitterly, even if she'd suddenly realised the things Jarret could do to her emotions. This morning at Giza ...

Was it only this same day? Not a million miles away in space? If Jarret had chosen to make love to her this morning he might have found a totally different response from the one of that unhappy wedding night. But he wouldn't have chosen to make love to her this morning, in broad daylight and in view of the coachload of about fifty tourists who'd rolled up as they were leaving.

Lissa opened the fridge door abruptly. She would be very foolish if she didn't come to terms with the fact that she was a paid employee. Only that way, and by quelling her foolish emotions before they got the upper hand, would bring acceptance of Jarret's lapses into brusque behaviour. But her new heightened emotions did not want to accept the dictate of common sense. They were re-membering the way Jarret had kissed her that first night in Cairo. They wanted to experience those kisses again, to discover what it would be like to surrender to them instead of fighting them . . .

Lissa compressed her lips tightly and tried to curb the disturbing sensations beginning to riot through her body. She had not wanted kisses or any kind of lovemaking from Jarret that night. She had been petrified at the thought of having a man she did not love take possession of her during a mood of temporary wildness. But now she was beginning to perceive just what passion and love were all about, and the thought of Jarret making love to her was tantalising beyond endurance.

She measured milk into the pan and tried to harden her heart. Did she want lovemaking without love? Did she want to be awakened fully to physical desire as well as the longing of the heart? Knowing that there was no commitment from Jarret, and knowing that a man could walk away from a woman he did not love and not even glance back, even though he had just possessed her?

Lissa knew the answer to this and it brought no balm to her spirit. Sighing, she looked for a tray on which to set the coffee and cups, and saw the note beside the bread-bin, weighted by a condiment pot. The note said it hoped three pints of milk would suffice, that there was butter, cheese and salami in the fridge, a toaster loaf in the bread-bin, and a home-made steak pie in the freezer, ready to warm through tomorrow. Then followed the initials M. R. This must be the housekeeper Jarret had mentioned, Mrs Ridge.

The note was a prosaic reminder that from now on she had a responsibility towards Jarret: the running of his home and the care of his child. Lissa picked up the tray and took a deep breath, determined to remain cool and not allow Jarret's needling to provoke her again. Pride must give way a little, for her own sake, and take the lesser line of resistance until the first strangeness of her new life wore off and she gained more confidence.

As she carried the tray through to the living room a telephone shrilled somewhere. She looked round, not seeing the source of the ringing in the still unfamiliar room, then heard Jarret's voice from the doorway. 'Okay, I'll take it through here.'

'Don't be long—the coffee's ready,' she called quickly.

But there was no reply. She set the tray down on a big square coffee table with a gleaming top of pale-coloured tiles that formed an Italianate pattern. For a moment she stood by the softly glowing fire, then turned restlessly and wandered across the room. The sound of the phone had reminded her that she must ring home as soon as she'd had her coffee. They'd be wondering if she was safely home. How would her father be ...?

She came to the broad window and peered out into the darkness. The rain had stopped and the sky was clear, showing pinpoints of stars emerging triumphantly where the dull clouds had hung sullenly an hour or so ago.

The view was panoramic. London lay like a carpet of lights glittering to the horizon. In daylight it would be fascinating to look out and try to pick out landmarks. At the moment everything was very strange, and the anonymous darkness heightened this feeling. She could be anywhere, Lissa thought, a wry smile curving her lips, and in all that fathomless city of light out there she knew not one soul. Only the man to whom she had delivered her fate for the next five years ...

It was a sobering thought, enough to bring the qualms and uncertainties back in full force, and she did not hear the light footfalls in the thick, sound-deadening carpet. When Jarret spoke she jumped with shock and spun round.

His brow flickered. 'Did I startle you?'

She managed an awkward laugh. 'I was miles away. What's the view like in daylight?'

'Well, there's a good view of concrete in various shapes and sizes,' he said dryly.

Her wide gaze obviously did not quite believe him, silently reproaching the cynical observation, and something flickered in his expression, something she could not read.

'Don't get too attached to the view, Lissa,' he said rather sharply. 'Or to the place itself. As I said before, you won't be here very long.'

Lissa experienced another kick of shock, and in lightning flashes her imagination supplied a series of disastrous answers. He'd changed his mind. He'd decided it wasn't going to work out after all. He was going to have the marriage annulled ...

He had turned away, moving down the room. 'I've finally made up my mind to get rid of this place,' he said over his shoulder. 'I want a proper home, a house with a garden round it and space for a child to play.'

The relief that flooded round Lissa's heart made her feel weak. She hurried to the table and picked up the coffee pot with a hand that trembled as she did so. 'Of course,' she said unsteadily, 'Emma ... she'll want somewhere with neighbouring children to play with.'

Jarret accepted the coffee. 'Yes, this is no place to rear a child. Nor can I live with ghosts.'

His dark head was bent, so that she could not make out his expression. He could only mean Claudine. He must have loved her very much ...

Lissa tried to quell the sadness of this thought. Of course he loved his dead wife; she must accept that and not think of the knell to her own fragile, burgeoning hopes that she hardly dare admit to in the deepest, most secret part of her heart. She must feel sadness and compassion only for the man and his loss.

'I'm sorry,' she murmured softly.

He made a small movement with one shoulder, almost dismissive, and stared at the flicker of crimson amid the glowing simulation of logs under the great canopy. For a moment Lissa had the impression that he was despising all artificiality, then he glanced at her and the impression fled.

'That was my secretary,' he said crisply. 'She's on her way here now, so would you rustle up some fresh coffee— she's strictly teetotal.'

'Yes, of course.' Lissa glanced at her watch, noting it showed a quarter after nine and reflecting that Jarret's secretary must be very devoted to duty to be prepared to turn out for her boss at nine o'clock on a Saturday evening. Then, inevitably, the stab of jealous suspicion. Was she a gorgeous, glamorous charmer who had no objection to assuaging her boss's loneliness when he needed her ...?

Lissa felt ashamed of the thought, and doubly so when Mrs Bell arrived shortly afterwards. Jarret's secretary was slim, chic, and definitely on the erring side of forty. Two minutes in her brisk friendly company was enough to banish any doubts about a possible sidekick in the office!

Mrs Bell was a little breathless as she sorted out a folder of papers. 'I'm so glad you got back because I really feel we'll have to move fast on this one. That is if you like it.'

The papers proved to be estate agents' details of houses, and it seemed she had spent a good deal of the past two weeks seeing properties that might measure up to Jarret's specifications. These had been winnowed down to three hopeful possibles, then unexpectedly another house had come on to the market which was rather special and exactly what Jarret required.

'It may not be quite large enough—you'd have to turn the small bedroom into a second bathroom on the first floor, but the top floor would make a splendid guest suite, or convert into a big playroom for Emma. It's period, about 1800, and there's a walled garden at the back and a dear coach house,' Mrs Bell hurried on enthusiastically. 'Right on the Heath, too. You could wait years for such a perfect gem to come on the market.'

'What about the others?'

'Well, the one at Kew is very nice. Edwardian, a bit Gothic, but well modernised. The price is hefty, and they're refusing offers, so it may stick for a while. The other is in Knightsbridge in a square, frightfully residential, prestige accommodation—short lease, though,' Mrs Bell laughed, 'I'm beginning to talk like an estate agent! Of course the price is astronomical.'

'I'd like to see the Richmond property.' Jarret frowned over the papers. 'Have you got the number?'

'Yes, I made a tentative appointment for Monday afternoon.' Mrs Bell hesitated. 'I also made arrangements for you to see the Hampstead place tomorrow morning. I hope I did the right thing.'

'I was planning on collecting Emma tomorrow,' he said, his brow furrowing. 'Is it as urgent as that?'

'Yes, you see it's one of these odd set-ups. It's one of those places lots of people have had their eye on for years, but after the owner died the heir had his own plans for it, but outline permission was refused and——'

'I'll make some coffee,' said Lissa, standing up. Suddenly she felt a little happier. Although Jarret's present home was luxurious to the last degree she suspected it could prove a very lonely spot to someone used to village life and the friendly gregariousness of neighbours, even if they did tend to be nosy about one's business. Here it might take years, if ever, to become acquainted with anyone other than the porter far below in that great palatial vestibule.

When she went back with the coffee, having discovered the ornate tea trolley with large wheels that glided like silk instead of the humpety-bump way the old trolley did at home, the discussion seemed to have ended. Jarret told her it was settled that they see the house next morning, then drive on down to Cranbrook after lunch to collect Emma.

Mrs Bell did not linger over her coffee and presently she rose, preparing to depart. Jarret insisted on calling a cab for her, and during the short time they waited until the porter buzzed to say the cab was there the conversation was general, impersonal. Then just before she turned to enter the lift Mrs Bell held out her hand to Lissa.

'I would like to wish you every happiness, Mrs Earle,' she said impulsively, 'and I do hope at least one of these houses will turn out to be your dream home.'

Touched, Lissa returned the warm handclasp with its unspoken offer of friendship and thanked her, while Jarret nodded gravely, making no comment. The lift sank, and Lissa and Jarret returned to the living room. The coffee things waited, and as Lissa piled them on the trolley some impulse made her look up at the great stretch of the room and exclaim: 'What a super place for parties! Loads of room to circulate.'

It was an innocent remark, an observation of fact made without thinking, but Jarret's face darkened and took on the set expression she had come to dread.

'I've gone off parties, I'm afraid,' he said coldly, 'so don't expect to have to play hostess at many of *those*.'

'I'm sorry.' The small glow died from her face and left it strained. 'I wasn't hinting that we ought to throw one.' She bent over the trolley, knowing she had not even begun to envisage herself hostessing the kind of revels this jet-plated apartment seemed to demand and unable to quell the smart of injustice.

'Oh, we used to have the fun people here, braying at one another over the din, consuming vast quantities of booze and shredding reputations for afters.' Jarret went to hold the door open for her and she glimpsed his cynical scorn. 'I could put up with that—and the bodies that wouldn't go home—but when it came to walking into one's own bedroom and finding a couple of guests had already staked their claim to the bed ...' his mouth went down at the corners. 'Is that the kind of life you imagined I led here?'

'Certainly not.' She looked at him and met his gaze levelly. 'I haven't presumed to imagine any kind of life you may have led prior to my knowing you. It's no concern of mine, Jarret, and you don't need to make any explanations.'

'I didn't intend to,' he returned coolly. 'I just don't want you to have any preconceived notions about my possible attachment to this place. Now,' his tone changed, became brisk, 'I suggest you ring your family and let them know you're back. Your father's bound to be anxious.'

Not for the first time Lissa wondered at his perception. How well he knew them, even though the sum total of actual acquaintance time was very short. He was well aware of how close was the affectionate relationship between father and daughter, and had no doubt discerned that Mrs Vayle was a practical woman who had never allowed sentiment to blind her to the hard realities of life.

Lissa felt a surge of love and joy when she heard her father's voice over the line a little while later. He said all was well and he was getting stronger every day, but there was a new dragon of a staff nurse on his ward who had been very sniffy about allowing him to take the call at that time of night. However, she had relented.

'I won't keep you,' Lissa said then, 'I have to phone Mummy as well.'

But when the second call was made she was aware of loneliness suddenly closing in on her. The sounds of family voices had come from across a gulf, the gulf that forms whenever a son or daughter marries and leaves the parental nest. Lissa had not felt it until now, there had been so much excitement, the journey, the wonders she had explored, and the not inconsequent preoccupation with the state of her own emotions. When at last she retired to the lilac and purple bedroom Jarret seemed to despise, Lissa was more conscious than ever of the lost feeling. Her girlhood roots had been pulled, and at present she was still in transit, in this luxurious, feminine bedroom that had belonged to another woman. Claudine ...

Lissa shivered, and concentrated on unpacking her cases, roughly sorting the contents and stowing them away. Perhaps tomorrow would bring new purpose and perhaps a more permanent home in which to begin afresh, without Jarret's ghosts ... And of course, there was Emma.

*   *   *

Lissa fell in love with the house the moment she stepped out of Jarret's car and took in the lovely warm old mellow brick lines of it, square, simple and satisfying, with four windows set each side of an elegant doorway and tall gracious central window. There was ivy at one side, neat box hedges screening the garden from the road, a sundial in the middle of the lawn, and curlicue iron boot-scrapers at the side of the three steps up to the front door with its half-moon fanlight above. But its atmosphere caught her immediately.

It was a happy house, it welcomed and shut out the cares of the world, and if it possessed ghosts they were serene, untroubled spirits. Lissa wandered from room to room while Jarret conferred with the agent. Except for slim, discreet radiators and the addition of a kitchen and bathroom wing the house still retained all its original period character, lovingly preserved by its former owners and kept in a state of remarkable good repair. Lissa could picture it curtained and furnished, softly lit and cosy against the dark cold winter nights, sunlit and airy and scented with the tangled roses and the straggling old lavender

bush by the back door in summer. There was the quaint
old timbered coach-house of which Mrs Bell had spoken,
and a large if somewhat ancient dog kennel in its sheltering
lee. There was even an old swing, its wooden seat worn
and polished by the generations of children who had slid
from it to run across the grass and into the house at the
bidding of mother, or nursemaid, or nanny. Lissa thrust
gently at it, trying to picture Emma sitting there.

If only Jarret chose this one!

Lissa tried to steel herself against the spell of the house.
She believed Jarret to be wealthy, but she could not imagine him being wealthy enough to contemplate buying a
house for which the asking price ran well into six figures.

'Well, what do you think of it?'

She caught the chain of the swing and stilled its motion,
not looking at Jarret.

'It's a very attractive house,' she said carefully. 'But
what a price!'

'Do you think Emma would like it?'

'I haven't met Emma,' she reminded him gently, 'but I
can't imagine her not liking it.'

He tested the support of the swing, pitting his strength
against it. He desisted, and looked down at her. 'Well?'

'I hope you're not asking me to make the decision.'

'I'm asking you if you like it?'

'I love it.' She turned to gaze at the house. 'I think
it's the most inviting and attractive house I've ever been
in. But ...'

'The economic climate worries you?' Jarret looked
amused. 'Go and wait in the car—the expression on your
face is liable to send the asking price up by another twenty
thousand!'

'I'd better try to look indifferent, I suppose.' She smiled
faintly and moved to obey.

The waiting time seemed to be an age while Lissa sat
in the car, trying not to look wistfully at the charming
old house and wonder what Jarret was saying to the agent.
At last the two men emerged from the front door, paused
a moment, then separated to get into their respective cars.
Jarret swung behind the wheel and drove off immediately
without speaking. When Lissa thought she couldn't bear

the suspense a moment longer Jarret said casually:

'I've taken an option on it.'

Lissa turned her head and studied his cool profile, unsure if this meant he'd made an offer for the house. As though aware of the unspoken doubt, he added, 'No one in their right senses plunges in headlong at that price before having a survey and independent valuation done. Of course it'll probably end up with a contract race.' His mouth lifted slightly at the corner. 'I suggest you put the matter out of your head for a few days. I'll let you know as soon as there's anything to report.'

And don't build up on getting it! She read the warning unspoken between the lines. How often had her father said to Pippa or herself: 'Now don't build up on it, lass ...' but somehow the longed-for treat had usually happened and all the secret building up had not led to disappointment.

But this was different. Lissa found it difficult to forget the house. It had made a tremendous impression on her, and not even the daunting reality that she rarely allowed herself to forget could banish the secret joyous hope that the miracle would happen and it would become their home. Even if she had to leave it all at the end of five years wouldn't those five years be well worth the wrench of parting?

The foolish, sad little figments of imagination could not be escaped. If only it were real! If only she and Jarret were really husband and wife, planning their dream home together, forging together a haven of enchantment in which the security of loving and sharing would be their shield against the world. Where they would weave the strands of their future, making Emma's world complete again, and hearing the laughter and scampering feet of a brother, and perhaps a sister, for Jarret's little girl ...

Dreams and whimsy kept Lissa preoccupied during the drive to Cranbrook where Emma's grandmother and aunt lived. They stopped for lunch on the way, and Jarret did not hurry, remarking that he did not want to arrive too early and find the family in the middle of lunch.

In Yalding they stopped for a little while to stroll by

the river and watch the boating enthusiasts taking full advantage of a mild, spring Sunday. As they got back into the car Jarret said abruptly, 'You're very quiet.'

'It—it isn't intentional,' she said after a hesitation.

'As long as you're not anticipating an ordeal.'

'I'm a bit nervous,' she admitted.

'I'd prefer you not to betray that, if possible.'

'I'll try not to—I only hope Emma isn't dreading *my* arrival.' Lissa's voice sounded as uncertain as she felt.

'It's possible that she is,' Jarret said in matter-of-fact tones. 'We have to be prepared for some uncertainty at least, but I don't anticipate any tantrums if that's what you're afraid of.'

He slowed, giving the courtesy of the road to a rider and receiving acknowledgement in return, then went on : 'I'm more concerned about your own reactions.'

'In what way?' Lissa was startled. Surely he didn't imagine she was going to be unkind to Emma! 'I promise you, I'll be very patient with her.'

'I'm not talking about Emma,' he said shortly. 'I'm talking about us. It hasn't mattered very much up till now, but in less than five minutes' time it's going to start mattering a great deal. Somehow, you have to try to pretend some vestige of affection for me, Lissa,' he added grimly.

The road had become narrow, and there was a high wall on the left. As Jarret's words impinged on her brain she saw the wide gates and felt the sway of pressure as he swung the car sharply into the drive that curved towards a big house half hidden behind trees. A few yards on and he halted the car, then turned to face her.

'A more virginal bride I've yet to see,' he almost groaned. 'For God's sake, Lissa, come here ...'

Before she realised his intention he snapped free of a confining seat belt and without waiting for his command to be obeyed he slewed across and reached for her.

The force of the movement brought his weight fully against her, his hands thrusting under her back. His breath fanned warmth on her cheek, then he swore under his breath : 'Damn seat belts!' and his hand sparked wild tremors through her as it slid over her thigh in its search for the belt release mechanism. Then the constriction gave and her body was free to be caught and curved pliantly up to the hard pressure of his.

For Lissa the world had stopped turning. When Jarret's mouth descended on hers she cared not that it brought the same impatience of the first time and the hint of suppressed violence. And when his mouth began to invade more intimately, with the kind of exploring kiss she'd never yet permitted any man to make, she felt only the fuse of a new desire spark to life and urge her body to seek for some strange hidden ecstasy hitherto only guessed at in the secret idealised romanticism of adolescence.

'Lissa ...' he said against her mouth, 'try putting your arms round me—it might help!'

Slowly, still uncertain, she raised her arms and slid her fingertips along the fine smooth stuff of his jacket, until they touched the thick dark hair just above the collar. Her fingertips wanted to ruffle and disturb the warm dark thickness, and then she felt the sigh that shivered through him. His hands parted her jacket fronts and homed to the slender shape of her beneath, drawing her insistently closer and deepening his kiss until her entire being seemed to be dissolving in a molten heat of desire.

Suddenly, as abruptly as he had initiated the embrace, Jarret released her and drew back, one hand rising to adjust the disturbed set of his tie. A faintly cynical smile touched his lips as Lissa sank back and weakly straightened her own disarray. She dared not look at him, not until she had regained her composure and the pounding drumbeat in her chest had subsided. But after a moment the slight smile left Jarret's mouth. He reached out and deliberately put a questioning finger along her jawline, turning her head and compelling her to meet his glance.

'Hm, a slight improvement, I think,' he said coolly. 'If you don't exactly have the look of a girl who's been thoroughly loved at least you appear to have given the matter some thought recently!'

With this sardonic observation he put the car into motion and drove the short remaining distance to the house. He got out and came swiftly round to the passenger side, to open the door and proffer a courteous hand.

'Come on,' he bade in a low voice, 'before the effect wears off!'

In silence she got out, to find a strong arm close instantly round her waist and fit her snugly into the contours of his side. Lissa did not resist; her limbs felt as though they moved through clouds of cottonwool. He walked her unhurriedly towards the front door, and to any casual or interested viewer they must surely seem like lovers closely enwrapped in their own private world of bliss.

But even the warm nearness of Jarret could not keep at bay the bitter chill of reality creeping back round her heart.

Appearances were often deceptive—as Lissa knew only too well.

CHAPTER FIVE

LISSA was not sure what or whom to expect as she stood beside Jarret waiting for a response to his tug at the old-fashioned bell pull. Somewhere in the depths of the house a dog barked furiously, then the heavy door swung back and a black Scottie shot out uttering challenging barks. A tall, dark-haired girl looked out blankly at Lissa for a split second before her gaze travelled to Jarret. Instantly her expression changed.

'Jarret! We didn't expect you so soon, after your call ... Whisky! *Shut up!*' With the exclamation she swayed forward and kissed Jarret, one hand going to his shoulder, and Lissa experienced a sharp stab of pure jealousy that she knew must be quite unfounded. 'But do come in,' the dark girl said. 'Mother's resting.'

Without waiting for introductions and ignoring the dog rushing irritably round their feet, she led the way through an inner hall and into a room on the right.

The place smelled distinctly doggy, and the reason was instantly discernible. An elderly black Labrador lay on a faded Turkey rug before the fire, a white poodle was curled up on one of the big armchairs, a second, smaller Labrador reclined on the settee, and Whisky, with a defiant yap at the newcomers, leapt on to the other armchair.

'Out! All of you!' The dark girl started tipping movements and the dogs began reluctantly to vacate their resting places.

'They're ruined, and Emma encourages them.' The dark girl looked at Lissa for the first time, and Jarret said hastily:

'My sister-in-law, Camilla. My wife, Lissa.'

The dark girl held out her hand formally, and Lissa felt her own inward reserve closing in. Despite the smell of the dogs, the slight, comfortable shabbiness of the gracious old house, there was the unmistakable air of what Pippa used to call 'very upper U!' It was in Camilla's finishing school accents, the cool hand that touched Lissa's almost limply, and the total self-confidence that just stopped short of arrogance as she waved Lissa to a chair. All a world away from the ambience of a daughter of a small-time country builder.

But Jarret did not sit down. 'Where's Emma?' he asked abruptly.

Camilla raised fine brows and pretended to look rueful. 'Don't sound like that, Jarret—please! She's gone to a party.'

'A party! But——'

'Didn't she tell you herself in her letters? My dear,' Camilla turned a glance to Lissa, as though seeking an ally, 'she's talked of nothing else for weeks. It's Jane's, her best friend! It was planned for yesterday, then Benjy developed a rash earlier this week and they thought it was measles and cancelled the bunfight, then it turned out to be something he'd eaten, so the party was hastily re-assembled for today, to give them a little more time to organise the eats. I hate to tell you Emma's reaction when she realised that the party was off as far as she was concerned.'

'I can guess,' said Jarret in dry tones.

'Now, Jarret, how could we refuse to allow her to go, after your call to say you were house-viewing and might not reach here till late afternoon?'

Jarret was silent, but the compression of his lips told the watching Lissa a great deal; Jarret was not pleased. He stood up and walked across to the window, then asked, 'What time will the shenanigans break up?'

'About six, or soon after.' Camilla hesitated. 'Jarret, why don't you leave her with us until the holidays are over?'

'Yes, why not do that, Jarret?'

The second voice came from the doorway. A tall, slender, older edition of Camilla stood there. Mrs de Rys walked into the room, her smile gracious but her eyes without warmth. She looked toward Lissa, waiting for a formal introduction to be made. When this was done she went on as though no interruption had occurred.

'Wouldn't it be a more satisfactory arrangement? I

gather you're house-hunting, so things are bound to be a trifle unsettled.' The older woman's voice was smooth, beautifully modulated, yet the timbre of steely determination was perceptible. Mrs de Rys was a woman unaccustomed to being crossed. 'Besides,' her glance slid to Lissa and she smiled, 'I should imagine your bride would be grateful for a few weeks' breathing space in which to adjust to her new life.'

Jarret inclined his head, and his expression had softened. 'Thank you—you've been wonderfully kind to Emma and I appreciate it more than I can say. But now,' he hesitated, glancing at Lissa, 'my wife is as anxious as I am to have Emma home with us at last.'

Perhaps he did not realise the particular significance his words might hold for Mrs de Rys, but Lissa was aware of it instantly, even before she saw the flicker of pain cross the older woman's features. Lissa's heart welled with sympathy for a mother who still grieved for the loss of her daughter, and for whom Emma must provide a doubly precious link. Lissa wanted to say to Jarret, let Emma stay a little longer, until her grandmother gets used to the idea of my taking her daughter's place ... Then she saw Jarret's eyes swing to her, cool and filled with warning, as though he had guessed her impulsive thought.

Mrs de Rys had turned away, her face closing, as though she regretted the brief display of emotion. She said tiredly, 'Of course. It's natural that you should want her with you. We're going to miss her quite a lot, though.'

Lissa could not remain silent any longer. 'But you'll be coming to visit her, and seeing our new home, whichever one we find eventually. And I'm sure Emma will be coming here to see you as often as possible.'

'You're very kind, my dear.' She smiled faintly. 'Three years is quite a long time, even though it seems to have passed remarkably quickly, and Emma has become very dear to me.'

Lissa was silent. Subtly, Mrs de Rys had put them both in the wrong by taking Emma from her, despite the fact that Emma's place was undoubtedly with her father and her new stepmother. The word in her consciousness broke Lissa's train of thought. She was receiving her first inkling of what Jarret had meant when he spoke vaguely of domestic problems. Now that she had met Camilla and Mrs de Rys she realised how possessive they were of Jarret's daughter. In a sense it was natural. Jarret had realised the difficulties faced by a man endeavouring to care for a four-year-old girl, and bowed to the inevitable by allowing the concern of her grandmother to prevail. But now he had realised how fleeting were the years of childhood, once gone never to be recalled, and so he had chosen Lissa to play her role. Now that the moment of parting was here Mrs de Rys did not want to yield control, and who could blame her? Nevertheless, Lissa knew where her true sympathies lay, despite her compassion for Emma's grandmother. After all, Lissa reflected, it wasn't as though they were taking Emma miles away. They would see her often, and Emma would probably spend holidays with them. But Lissa did not realise at that moment that it would not be as simple as that.

Mrs de Rys, apparently reconciled to the idea, suggested tea. The conversation inevitably turned to Emma, how well she was doing at school, her emerging talent for music and her tremendous spirit of independence. But during this Lissa was conscious of strain in the atmosphere, puzzling because it was difficult to pinpoint the source.

She was thankful when the play with bone china and slivers of lemon was over and Camilla asked if she rode. Lissa shook her head, and could not do anything but assent when Camilla expressed a wish for Jarret's opinion on a new hunter she had recently acquired. Camilla bore him off stablewards, leaving Lissa in the company of Mrs de Rys.

'My daughter is crazy about horses. So was my darling Claudine,' Mrs de Rys mused. 'But Emma shows no inclination at all to follow in her mother's footsteps—if that's the right way to express it,' she added wryly. 'Would you care to see the garden, my dear?'

She showed Lissa through the french windows which gave out on to a terrace overlooking spacious lawns and shrubberies at the rear of the long, rambling house. The dogs appeared, gambolling round their feet and begging to be played with or taken for a walk. Mrs de Rys picked

up a well chewed ball from the grass and tossed it a little
way. 'Go on, I haven't the energy to amuse you today.'

She strolled along the pathways, chatting easily with
the effortless expertise of good breeding and long practice
of entertaining visitors without giving away for one moment
anything of her own true personal warmth. The kind of
sociality like a picture drawn in sand, reflected Lissa, then
the waves lap it away, leaving nothing. But it was unfair
to judge by the first meeting, Lissa amended, as Mrs
de Rys pointed to a quaint little bell-shaped building that
stood across the lawn.

'We call it our folly. Generations of de Ryses have done
their courting there—slipping out by the side door there.'

They had reached the side of the house, where the drive
curved round and under a mellow brick archway into a
courtyard where the stables and old coach-house were situ-
ated. A high clipped hedge screened one side, and a narrow
pathway led towards the folly. Mrs de Ryse was about to
step along it when a telephone began to ring somewhere
inside the house.

She gave an exclamation and turned back. 'Do excuse
me, my dear. And do explore.' She hurried towards the
side door, leaving Lissa alone.

After a moment's hesitation Lissa began to walk along
the path leading to the folly. Under its cupola roof it
appeared to be divided into three sections, each with its
old wooden seat that would be sheltered from chilly breezes.
It was not difficult to imagine the ladies with their parasols
and the dashing beaux in striped blazers and boaters.
Lissa smiled to herself at the thought as she reached the
grassy circle surrounding it, then, about to step up into
the nearest section, she heard voices and froze.

There was no mistaking Jarret's tones, and the quick,
angry voice of Camilla. Horror overtook Lissa as she realised her predicament. There was another path at the far
side of the folly, one that led to an opening in the tall hedge
and was probably a short cut from the far end of the stable
block; Jarret and Camilla must have emerged at the pre-
cise moment Lissa reached the folly, and the little building
cut off all line of sight at that angle. She heard Jarret say

coldly, 'I've told you, Camilla, it's impossible. No!' and she looked round desperately for a way out of the trap. She did not wish to hear their argument, which would almost certainly be over Emma.

But there seemed no escape. If she moved they might hear her. If she tried to back away quietly they might see her. And the sound of them definitely precluded a normal, casual, bright appearance in their path.

A moment later her unwilling ears proved the accuracy of her surmise as Camilla's raised voice came clearly:

'How can you take her back like this? It's disgusting! After three years. You were quite happy to let her stay here while it suited your convenience.'

'You know perfectly well why.' His voice was tightly controlled, but Lissa knew the anger was simmering beneath. But Camilla apparently chose to ignore the warning.

'Yes, I know,' she cried bitterly, 'but I never thought you'd take revenge in this way. It will break my mother's heart. She adores Emma.'

'I'm aware of that.' His voice was icy. 'But I thought I'd already made it clear. Isn't it natural that my wife and I should wish to have our daughter at home with us?'

'*Our*?' There was a ring of scorn in Camilla's tone that made Lissa feel cold. The bitter echo of that one little word seemed to encompass the whole truth about herself and her relationship with Jarret. That her own claim to the child she had not yet even seen was nil, a paper link that would be broken in five years' time.

She wrapped her arms across herself to try to still the shivers that beset her. What did Camilla mean by revenge?

'I don't believe you care a scrap for Emma!' she heard Camilla accuse. 'If you did you would leave her here where she's happy. If the truth was known, you hate her be-cause——'

Suddenly Lissa could bear no more. She had to escape the bitter revelations of a past that did not concern her. She sped from the folly, casting one hurried glance over her shoulder before she ran towards the house. When she reached the french window she paused, catching at her racing breath. But the big room was empty, and the folly appeared deserted against the green shadows of the shrubbery.

She started with shock at the sudden movement against her legs and the cold thrust of a wet nose. Then she laughed shakily and stooped to pet Bess, the smaller of the two Labradors, who had taken a fancy to her the moment she arrived. When Lissa straightened from stroking the silky black head Camilla was striding across the lawn, head imperiously high, with Jarret at her side, looking as black of visage as Lissa had ever seen him.

'Where's Mother?' Camilla demanded when she entered, almost as though she suspected Lissa of spiriting the older woman away.

'The telephone rang a few minutes ago,' Lissa said quietly, conscious of the bottled-up anger still in the other girl and that some of it was going to be directed against herself. 'Your mother must still be talking.'

'If it's Thea she'll be there all evening.' Camilla glanced at her watch and made a visible effort to resume the façade worn for guests. 'Would you like a drink or anything?' she asked. 'I don't suppose we'll see Emma for another hour, at least. So boring, waiting for something, isn't it?' She smiled superficially.

Boring was hardly the word Lissa would have chosen to describe the atmosphere now prevailing. Jarret had refused a drink and was pacing restlessly over to the window, and Camilla did not repeat the invitation to Lissa. Fortunately, Mrs de Rys came back at that moment, apologising for her absence and giving a blow-by-blow résumé of her telephone conversation with the unknown Thea. But at least the 'I saids' and 'she saids' broke the ice, and then Mrs de Rys produced a large, leather-bound photograph album filled with family pictures, of which quite a number depicted Emma. It seemed the late Mr de Rys had been an ardent camera buff and the resultant record of his family went back quite a number of years, and at last Lissa saw the face of Claudine.

To say that Jarret's first wife was beautiful was an understatement. A lovely colour study showed her oval features to be flawless, and the bone structure beneath them of the kind to keep those features still lovely when youth had gone—except that fate had not allowed that test of time. The photograph held Lissa like a magnet and she could not stop herself studying the face of the woman Jarret had loved, the dark vitality that glowed in the wide eyes, the hint of mystery in the expression and the sensuous invitation lingering round the mouth. The face of a woman no man could help loving ...

Suddenly Lissa found that Mrs de Rys no longer sat at her shoulder, adding small commentaries on the photographs. Camilla exclaimed, 'Here they are,' and there was a car door slamming, then a general movement out into the hall.

Lissa followed, her heart beating faster even as she told herself it was foolish to feel afraid or nervous of meeting a child. But this was no ordinary child; this was Jarret's daughter, and it was already obvious that she was the central figure in a threatened battle for possession.

She was a straight, thin little girl with wide grey eyes and long, very fine soft brown hair that framed her small serious face and pointed chin. She was wearing an ankle-length dress of soft blue with sprays of white daisies making a chain round the hem and the neat square neck, and she clutched a bulging carrier bag that said Sainsburys. Her small, silver-shoed feet hurried towards the door, but even in excitement Emma did not laugh.

'Daddy! There was a treasure hunt and I won it! Look!' She delved into the plastic bag and hauled out an oblong, brightly coloured box. 'And I got a Paddington notebook out of the lucky dip! Though actually I got a pen that wrote in four different colours, but I exchanged with Lorna because she didn't want Paddington and I've got a pen already that writes in four colours.' Emma drew a rapid breath. 'And Uncle Neil stayed at the party as well.'

'Did he?' Jarret scooped his daughter, prizes and all, high in his arms, hugging her closely to him.

Lissa watched the slender arms fasten round his neck and the small profile press against his dark head. Then her gaze went to the man coming round the front of the white car.

He was not as tall as Jarret, nor so dark, dressed casually in light blue pants and a matching blouson worn open over a dark blue shirt. His brown hair was ruffled, and his suede shoes scuffed, as though he had indeed been through the mêlée of a celebration for a crowd of small, excited children. But judging by the smile he wore he had thoroughly enjoyed every minute of it. Camilla went to meet him, received an arm round her shoulders and an easy kiss on her mouth that bore no trace of abashment in front of onlookers.

Jarret lowered Emma to the ground, and Mrs de Rys said brightly, 'My, you've won some bounty, haven't you, darling?'

'Yes.' Emma's head turned now to look at the silent Lissa in the background. Some of the excitement ebbed from her face and the tiny bones of her fist stood out whitely as she clutched at her bounty.

Jarret drew her forward, and for a moment Lissa fancied the air had stilled around them. He said unsmilingly, 'Lissa, this is my daughter Emma.' Then he bent down, saying quietly to the waiting child, 'This is the lady I've married, Emma, but shall we wait until we get home before we start getting to know each other?'

'If you like, Daddy.' Emma looked as uncertain as Lissa felt, and yet there was relief there. Lissa felt sure that Jarret's approach had been the best in the circumstances, sparing the child the ordeal of attempting an affectionate greeting to a total stranger. So Lissa smiled and said, 'Hello, Emma. I hope you'll tell me about the party while we're driving home.'

Emma said, 'Yes,' in a stiff, polite little voice, and then Camilla broke in:

'Lissa, meet my fiancé, Neil Hargill. Neil, this is Lissa, Jarret's new wife.'

'How do you do.' The words were formal, but there was nothing formal about Neil Hargill's smile or the warm clasp of his hand that closed over Lissa's and held it far longer than was necessary. His eyes grinned down into hers, openly saying that he'd like to kiss her, that he liked to kiss all pretty girls, but her husband and his fiancée certainly would not approve.

He had the kind of charm that few women could resist basking in. Not wolfish, not raffish, just an unfair share of sheer male attractiveness coupled with a generous desire to lavish it on the feminine sex.

During the brief time before their departure it was plain to see that Emma adored him, Mrs de Rys was anything but immune and Camilla wore a self-satisfied expression every time her gaze lighted on his handsome face. Equally obvious, though, was the fact that Neil Hargill was not a man's man. He and Jarret had absolutely nothing to say to one another apart from the sparsest of civilities, and when at last Emma's cases were brought down and stowed in the car and it was time to say goodbye Jarret's was a mere nod and Neil's the same.

The waving and the farewells finally ended and Emma turned reluctantly from her craning position at the window as the house dropped away out of sight. She settled down in her seat, adjusted the folds of the party frock which she had refused to change before they left, and lapsed into a silence unusual for a child.

'Well,' said Jarret, not troubling to disguise the note of relief in his voice, 'so it was a good party.'

'Yes,' said Emma, not moving.

'What was your prize, Emma?' Lissa ventured, deciding she had to break the ice between Emma and herself sooner or later and there didn't seem much point in putting off the moment.

'A game.' Emma's intense little profile remained at the same angle. 'A—a compen-dium.' She did not enlarge any further.

'Perhaps we can have fun playing them when we get home,' Lissa suggested, after a pause.

Emma appeared to consider this possibility, then she said flatly, 'They're children's games.'

There was another little silence, then Jarret said calmly, 'That doesn't mean grown-ups can't learn them too.'

'I suppose so.'

Emma lapsed into silence once more, turning her head to stared fixedly through the window at the charm of the Kent countryside in spring. As though Jarret sensed his daughter's withdrawal and accepted it, he quickened the speed of the powerful car and the miles began to race away.

Lissa sighed softly to herself. Her sympathy was with Emma. It must be a tremendous ordeal for a child to be pitchforked into the company of a total stranger, a stranger moreover who seemed about to take on the role of a mother. Not for the first time Lissa thought that Jarret had approached the matter completely without understanding and compassion for his motherless daughter. Why hadn't he allowed her to meet Emma before the wedding? Even if only a couple of times, so that the child's ordeal was lessened? Gaining Emma's trust was going to require a great deal of patience, and Lissa could not help fearing that there might be quite a few problems to sort out on the way to understanding.

Lissa's fear proved not unfounded sooner than she had expected.

They reached home just before eight. Emma walked into that vast jet-set living room and stood in the centre of it, still huddled in her dark blue coat, and looked so small and lost and forlorn that Lissa longed to throw her arms round the slight little figure and try to instil reassurance. But there was a wary, remote air like an invisible barrier round Emma, and Lissa stayed uncertainly outside its confines.

'What would you like for your supper, Emma?'

Emma thought for a moment. 'Could I have a pâté on toast?'

'Have a heart!' Jarret came into the room, having deposited Emma's belongings in her bedroom. 'We only got back from Egypt last night. Give us a chance to get re-organised, poppet.'

'Oh, I forgot. Is there any cereal?'

'There should be—I haven't explored the store cupboards myself yet,' Lissa laughed, trying to put the child at her ease. 'Take your coat off, Emma, while I investigate.'

But Emma stood there, her face pale and serious. She looked at Lissa. 'I don't know what I have to call you.'

For a moment Lissa was perplexed. She was not prepared for this poser, then Emma said uncertainly: Should I call you Aunty?'

'Don't be so silly, Emma,' exclaimed Jarret, pouring himself a drink at the miniature cocktail bar. 'Lissa is now my wife, and therefore she's now your stepmother.'

'I don't like stepmother. It's a horrid word.'

'Well, I wasn't suggesting that you address Lissa as Stepmother!'

Emma stood her ground, her small pointed chin stubborn, even though there was a tiny quiver of the taut little lip above it. 'I—I can't say Mummy,' she stammered at last.

'Of course you can't!' Lissa could not contain her warm-hearted sympathy a moment longer. She dropped to one knee in front of the child and put out her hands to slip the coat from her shoulders. 'I think you'd better call me Lissa, then there'll be no mistake about who you're talking about.' She straightened, the coat over her arm. 'Now suppose you come into the kitchen with me and we'll see what there is for supper?'

Fortunately, Mrs Ridge, acting on Jarret's instructions, had stocked the store cupboards generously, and after a frowning deliberation along the shelf of assorted tinned foods Emma settled on the perennial favourite—baked beans.

She must have been hungry because she tucked into a fair-sized plateful, along with two slices of toast and the lot garnished liberally with tomato ketchup. Jarret pulled a face of revulsion when he saw his daughter's choice of fare.

'Didn't they feed you at that party?'

'Yes, but there were a lot of gooey cream cakes. I only got one sausage roll and one weeny tongue sandwich, then there was none left,' Emma said disgustedly, mopping up the last drop of ketchup, 'and I don't eat cakes. Aunt Camilla says I must never eat cakes or I'll get fat.'

Jarret raised his brows but made no comment.

'I don't think you're the type to get fat,' said Lissa, pouring out a glass of orange juice to wash it down with, having been informed by Emma that she didn't like milk and didn't like tea because Aunt Camilla wouldn't let her drink tea unless it had a lot of milk in it.

'She won't let me have tomato sauce, either,' Emma took

a thirsty swig of juice and sighed, 'and I like it on everything.'

'Who's "she"?' reprimanded Lissa gently.

Emma made a face. 'Sorry—Aunt Camilla. She says tomato sauce is vulgar.'

Jarret's mouth twitched and his brows quirked again before he went through into the living room. A short while later Emma was snug in clean pyjamas which Lissa had left to warm in the airing cupboard since that morning. Paddington was settled in his chair, Emma said her prayers, and then climbed into bed.

Lissa tucked her in, smiled, and Emma looked up at her.

'There's a girl at school who calls her parents by their first names, but Grannie says it isn't right.' Emma hesitated. 'Are you sure it's all right, really, to call you Lissa?'

'Of course. I wouldn't have suggested it otherwise.' Lissa sat on the edge of the bed. 'It's quite a problem, isn't it? Because it would sound awfully funny if you called me Mrs Earle. But I agree, we don't know each other well enough yet for you to call me a family name.'

'Did you know Daddy a long time before you married him?'

'No, just for a little while.'

'Oh.' Emma looked up at the ceiling. 'Why didn't he let me see you first?'

Lissa was saved from this virtually unanswerable poser by the advent of Jarret, just in time to hear his daughter's perfectly natural question.

'Because if I'd let you two meet and you hadn't liked each other I might not have been able to marry Lissa.' He paused, his face enigmatic. 'Time you put the light out, young lady.'

'I hope you're not going to spoil her,' Jarret said when they were out of earshot and back in the living room. 'This allowing her to address you by your first name.'

'Have you a better suggestion?' she asked quietly.

'No, and I agree, it's awkward. But I dislike precocious brats.'

'I don't think you need have any fear in that respect

concerning Emma.' Lissa paused, then faced him with determination. 'Jarret, I think we should get some points clear straight away.'

'Well?' He sat down and lounged back, long legs crossed, waiting.

She took a deep breath. 'To date I'm under the impression that the principal reason for my being here is to care for Emma.'

'I'm not disputing that.' He eyed her from under shadowing lids, a look that always had the effect of disconcerting Lissa. 'What's worrying you? I merely passed a personal opinion regarding children's behaviour.'

'Yes, I realise that.' Lissa bit her lip. 'But I couldn't help getting the impression that you didn't want me to—to show Emma too much affection.'

'Ye gods! The thought never entered my head,' he exclaimed impatiently. 'You're certainly reversing the classic stepmother situation. Do you think Emma's starving for affection?'

'No, not exactly,' Lissa said slowly.

'Well then?' he demanded.

She looked so strained this afternoon, and when we got here,' Lissa went on, caution making her choose her words with care. 'I can't help thinking that she must be feeling insecure.'

Jarret regarded her with a long, level stare until she finished speaking. Then he said, 'Exactly. Why do you think I brought you into our lives? Go ahead, love her as much as you want.'

Lissa was not prepared for this total capitulation. To her dismay she was discovering that there was no sense of joy or triumph in the moment that seemed to give her carte blanche to lavish on and win from Emma the warm caring and love her nature dictated. The cold voice of logic that was never far away came to remind her of the danger this could bring, the danger of heartbreak. She turned away, aghast at the thought, and Jarret said abruptly:

'Now what's the matter? What have I said?'

'You haven't said anything,' she whispered. 'I was wrong —I've just realised how—how unfair it is.'

'How unfair what is?' He stood up. 'What are you talking about, Lissa?'

'To encourage Emma, to let her get too close to me, when in five years' time it'll be all over,' she said in a low voice, then whirled to face him. 'It's wrong, Jarret!'

'What are you suggesting? An extension of the contract?'

'No!' The expression on his mouth looked cynical and she flung the denial at him. 'I'm not suggesting anything! I just want to do what's best for Emma's future.'

'And so do I,' he said in clipped tones. 'We've been through all this before. Emma will be twelve when these five years have gone. She'll be at boarding school, where I've no doubt she'll discover that the problem of divorced or separated parents is not an uncommon one. It's the present I want you to concentrate on, not the future.'

There was a finality in his words that told her the subject was now closed as far as she was concerned. But even her secret, burgeoning love for him could not mask the shock and incredulity with which she listened to his callous dismissal of her concern. Nor could it dull her anger. She stared at him. 'Don't you realise that the present makes the future in a child's life?' she cried. 'Don't you care at all for Emma's future happiness?'

He moved so fast there was no time to back away. He seized her arms, his fingers biting into the soft flesh like clamps, and his eyes smouldered with anger. 'Don't you ever dare say that again!' he hissed. 'Do you hear?'

Tears of pain forced their way into Lissa's eyes, but she refused to retract. 'Do you?' she whispered fiercely. '*Do you?*'

For a dreadful moment she thought he would strike her. His features were a dark mass in which only the eyes burned. Then with a muttered profanity he flung away from her and stormed across to the cocktail bar. With jerky, clinking movements he fixed a drink and stood with his back to the stricken Lissa.

'What kind of monster do you think I am?' He tossed back half the glassful and swung round, obviously fighting to master his anger. 'Do you seriously believe I would deliberately hurt a child?'

'I—I don't know,' she whispered, trying to stop her

hands going to rub the smarting, bruised flesh of her upper arms. 'I—I think you misunderstood what I was trying to say.'

'Did I?' There was more control in his voice. 'I think you did your share of misunderstanding, Lissa.'

She was silent, trying to control her own trembling, and then she heard the softer chime of the glass being set down on the opaline shelf.

'Lissa,' he said, almost wearily, 'this isn't going to get us anywhere. Let's try again.'

'Yes, I think we'd better,' she said unsteadily.

'I never intended that you should not make decisions concerning Emma's welfare,' he said heavily. 'That was the whole idea in the first place.'

'Yes. But what if I were to make a decision with which you disagree?'

He did not immediately reply to her question. His glance had discovered the patches of reddening skin below the line of the short sleeve of her white top. 'Did I hurt you?' he asked.

'No.' She looked away, unwilling to be drawn so easily back into his spell by a facile changing mood.

He reached out and drew the sleeve up, revealing the dull, darkening imprints of his fingers. Those same fingers slid up caressingly under the yielding material, warm and gentle now, and evoking sensations as disturbing as their previous attack.

'I'm sorry,' he said, 'I lost my temper.'

Suddenly she could not bear the torment of his touch. 'It doesn't matter,' she said sharply, jerking her arm free.

'Doesn't it?' He gave her a curious glance, but made no further comment. 'Are we agreed, then? I don't expect you to consult me on every minor day-to-day decision concerning Emma. I trust your logic and common sense to deal with any small emergencies which may arise.'

'Do you?' Lissa shivered a little, though why she didn't know; the room was warm enough. 'I hope you won't be disappointed.'

'I don't think so. I believe you to be the most truthful and conscientous girl I've ever known,' he said slowly, and distinctly, and watched the quick rush of rose to her cheeks. 'You may be emotional in your approach, but I see no reason to doubt your common sense in caring for Emma.' He paused, and the suggestion of a wry smile touched the corners of his mouth. 'Does that make you any happier?'

She sighed, and avoided his gaze. 'I don't think my personal happiness comes into it.'

'Doesn't it?' He reached out to switch on a big floor lamp, the radiance of which flowed out to Lissa. 'I see no reason to preclude happiness entirely from our lives. It wasn't written out of our contract, you know.'

'I suppose not.' She turned away from the revealing glow of the lamp. 'I hadn't thought of it that way.'

'Neither had I—until this moment. But I certainly never envisaged five years of chill formality.'

He sounded impatient again, and she remembered the moments in the car, when they arrived to collect Emma. It had all been deliberate, an act for a definite purpose, to convince ... Suddenly Lissa felt sick at heart and desperately tired. She tried to make her voice casual as she said, 'Neither did I, but I don't think we've been exactly chilly or formal to date.' She forced an impersonal smile. 'I'd better make a start on the evening meal. Is there anything in particular you'd like to eat?'

He glanced at his watch. 'Do you have to bother?'

She shrugged.

'Would you like to go out for a meal?'

'No. We can't leave Emma alone. And if she woke up alone, on her first night back here, she might be terribly scared.'

He nodded. 'Of course you're right. I'd forgotten for a moment.' The wry smile flashed back. 'You see! Your conscientiousness is second nature!'

She smiled faintly, waiting.

'Oh—food.' He frowned, then half turned away, indifferent. 'I'm not terribly hungry. A couple of cheese sandwiches would do for me.'

She nodded, thankful not to have to start preparing an elaborate meal. Normally she enjoyed creative cookery and had looked forward to making her first full-scale evening meal for Jarret. But when she did she wanted to feel alert and capable, not jaded and dispirited as she felt now. At least there was one consolation, she told herself as she fixed the simple repast: he had virtually given her a free hand to care for Emma.

She set the trolley, her mind going over that recent exchange. What exactly had he implied by those remarks on happiness and chill formality? She had thought him condescending in those observations about her common sense, yet now she thought back on them she was suddenly convinced he had been perfectly sincere.

A disturbing change in more ways than one, she sighed as she wheeled the trolley into the living room, but at least she had cleared the air regarding Emma.

It was the one tiny score to chalk up against the total unpredictability of Jarret Earle.

CHAPTER SIX

THE following weeks slowly formed a pattern for Lissa, and as this took shape she began to gain confidence and feel less as though she had been plunged into a new job for which she had had little preparation. But after the initial stiffness wore off and the inevitable sounding out of each other's personality took place the first delicate strands of a relationship could begin to be woven between Lissa and Jarret's daughter.

Gradually Emma seemed to be accepting Lissa quite naturally as part of her life, and the first time that a tearful Emma ran headlong into Lissa's arms, sobbing out one of the heart-breaks of school life, so trivial in retrospect to an adult yet so world-shattering to a seven-year-old, Lissa comforted her and dried her tears, finding a tender, poignant happiness in knowing that Emma had bestowed her trust.

She settled down quite quickly at her new school and made friends, although she missed Jane, her 'best' friend in Cranbrook, dreadfully, and she missed the dogs. Often she spoke wistfully of her Uncle Daniel, who had died a few months previously.

'He got pneumonia. Grannie didn't call the doctor soon enough,' Emma said, with unconscious reproach in her young voice. However, there were so many new things happening in her life that Emma had little time to fret.

The most exciting was the House.

About two weeks after they'd brought Emma home Jarret broke the glad news that the dream house was theirs —'Or will be as soon as the legal part of the transaction is completed,' he qualified. 'I'm hoping to take possession before the end of May.'

Emma fell in love with the house, especially the swing, as Lissa had guessed she would. She wanted to know if she could have a puppy, a black one that would grow up to look exactly like Bess. And could she invite Jane to stay with her the moment they moved in.

'Because Jane's asked me to go to Scotland with her in July. And you said I could, Daddy.'

Jarret regarded the appealing face of his daughter and admitted that this arrangement had indeed been settled before he brought Emma back home and of course it would stand. 'But you must ask Lissa's permission before issuing any invitations yourself. Lissa will have to look after both of you. As for a dog...' Jarret looked doubtful. 'We'll see.'

With that Emma had to be content, but Lissa had a strong suspicion that it would only be a matter of time before a black Labrador puppy would be gambolling about in their new home. Meanwhile, there seemed a thousand and one things lining up to be done. Decisions on which of their present furnishings were to be kept, and which would have to be disposed of when they moved. Decisions to be made regarding the layout of the new bathroom and the kitchen fittings. All of which had to be settled before the plumber and electricians and builders could start work on the alterations. And of course there was the planning permission to be sorted out.

Jarret was inclined to hand over the whole job to an interior designer and colour consultant, on the premise that the whole scheme was to be totally in keeping with the period of the house. Lissa was horrified at the thought. She fully realised that the ultra-modern pieces in their present home would have to go, but she could not bear the idea of a professional expert superimposing a stranger's personality on the new home, no matter how skilful or tasteful.

'It'll take days, never mind hours, of foot-slogging round the stores, going through pattern books and matching things,' Jarret reminded her.

'I don't mind.'

'And I've got to go to Germany next month. I can't put it off.'

'I'll do all the preliminary searching and work out some schemes, then you can see which you approve. Oh, Jarret,' she was unconscious of the wistful appeal in her wide blue eyes and the gentle curve of her mouth, 'do let's choose our own decor. It'll be such fun—I've never worked out schemes for a whole house before. Besides, Emma has already decided on her own colour scheme!'

Jarret yielded, and Lissa tried to hide her relief; the idea of home-making had become very precious to her, and no matter how much time and energy the task would entail she would love every moment it consumed.

On the twenty-third of May Emma celebrated her eighth birthday, and on the twenty-fourth the key of the house came into Jarret's possession. The next few weeks were hectic, and the gracious old house began to look as though a demolition squad had passed that way and paused there, for a brief practice run. It was a relief to wave goodbye to the builders, who had worked remarkably quickly, and see the gleaming new pale green onyx bathroom suite arrive with the men who would install it.

Lissa had chosen all the bedroom colour schemes first; white with warm toning browns for Jarret's room, Wedgwood blue and white for her own, spring green and primrose and white with a gingham motif for Emma's, white and rose for the main guest room, and Adam's green for the other two spare rooms. Carpeting throughout the upper floors of the house was to be cream, to keep a tranquil note of continuity that would not disturb the gracious proportions of the lovely old house. As soon as the interior decorators moved in to start on all this Lissa took the opportunity of overhauling Emma's wardrobe. There was also the Scottish holiday coming very near, as Emma reminded her on an average of half a dozen times a day, with the added injunction that some new clothes were indicated for this event.

'Shall we have a look at what you have?' Lissa suggested, for some time now secretly aghast and not a little scared at the vast amount of money the house was swallowing and determined to make such other economies as possible.

'None of last year's will be any good,' Emma announced firmly.' 'They're all too babyish, anyway, except for my red and white set. It's my favourite—Aunt Camilla brought it from Paris.'

Lissa watched her skip to the wardrobe and reach down a hanger, from which she hauled off the plastic dust cover to reveal a most attractive outfit. It consisted of a white linen pleated skirt, a silky scarlet matelot top, a cute little white jacket and a jaunty matching cap. The Paris look was unmistakable, and the price tag anyone's guess. Emma proceeded to try it on, pirouetting wildly to demonstrate how far out the pleats would swirl, then she caught sight of herself in the mirror.

'It's too short!' she wailed. 'Look! You can see my knickers!' She dragged up her briefs and tried to pull down the skirt, tragedy written all over her small expressive face, 'I only wore it twice because summer was nearly over when I got it.'

And Aunt Camilla had forgotten how quickly children grow, thought Lissa; Emma had probably shot up three inches since last summer.

'All the others will be too short as well,' Emma cried frantically. 'And my white shoes are too tight.'

'Keep still—let me see that skirt.' Two lines of concentration formed between Lissa's fine brows. It seemed so extravagant to replace the expensive clothes in Emma's generously sized wardrobe. 'The jacket's all right,' she smiled. 'You haven't got wider—only longer!'

But Emma did not giggle. 'I can't wear the jacket by itself,' she protested with a petulant stamp.

'I didn't say you should,' Lissa said patiently, 'but I think I can make the kilt fit you again.'

'Oh, could you?' Emma was all smiles again. 'It doesn't matter about the others, just this outfit.'

'Doesn't it?' asked Lissa dryly. 'You can start trying them all on, and we'll see what fits and what doesn't.' Her voice was more confident now that she had discovered generous seams and an amply deep hem that would yield another three inches to her needle.

'It's next week,' Emma reminded her, when a formidable heap of garments needing altering lay on the bed. Can you sew them all by then?'

'Those that you'll need, yes. I'll finish the rest while you're away.'

Lissa was a competent dressmaker, having made quite a lot of clothes for herself and Pippa in the past, but as soon as she began on the alterations for Emma she realised how much she missed her old sewing machine at home.

She switched off the lamp at her elbow and glanced

across the room at Jarret, who was watching a documentary on television. It was almost over, and when the credits began to roll she said softly, 'Jarret ...?'

'Hm.' He did not turn his head.

'Would you mind if I went home for this weekend?'

He frowned slightly, then it cleared. 'No, of course not. Nothing wrong, is there? Your father ... ?'

'No, nothing like that.' She picked up her sewing and switched on the lamp again, far enough away not to disturb Jarret when he resumed his viewing. 'I've a sewing machine there and I could clear all these in a couple of days.'

'It would be a better idea to invest in a new machine here,' he suggested, 'if you intend to do much sewing.'

She knew that to Jarret this meant one of the latest luxury electric models with every conceivable gadget. But she could not help worrying about the considerable expense of the house, and felt that this was a luxury that could be deferred. She said so, and he gave a wry, acquiescent nod of his dark head, murmuring something about an economical wife that Lissa could not quite discern above the sound of the television. Then he said he would run her and Emma to Lissa's home and returned his attention to the news.

Suddenly the room had a happy atmosphere, as though it held one of the quiet, contented interludes of a happy marriage. If only it were truly so, she sighed to herself. If only it were a true marriage. Sadly, trying to forget the ache that tugged at her heart-strings with the thought, she bent her head again to the task in hand.

*   *   *

Emma thoroughly enjoyed the weekend at Lissa's home, and Lissa herself was heartened at the improvement she saw in her father's health.

He was walking by now, slowly it was true, but this was a tremendous step forward from a wheelchair. His speech was almost back to normal, and he seemed so cheerful, full of plans for when he was able to take up the reins of his business again. But he looked very searchingly at Lissa, as though to reassure himself that all was well with his much-loved daughter, and in the first moment they were alone together he asked bluntly: 'Are you truly happy, my love?'

Never before her marriage had Lissa tried to dissemble in any way with her father; now she knew she must, and that her quiet affirmative had to carry the full conviction he wanted.

'It was a bit more sudden than I'd expected for you,' Mr Vayle went on, his eyes still keenly probing her face. 'I know your mother thought it a splendid match for you, but all the same ...' He paused, and shook his head. 'Money isn't everything, though a lot thinks it is.'

'I'm fine. But I miss you tremendously, you know,' she told him, putting impulsive arms round his neck. 'Don't worry, Daddy. I'm happy. And Emma's a darling.'

In a strange way it was true. She was happy. Happy just being near to Jarret, discovering her love for him, and loving Emma even more just because she was his. It was a borderline she trod, though—the borderline between a mirage of heaven and the hell of knowing that it must all come to an end one day, even the little she had, when the debt was repaid. Often she dreamed, weaving the fantasies of what might have been, only to have the sweet pretences change into dreadful moments of longing, when she craved Jarret's love more than anything else in the world. When these descents into her own private nadir took her to the brink of despair she forced herself to seek physical activity in which she could find sublimation. At the present so much was going on that it wasn't impossible to find a measure of forgetfulness, and Jarret himself unknowingly seemed to contribute towards this. He had become more relaxed in her company, and since that night when they brought Emma home he had ceased to needle her and misread the most innocent of remarks. Certainly he was more equable in temperament. Perhaps it was Emma's influence, she thought, or perhaps he had simply lost interest in herself now that his objective had been achieved.

She pushed the thought away; it was one of the leading beckoners down into that small hell that waited in the dark lonely hours of the night.

Emma returned from her Scottish holiday well sunburnt and armed with souvenirs. After being assured that they had missed her every minute of her absence she delved into her case, scattering belongings all over the carpet, and produced presents from Bonnie Scotland. There was a little tartan chair designed to be used as a pin cushion for Lissa, and a tartan tie for her father. Jarret blanched, but managed to appear suitably overwhelmed with delight, even as Jane, a rosy flaxen-haired child of a rather more practical disposition than Emma, announced that she'd told Emma while they were in the shop that a green tweed plaid might prove a more amiable match in her father's wardrobe than Stuart tartan.

Lissa and Jarret had made full use of the ten days of Emma's absence, and the house was almost ready for occupation. Only the hall and dining room carpets remained to be fitted, and the furniture put into place. Then Lissa could start unpacking the innumerable boxes and crates that filled the utility room.

Exactly one week later the great day dawned and by sunset they were actually in residence in the new home. Emma had her swing, nobody could find anything, and Lissa had never felt so tired in her life.

But the hectic pace did not settle once the move was completed, rather did it seem to increase. They lost Mrs Ridge because they were now living too far from where she lived and she refused to consider coming to live in as full-time housekeeper. Jarret said confidently that they would find somebody; meanwhile Lissa coped. Then the visitors began.

Emma's grandmother and Camilla and Neil could not wait for an invitation and gave no warning of their intended call, three days after the move.

'Forgive me, I should have telephoned, but we mislaid your card with the new address.' Mrs de Rys smiled apologetically proffered a charming sheaf of pink carnations and feathery maidenhair fern. 'We were in town and we couldn't stay away!'

Lissa accepted the flowers, trying to smile her thanks but bitterly conscious of her flushed face, hair flying into untidy wisps, and the traces of the garden on her oldest and shabbiest slacks. 'Do come in,' she invited. 'I'll make some coffee.'

Mrs de Rys protested, but of course the coffee was made and the visitors were shown over the house and garden. Emma dragged 'Uncle' Neil out to see her swing, where he was promptly commandeered for obvious reasons, to which he did not seem to object in the least.

'Emma adores him,' said Mrs de Rys fondly. 'He really is wonderful with children. Why he hasn't settled down before now I really do not know.'

Camilla was standing by the window, looking across the garden to where Emma screamed joyously as Neil pushed her even higher. Camilla turned, her face unreadable in the shadowy outline she made against the sunlit oblong. 'Perhaps he—' she began, and got no further as the thud of the front door closing echoed through the house.

Lissa hurried to greet Jarret and give him those few moments of warning about the visitors which she herself had been denied. When he followed her into the sunny morning room his expression was a smooth mask.

He was suave and affable, but the sense of strain Lissa remembered from the first meeting was taut in the air. Mrs de Rys seemed to sense it, for within a short time she glanced at her heavy gold wristwatch and stood up. Jarret went to call Emma, his voice peremptory when he had to call her a second time, and Lissa could not help but notice the rays of antagonism that leapt invisibly yet perceptibly between the two men.

'My dear . . .'

Lissa turned with a start to find Mrs de Rys at her side, taking swift advantage of the few moments they were alone, for Camilla had followed Jarret from the room.

'I appreciate that there could be a certain sensitivity about our forming a relationship,' the older woman said with delicacy. 'We belong to a part of your husband's life you may wish to forget. It would be quite natural, and I understand this. But I do hope you'll understand our feelings for Emma; we love her very dearly.'

'Yes, of course I understand,' Lissa said gently, somehow glad that Mrs de Rys had had the courage to bring the matter out into the open. Impulsively she touched Mrs

de Rys's arm. 'Please don't be afraid ... it won't make
any difference, not as far as I'm concerned. Emma will still
come to see you, and you must feel free to visit us whenever you want to see her.'

'Thank you, this is more than I dared hope for. You're
a sweet child, I hope you'll be very happy.' Unexpectedly
Mrs de Rys brushed cool lips across Lissa's cheek, then
added, 'And I hope you will feel that we are your family
in future as well as Emma's.'

'And what was all that about?' Jarret asked, after he
had given Emma a dismissive push and released Lissa from
the rather possessively close embrace in which he had
held wife and daughter as he watched the visitors depart.

'What was what about?' parried Lissa, still tingling from
the unexpected pressure of Jarret's body against her.

'The huddle with my former mother-in-law,' he said
dryly.

'Oh, that.' Lissa told him, and added, 'I was rather
surprised. I got the impression she was cold and stand-
offish the first time I met her, but actually I think she's
very sweet once you get to know her.'

Her voice faltered away unhappily. There could be
no mistaking the displeasure in Jarret's face. 'Please don't
look like that—I felt sorry for her.'

'You've no need to,' he said brusquely. 'When are you
planning to invite your parents and sister?'

'I don't know—I've hardly got my breath back after
the move,' she laughed unsteadily, so thankful that he
had changed the subject. 'Do you want to have a house-
warming?'

He shrugged indifferently. 'I suppose it would get it all
over at once.'

'Yes.' Her eyes filled with sadness and she turned away.
It was no use denying it, she told herself wearily as she
wandered out into the garden to resume her interrupted
weeding, being foolish enough to fall hopelessly in love
with Jarret had made her acutely sensitive to his every
mood and she was instantly conscious of his displeasure,
even when he was in sufficiently controlled a mood not
to voice it. But it wasn't fair! she cried inwardly. He was
possessive of his child, and obviously the de Rys family

were too. But it wasn't her fault. How could she avoid saying or doing things that displeased him until she knew exactly why he'd suddenly decided to remove Emma as far out of their ken as possible? And wasn't his attitude just a little ungrateful? After all, it hadn't been convenient for him to care for a four-year-old. Obviously he'd tried and failed. His mother who might have helped, was in New Zealand, a somewhat inconvenient distance for any baby-sitting, Lissa thought bitterly, so it could have been very awkward for Jarret had his mother-in-law not offered to help with caring for Emma. Anyway, it was hard and cruel to take Emma away from her grandmother altogether. But Jarret could be hard and cruel when he felt so inclined. 'Oh *damn*!'

Lissa had tugged furiously at a stubborn trail of something that seemed to be a woody root. It came away, but left its revenge in the shape of a large splinter in Lissa's palm. It was just too much! She was having one of those days when she felt weepy and all egg shells to start with; she'd been caught looking a wreck; she was so tired she ached all over, and Jarret didn't care a damn. She nursed her pain-filled hand, trying to pluck up courage to pluck out that long vicious splinter, and the tears wouldn't let her even see. A strangled little sob escaped her, then small warm arms went fiercely round her neck.

'What's the matter? Why are you crying?' Emma's warm little cheek tried to nestle in curiously to Lissa's bowed head. Then Emma gave a squeal. 'Ooh! You've got a great big splinter in your hand, Lissa! Shall I get it out for you?'

Lissa scrambled to her feet, cursing her foolishness in not wearing gloves. 'I think we'd better go and find the tweezers, Emma.'

'I'll fetch them! They're in your manicure set!' Emma rushed into the house, and Lissa followed more slowly, trying surreptitiously to brush away the foolish tears with the back of her hand. What was the matter with her today? Weeping because of a silly splinter in her hand!

She went into the utility room, not wanting to trail her grubby self upstairs to the bathroom, and washed the soil off her hands before she looked at her palm. It stabbed painfully with every movement or touch, and too impatient to wait for Emma's return, she tried to pinch the tip of the splinter and draw it out of her flesh.

'What's the matter? Emma just shot in like an express train——'

Jarret's voice startled her and she exclaimed as the splinter broke, leaving half still embedded and blood welling up. He grabbed her hand. 'A cut?'

'No, just a——' She was interrupted by Emma, full of importance and the information her father had sought.

'I've brought the tweezers! Shall I try to get it out for you?'

'I think not,' Jarret said firmly, and dispatched his daughter in search of cotton wool and antiseptic lotion. 'And wash your filthy paws first!' he called after her small, scurrying figure.

It took several minutes of painful probing before Jarret succeeded in removing the rest of the splinter. Lissa stayed silent during the small ordeal, not so much with stoicism but because the strain of being so near to him made her tense and shaky. She could see the determined line of his jaw, the intentness of his eyes, and feel the light stirring warmth of his breath against her hair. The temptation, just to lay her head against his shoulder was overwhelming, and she was experiencing those same tormenting longings first known that morning before they left Egypt. Then he gave an abrupt exclamation and reached for the antiseptic.

'Sorry that took so long—I must have hurt you.'

'No, you didn't.' She allowed a long pent-up sigh to escape as he pressed the cool soaked pad of cottonwool into her palm, his fingers staying curved over her wrist and making her responding pulses cancel out the sting of the lotion. Suddenly it became intolerable and she snatched her hand out of his grasp. 'Thank you—it's fine now.'

'Is it?'

'Yes,' her face was averted. 'I—I have to see about lunch now.'

She wondered if she imagined the air of restraint during the subsequent meal. Emma chattered brightly enough, but Jarret's responses seemed rather automatic, and once or twice Lissa became conscious of his glance resting rather curiously on her, although he made no comment other than to enquire if the minor injury still troubled her.

She denied this, as she also denied his observation later that evening that she looked tired.

'Well, I certainly am,' he said flatly. 'I think it's time we had a break.'

She looked at him with surprise. 'But we can't! Not with all the jobs still to do in the house, and especially the garden.'

'One can't transform a house and garden into one's own preconceived vision of it in a few weeks,' he reminded her, 'so don't try. But to get back to a holiday ...' He paused, his lean hands fixing after dinner drinks with smooth, unhurried movements before he went on: 'Courtesy demands we return a holiday invitation to Emma's friend, but to be candid I don't feel very enthusiastic about taking a couple of kids abroad during the high season hassle and coping with the inevitable holiday tummy and all the rest of it.' He swirled the amber liquid in his glass and looked at it reflectively before he glanced up at her. 'Do you like Cornwall?'

'Devon's as far west as I've been,' she said wryly, 'and that was only a weekend.'

'A colleague of mine owns a small estate near Trevarron. There's always been an understanding that if ever I wanted the use of Cove Cottage I'd only to say. But it's isolated, above a private beach, and the nearest shop is about a mile away. It's a lovely spot, but if the weather doesn't hold ...'

Visions of being cooped up in a small cottage with two children, watching the rain lashing against the window, flashed into Lissa's mind. But this was a risk one ran when taking a holiday in Britain, she reminded herself with a faint smile.

Jarret noticed the smile, and perhaps misread it. 'There could be snags,' he pointed out, 'and I have to be honest; the arrangement would suit me because I've a project in line in the area. I could mix the two very well. But it means there'll be days you'll be left with the children.'

The unspoken questions hung in the air. How did she feel about this? Could she cope?

'The children won't worry me—and we'll deal with the weather problem if it arises. I'm looking forward to it already,' she said with assurance.

And so it was settled. Jarret would contact his friend immediately and fix a convenient date, then Emma could make her invitation to Jane.

Lissa lay awake a long time that night, thinking of the cottage as Jarret had described it and the intimacy it could not help but engender in so isolated a place. Certainly, he would be absent at times, but there would be the long evenings after the children had been dispatched to bed. Three weeks . . .

Her imagination bounded ahead despite the control she always endeavoured to place on it and started to explore the possibilities—and the dangers. In Egypt it had been different; they had not become accustomed to living in the close state of marriage—without the physical bond that broke down the barriers of reserve. Since then they had moved carefully towards an amicable if guarded relationship, one which Emma had stabilised, and the excitement of the move, with all the work this had entailed, had imperceptibly smoothed away much of the strangeness and awkwardness that had persisted. But now . . .

Lissa turned her face abruptly into the pillow. How much longer could she hide her love? If she should ever give herself away, if Jarret were ever to learn the truth of how she felt about him it would ruin everything. Because she couldn't bear it if he did.

She shivered and closed her eyes, trying to ignore the traitorous, sensuous thrill of anticipation that tingled through her body. For the moment it was strong enough to drive out all fear.

Desire was all that mattered.

CHAPTER SEVEN

THE cottage was a dream: and so was the weather.

A warm, benevolent sun poured its gold down from an azure sky dotted with clouds like drifts of swansdown, and the sea glistened like a sparkling blue mirror the afternoon Lissa and the two children clambered excitedly out of the car.

Emma looked round. 'Is that ours?' She pointed to the long, low white cottage planted sturdily in the green fold above the cove.

'There aren't any more, so it must be—silly!' Jane capered and dodged Emma's attempts at retaliation. 'Race you!'

They had sparred amicably for most of the long drive to the West Country, and now they released some of the energy that had built up during the journey. Jarret gave a peremptory shout as they tore away down the winding path, a command which met with brief glances back at him and shaken heads. Jarret looked at Lissa, and then at the motley assortment of bags, carriers, buckets and spades and balls and sunhats, camera, binoculars, picnic box and suitcases revealed when he opened the trunk of the car. 'They can expound some of that surplus energy toting their own gear,' he said with mock grimness, heaving the two largest cases out.

It was a small snag, that the gated road through the estate stopped slightly short of journey's end, leaving about fifty yards to carry everything to the cottage. But it was worth it, Lissa thought happily when she began the first exploration of their holiday home for the next three weeks.

It had all the traditional dream-cottage features. Low casement windows with the quaint bottle-glass panes, window seats covered in chintz, Suffolk latches on heavy old oaken doors set in whitewashed walls fifteen inches thick. There were spindle chairs and horse-brass and a wide hearth

with an inglenook in the sitting room, narrow winding stairs
that led up to the bedrooms, one of which held a fourposter,
dormer windows which vied with one another for the love-
liest view, and age-blacked beams everywhere that Jarret
was going to have to watch didn't make too close contact
with his head during the sojourn. There was a tiny bathroom with a floor that sloped downwards, two of the bedrooms were linked, requiring a journey through the first
one to reach the second, and the third bedroom contained a wardrobe of such vast and cavernous size there
was scarcely room for much else than the essential bed.

It worked out very well, really. Jarret announced that
he would sleep in the wardrobe, which brought howls of
mirth from the kids, Lissa was to have the fourposter, and
Emma and Jane could share the adjoining room.

Most of the time the weather was kind. There was one
storm, and one night a gale roared round the cottage,
huffing and puffing in from the ocean, as though it would
fell even granite and slate in its path. When a slate did go
flying there were squeals from the children, who finished up
that night in the fourposter with Lissa.

She was alternately happy and sad during those long,
sunlit days. The simple, age-old pursuits of the children,
building sand-castles, shrimping, gathering shells and cart-
ing buckets of assorted marine specimens back to the cottage—buckets that tended to take on an anything but
ozone freshness by the next morning!—all brought back
happy memories of her own childhood holidays. The first
sad mood came when she realised she had been married
four months. A third of a year, of the first year. The next
third would bring their first Christmas, then New Year,
then Easter, the milestones which inexorably marked the
march of the seasons. And would deepen love fated to be
denied.

The thought haunted Lissa in those moments of quiet,
and cast a shadow over the times of joy when she could
not quite forget. It was the bitter-sweet highlights of that
holiday which gave her such a poignant insight to what
it would be like to be truly the wife of Jarret and the
mother of his children. The glimpses of the small, tender
intimacies, the tears, the little dramas, the laughter and

the prickly moments, all the things that went to make up the pattern of family life.

There was the day that Emma went missing. One minute she was there, trailing big circles in the smooth sand with a long seaweed stick, the next moment the beach seemed empty apart from herself and Jarret, who was sprawled on the sand, enjoying the heat of the sun on his tanned back.

Lissa put down her book and stared round uneasily. Emma must have gone up to the cottage to meet Jane, who had dashed back because she'd left her sunglasses somewhere. Both children had the new crazy-crackle specs, which Jarret had bought for them during a visit to Truro the previous day, and neither could bear to be seen without them—the sunglasses had been worn during bathtime the night before, and only removed for bed after an argument and a great deal of giggling.

But the path was deserted. Lissa got up stealthily, not wanting to worry Jarret yet, and moved up the incline of the beach, shading her eyes as she scanned the steep sides of the cove, and then the green fold where the cottage nestled under the lee of a thick copse. Where could she be?

The two promontories enclosed the cove completely, reaching out their jagged rock arms into deep water that made access from the neighbouring sections of coast impossible, even at low tide. Then she glimpsed a quick movement and the flash of scarlet in front of the cottage; Jane in her scarlet shorts and white top, and alone. Lissa rushed to meet her, and met surprise. No, Emma hadn't gone with her. Emma was still on the beach.

'What's the matter?' Jarret had arrived.

Lissa told him, and he frowned. 'But where could she go?'

'She'll be hiding?' said Jane.

'Where?'

'Among the rocks, or she might be in the caves!' Jane darted away, and Lissa hurried after her.

There were a couple of small caves at the northern side of the cove, more like shallow crevices in the cliff face than deep, tortuous caverns, and it took only a glance to see that they were empty. A large sand-castle stood at the entrance to one, and bore the artistic prints of small toes round its battlements, and a comic had been weighted down with a large stone, but of the owner there wasn't a sign.

Lissa turned, really worried now, and saw that Jarret was loping up the path to the cottage. He would be making sure that Emma hadn't gone there and somehow managed to miss her friend. But she would have run down to the beach again by now, Lissa told herself and looked round for Jane.

Jane had taken herself up on to the rocks of the point, and was leaping from one to another where they stretched out into the sea like a miniature Land's End, until she was poised daringly on the farthermost pinnacle.

'Jane! Come back!' Lissa cried sharply. 'We don't want to lose you as well.'

'Sorry, Auntie Lissa. But it's quite safe really,' Jane assured her with the superb confidence of childhood.

'Maybe, but we're not risking it any more.' Lissa went to the base of the rocks and held out her hand, to have a small wet sandy one put trustingly into it. Thank goodness Jane was a biddable child, she reflected as Jane leaped down and trotted at her side across the beach.

They could hear Jarret's voice on the clear air as he called Emma's name. Then he emerged from the tangle of woodland behind the cottage, alone. His tall figure began to return down the path to the beach, and then Lissa's attention was diverted by a stifled sneeze nearby.

'Bless you,' she murmured automatically, thinking it was Jane, and the sound was repeated.

'It wasn't me,' said Jane, 'it must be—*Oh!*' She stopped dead, pointed, and dissolved into giggles. 'Look!'

Immediately ahead, a small sand hummock seemed to be moving in a very odd way, shedding strands of seaweed and the remains of Jarret's morning paper. The hummock rose, transforming itself into the shape of Emma, an Emma smothered in sand, helpless with laughter, and eyes agleam with triumph through her sandy mask.

'You never spotted me! You walked right past me twice! Daddy nearly *stood* on me!'

'Emma, you might have been smothered!' Lissa's voice

was unsteady with mingled relief and anger. 'Whatever made you do such a silly thing?'

'I was all right. I made a funnel to breathe through with the paper.' Emma seemed unaware of anything other than fun in her prank. 'I thought you'd never find me.'

'Yes, and soon you're going to wish we hadn't!'

Jarret loomed over the child, his expression furious. He pointed to the cottage. 'Bath, then bed.'

Emma's face changed from mirth to shock in a second. 'B-but it's not tea-time yet. I stay up until nine o'clock now, Daddy.'

'Not today,' he said grimly. 'This is punishment for playing such a stupid trick and worrying Lissa—and me. Now,' he lifted his hand threateningly, 'are you going, or do I smack you until you obey?'

Lissa held her breath, realising that Jarret would carry out his threat and willing Emma not to defy him. Slowly and despondently the child turned and trailed disconsolately over the sand. Lissa bit her lip. 'Jarret,' she ventured, 'it was a childish joke. She didn't mean to worry us.'

'She could have smothered herself.' His tone was brusque. 'And surely you realise that I have to keep my word, or I'll never maintain discipline again.'

She knew he was right, but it cast a cloud over the day. Emma wept when she came out of the bath and found she really did have to don her nightie and go to bed in the middle of the afternoon. Jane valiantly offered to do the same, and it was only a short time before there were muffled giggles coming from the fourposter. Jarret relented at teatime, and took them out for a meal and an evening drive, and by the following morning the incident was forgotten.

That was the morning the Cornish mizzle crept in from the sea, leaving its ghostly veil over the cove. There wasn't a breath of breeze to disperse it, nor even a sign of a good fall of rain to help wash it away; only the still white dampness that settled on one's hair and enclosed one in an eerie isolation. Jarret had no inclination for driving in it, so perforce, a day of indoor amusement was required. There was no television, and somehow the radio did not hold the children's attention for long. So Lissa devised such pastimes as could be improvised from materials to hand.

They did the cards, and Lissa, putting them in her bag ready for the next pillar-box, could not help noticing that Emma's carefully printed message to her Aunt Camilla was a very stilted affair, but a card to Uncle Neil overflowed with scribbles of affection and crosses that continued into the address side. She suggested they might sort the considerable amount of shells already gathered, and this passed away another hour, the children's heads and Lissa's bent earnestly to the task. Once Jarret came over to see what was happening and put his arms round the close little group.

Instantly Lissa was caught in that indefinable aura he seemed to exert for her. When he bent over from behind her chair to look at a special shell Emma held up his chin brushed against Lissa's hair and she felt his closeness acutely. But she had to play her part of the amicable but passionless wife. She too held up a shell for his inspection, one which Jane had found, and when she turned her head to glance up at him the smile ebbed from her face. Because his smile had gone and he was looking down into her eyes with that strange shuttered glance she found so disturbing.

'It's beautiful,' he said, but he had not even looked at the shell. His hands fell from the children's shoulders and for a moment rested on Lissa's. His fingertips burned through her thin muslin blouse, and called up all the responses within her that she tried so hard to defy. She wanted to stay there, under his hands, but she knew she must break the spell before her own hands moved to meet his. If only she could lean back and lay her head against his shoulder, evoke his caresses ...

'The sun's out!'

Jane's exuberant cry broke the tension. The children rushed to the window, and Jarret moved away from Lissa. 'Come on, we'll go for a walk,' he said. 'We've a lot of energy to work off after being in all day.'

He walked them for miles, until the sun had gone down and the sky reflected its rose and amber tints over the landscape. It was dark when they got back, and, as far as Lissa and the children were concerned, they were so tired they were falling asleep over the supper-time snack.

'We'll have a sand-castle competition this morning, I think,' announced Jarret at breakfast next morning.

'Is there a prize, Daddy?'

'Of course there'll be a prize.'

'How much?'

'Fifty pence for the biggest one.'

Their eyes glistened and they were ready to take off for the beach that very moment.

'I'll give a prize too, for the one that's best decorated,' added Lissa, just in case Jarret forgot about the poor loser.

Never were the chores of bed-making and dish-washing so quickly accomplished. The children raced happily down to the beach, where Jarret staked out two large sites, one at each side so that the whole width of the cove separated the contestants and the furious digging began.

He set a time limit of one hour, forbade them to cross to each other's site, and then retired with Lissa to a secluded hollow further up the beach, remarking that an hour of peace should be guaranteed.

'Did you bring the sun lotion?' he asked, as Lissa searched in the beach bag for her novel and her sunglasses.

She handed it over, reflecting that it was going to be needed. The sun was hot already, in a cloudless sky with a slight haze in it; the promise of heat to come.

She relaxed back, and Jarret applied the lotion liberally over his arms, chest and shoulders. Already he was deeply tanned, as were the children, but Lissa, whose fair skin needed a slower acclimatisation, had been cautious about her sunbathing during the first few days.

'Like to do the honours?' There was a sardonic note in his voice as he lay prone and held out the bottle of lotion.

Silently she took it and knelt by his side. Emma had done the anointing of her father's back on previous occasions, ladling the lotion on with small, liberal hands. Lissa poured some of it into her palm and hesitated, looking down on the broad, muscular expanse of Jarret's back. She had never touched his body before and she felt strangely nervous.

'What's the hold-up—are you reading the instructions?'

he enquired, in the same dry, sardonic tone, his head pillowed lazily on his forearms.

'Shouldn't I?' she said lightly, and essayed the first application.

The feel of his warm firm flesh under her hand was instantly sensuous and exciting. When she had covered his shoulders and his back right down to the top of his brief blue shorts, she did not want to stop. Almost reluctantly she capped the bottle and sank back on the beach towel. 'You'll do,' she said in a strained little voice.

'Thanks.'

His eyes were closed, his dark hair smudged with a streak of sand, and he seemed on the verge of a lazy sleep in the sun. With a small sigh Lissa put the lotion back in the bag, then changed her mind and took it out again. The power of that sun was not to be ignored.

She had donned a bikini that morning with the intention of having a swim as soon as her breakfast had settled, and over it she had carelessly slipped a thin white embroidered cotton smock that was barely fingertip length. Perhaps her innate modesty might have dictated another choice, had she been able to see her reflection more clearly. But the mirror in her bedroom was not ideally placed for light, and the room itself tended to be shadowy under the overhanging eaves. As she began to apply the sun lotion to her long slender legs she was blissfully unaware that the brilliant light revealed every line of her body beneath the diaphanous cotton, or that the pale lemon tint of her bikini glowed through and somehow made a far more revealing and provocative picture than the frank bareness of the bikini by itself. She pushed up the loose sleeves of the smock and laved her arms, and Jarret's voice said sleepily: 'Take it off.'

'*What?*'

'How can you put on the stuff wearing that thing?' He sounded more awake. 'It's like trying to undress while you keep your coat on.'

'You've made me spill it!' She dabbed at the rivulets of lotion now making oily blotches among the pretty Indian embroidery.

'What did you expect?' He sat up and took the bottle

from her. 'You'd better let me return the compliment.'

There was no way she could refuse, even though one small inner voice was saying no and another was saying why not. Slowly she slipped the smock over her head and presented her back to the waiting Jarret.

'It'll be easier if you lie flat.'

Silently she stretched herself out and pillowed her forehead on her arms, much in the way he had done a few minutes previously. She tensed every nerve for his touch, but despite her control a contraction ran through her limbs at the first moment of contact. His touch was surprisingly gentle, and unaccountably soothing. After a few moments she was lulled into sensuous acceptance of those long smooth silken strokes down her body. Until they stopped for an instant, unconversant fingers fumbled between her shoulder blades, and released the fastener of her bra top.

'It's in the way,' he said softly and casually, and sounded so innocently matter-of-fact she relaxed again.

Afterwards she could not pinpoint the moment when the leisurely smoothing application of sun lotion changed to long sensuous caresses that swept the length of her body. She did not move, aware that Jarret had become very intent even though she dared not turn her head up sufficiently to see him. Her pulses began to throb and her heartbeat became a wild, hammering thud.

She drew in a shuddering breath, and the caresses became more insistent, exploring the shadowy hollows under her tumbled hair, then smoothing the long sweep from shoulder to thigh, lingering in the warm concave just above her hip. Then he moved, and she felt the hard pressure of his thigh thrust against her own.

The sudden movement made her start up a little, and his hand slipped under her waist, homing to her breast, and there discovering the tell-tale reaction to his touch that all the will-power in the world could not prevent.

'Do you know how beautiful you are, Lissa?' The question was unsteady, as though he too strove to seem flippant.

She could not speak, and the warm, insistent pressure of his hand was bringing to a peak the surge of desire he had invoked in her body. She wanted to turn to face him and arch herself up to the magnetic force of his body, to press and cling until nothing divided them, until spent passion would somehow, magically, sate this turbulent hunger that burned in her body like a fever.

'Lissa . . .'

He bent over her, the word stirring against her ear, and his hand ran over the taut curve of her abdomen, seeking the most intimate caress of all.

Frissons coursed down her spine into a wild sweet fire, and she turned towards him, her mouth softly parted and her whole being pliant. Then a flash of scarlet beyond his shoulder and a young excited voice pierced the spell of desire.

Lissa crashed back into sanity, frantically scrabbling for her bra top, but Jarret had already snatched it and held it to her, shielding her until her shaking fingers managed the fastening.

'I've finished, Uncle Jarret! It's super! Emma hasn't finished yet!'

Jane raced up to the two rather flushed adults, her small chubby features alight with triumph. 'Are you going to judge them now?' she added eagerly.

Jarret sought his watch. 'The hour isn't over yet, Jane, so we mustn't judge them until it is.'

She nodded unquestioningly, and knelt on the sand. 'You've spilt the sun-tan stuff, Auntie Lissa.'

Sure enough, the lotion was draining away into the sand where Jarret had set the bottle without thinking. Lissa gathered it up and pressed the cap on to salvage the little that remained, thankful for the small actions to tide her over those feverish moments while she tried to recapture composure. She did not dare look at Jarret, lest the scarlet tides race into her cheeks.

But he appeared to have regained equilibrium with remarkable ease.

'Like a drink of squash?' he asked Jane.

The child's eyes rounded eagerly and thirstily. He pulled the bottle of orange out of the bag, poured it into a beaker, dropped in a couple of ice-cubes out of the pineapple ice box, and then settled himself face down again on the sand.

Lissa, not because she was thirsty, but to occupy her hands, mixed one for herself, and a few minutes later Emma arrived to announce that her castle was finished and it was super.

Jarret got to his feet, and now there was no indication that he too had shared a sensuous and frustrating incident only a few minutes ago. He held out his hand to Lissa in much the same way he would to the children and hauled her up to her feet. He tossed a coin to decide which castle to view first and the judging began.

There was no problem in allotting the prizes! Jane had finished first and allowed herself ample time in which to decorate her fortress with extravagant patterns of pebbles and shells and artistic trails of seaweed. It had elaborate battlements and a moat complete with drawbridge made from driftwood; unfortunately she had failed to keep the moat afloat.

Emma had worked till the last minute, and the great pits beside her castle testified to the amount of excavation the vast pile had entailed. Sadly, the final touches showed every sign of frantic last-minute slapdash.

She received her fifty-pence piece from her father, and Lissa solemnly presented an identical coin to Jane. Honour was satisfied. Emma gave an exuberant whoop and leapt on top of her castle, jumping up and down until it started to disintegrate. 'I'm going to buy a castle to live in when I grow up!' she cried.

'You won't have enough money, silly,' pointed out the more practical Jane.

'I will!' Emma jumped to the other end of her crumbling edifice. 'I'm going to be rich when I'm eighteen!'

'So you say,' Jane said placidly, daring to start a little demolition aid.

'Don't touch my castle! It's true. Isn't it, Daddy?'

Appealed to, Jarret frowned. 'Yes,' he said with a trace of unwillingness, 'but it's a long way off and you won't be a millionairess, my girl, so forget about it until the time comes.'

Lissa felt puzzled. This was the first she had heard of possible wealth to come for Emma. The child had made quite a lot of endearing little confidences as she got to know

Lissa, but she had never uttered the boast of a few minutes ago, and Jarret had never volunteered a word of it. But it really wasn't any business of hers, Lissa told herself, and probably it would be a legacy from a relative, which didn't seem cause for Jarret's distinct frown of displeasure.

The subject was forgotten as the day went on, and Lissa was too conscious of the perceptible air of strain between herself and Jarret to concern herself with speculation regarding Emma's future expectations. It wasn't so bad when the children were present, their high spirits and exhausting energy soon dispersed thoughts of self, but the moment she was alone with him the memories of that morning rushed back, bringing bitter humiliation at the way her traitorous body had almost betrayed her.

The children's bedtime came too soon for her peace of mind, but even Lissa realised that her own retirement up-stairs would lead to enquiries which might easily encroach on dangerous ground. Outwardly calm when she returned downstairs after settling Emma and Jane for the night, she listened to the news on radio and then said as casually as she was able: 'I'm going to have a bath, then I think I'll have an early night.'

Jarret looked up. 'Come downstairs again before you turn in. I want to talk to you.'

He sounded cool and peremptory. Lissa frowned. 'You're making me feel like one of the children,' she protested.

His gaze roamed deliberately over her and returned to her face. 'You don't look like one of the children,' he observed dryly.

'I'd hardly be here if I did.' Without waiting for any response she went from the room and upstairs to run her bath. She locked the door very carefully, and then indulged in a heartbreaking little fantasy in which she drifted down to him in a shimmery, misty nightdress and in the soft golden glow of the Victorian oil lamps he declared his love for her, whispering against her hair that they would have the perfect marriage and live happily ever after. And then he would kiss her ...

Lissa splashed her face savagely with cold water and scrubbed herself dry. Happy endings like that belonged between the pages of novels, and in the misty fade-outs of two profiles enjoined in chaste kiss beloved of the ancient movies. Her own particular situation was very clear and had been spelled out right at the start. She'd be all kinds of a fool if she started kidding herself that Jarret was becoming attracted to her just because he'd felt inclined to venture a spot of petting this morning. It didn't mean a thing. Hadn't he avowed from the start that he had no intention of expecting her to make the marriage a complete one? Anyway, none of her nighties was exactly the style to which a seductress was accustomed!

She pinned up her hair and donned a pair of clean denims and a blue cotton blouson before she went downstairs to make their supper drinks and hear what Jarret wanted to say. But he did not want a drink or snack, only something a bit stronger. He followed her to the little cottage kitchen with its gleaming copper-ware and watched as she made her own cup of tea.

He was moody and restless, with a betrayal of pent-up energy surging under a strict rein. She knew the mood well enough by now and sighed inwardly, preparing herself for the conflict that was about to come. It had been too much to hope for that the fragile rapprochement of the past few weeks would endure indefinitely.

She turned and leaned back against the cupboard, cradling the beaker of tea between her hands. The warning bells were starting their clamour, but she forced herself to take the initiative and look at him calmly. 'Well, Jarret, what is it?'

'You.'

'Me?' The bells clamoured louder than ever, but she maintained her steady regard of him, resolutely closing her mind to the day's incident. 'What have I done, for goodness' sake?'

He took a mouthful of whisky. 'You haven't done anything, and you're perfectly well aware of it. Lissa, is something worrying you?'

She hesitated. 'Not at the moment.' Her tone was guarded; she hadn't forgotten the night she had dared to voice her fear that there might be a reckoning in five years' time when she had to walk out of Emma's life. His response that night had hardened her resolve never to broach that subject again.

'I'm not convinced, Lissa.' He walked past her and put the empty glass on the draining board. 'I've been taking note lately, and I can't entirely fathom it. One moment you look as though you hadn't a care in the world, and the next . . .' he shook his head. 'What is it?'

'I think you're imagining it,' she said flatly.

'Maybe.' He was facing her now, his gaze intent. 'By the way, did this morning upset you?'

'*Of course not!*'

'I'm glad to hear it,' he said dryly. 'I wondered afterwards if you were worried in case the kids saw you minus your bra.'

She had not expected so direct a reference and the scarlet colour welled up into her cheeks. His mouth went down at the corners and he said, 'I thought so.'

'Don't be ridiculous!' She turned away and almost ran through the arched opening into the sitting room. 'That happened today! You give the impression I've been having wet-week moods for months.'

'And so you have! Stop it, and listen to me!' He caught up with her with incredible swiftness and clamped his hands on her shoulders. 'I've had my suspicions for some weeks now, and this morning confirmed them.'

'W-what do you mean?' she stammered, clutching the beaker as though it were a lifeline.'

'Put that damn tea down before you spill it! And for God's sake, do I have to spell it out?' His eyes raked her face now, as though he would strip away the last vestige of her defence. 'Surely you realise that living with a man can prove to be totally different in reality from theory? That the unpredictable element is bound to be present?'

Apprehension came into her eyes. She turned away and began feverishly rinsing the glass he had just used. 'I thought we'd settled all that.'

'You can't settle human nature. Lissa, I have to say this, because I don't want you to be caused unhappiness, and frustration, through something neither of us had foreseen.'

She was beginning to tremble inwardly and the scarlet flush had long since drained from her cheeks, leaving the skin white and translucent under its faint golden touch of tan.

'I'm well aware of how you approached this marriage,' he went on doggedly, 'more or less as I expected you to, and I respected your wishes. But time and circumstances change.'

'What are you trying to say to me, Jarret?' she whispered.

'I'm trying to tell you that if you want me, for heaven's sake don't be afraid to say so.'

'Want you ...?' Her voice seemed to be choking in her throat. 'You mean—you think——'

'I think you've been aware of me in the physical sense for some time now.' His glance never wavered. 'Or, even if you won't admit it, your body has. And why not? It's a perfectly natural reaction. Certainly the last thing to feel ashamed of.'

When she spoke her own voice sounded a long way away, as though it didn't belong to her. 'I don't think I've done anything of which to be ashamed.'

'I didn't say you had!' he said sharply. 'But I wonder if you realise how compulsive is the physical need once it's awakened. And how hard to deny.'

'Aren't you perhaps concerned with your own problems?' She avoided his gaze.

'I can take care of my own problems, but with the farthest stretch of imagination I can't see you taking care of your own.'

She recoiled from the harshness in his voice. 'How can you talk about love as if—as if it were a commodity one bought off a supermarket shelf?'

'I don't think love comes into it. It's possible to love without sex—and have sex without love. But both of them can make life a hell if their need isn't satisfied.'

Lissa was aghast. 'You make it all sound so cold-blooded!'

He shrugged, and the cynical little twist took his mouth again. 'There's nothing cold-blooded about it, my dear Lissa, and it's the last word I'd choose to describe your particular charm. Have you honestly no idea of your own attraction?'

She looked down stubbornly, remaining silent, and he gave a short laugh.

'A more unassuming girl I've yet to meet—or a less demanding one. Did I leave you in any doubt this morning that I find you attractive?'

'Not exactly.' Her cheeks began to glow again.

'Well then?'

She shook her head and almost blindly opened the drawer of the oak dresser, seeking the bright checked tablecloth to start setting out the breakfast places.

'Lissa ...' deliberately he pulled the cloth out of her hands and threw it on the table, where it skidded on the polished surface and fell to the floor, 'no—leave it,' he seized her wrist. 'Have you ever wondered about *my* sexual need?'

Alarm thudded dully into the pit of her stomach and she tensed. 'No,' her mouth hardened, 'it didn't occur to me. I didn't know you well enough to speculate on so personal a matter. We made a formal arrangement.'

'Yes—too damned formal—like this discussion. Oh, Lissa—come into my arms for just two minutes and I'll prove beyond all doubt that you need me as much as I need you.'

For long moments she stared at him, and an unbearable feeling of sadness washed over her. 'No, Jarret.'

'Then I must come to you.' Imperceptibly his voice had softened and something like tender amusement curved his mouth. 'Never heard of body language, my pet? I'm sorry to disillusion you, but I'd be blind and deaf if I couldn't read the message.'

She steeled herself against traitorous temptation, trying to inject amusement into her voice. 'You're reading the wrong book—or something that isn't there.'

'And you're behaving like the most provocative foolish virgin in history.' With the softly spoken words his arms caught her before her disturbed reactions could counsel evasion. He pulled her against him and stopped the protest on her lips with the force of his mouth.

Lissa's heart began to pound like a hammer under her

ribs. She was acutely aware of how small and slender she was when measured against Jarret's height and strength. His kiss was a challenge and a demand and a plea; his masculinity an irresistible force drawing her into his power. Her arms wanted to curve around his shoulders, not make a feeble thrusting protest against his shirt-front, and then under his hands the soft blouson glided over her talcum-smooth skin, and she knew this betrayed that she wore nothing beneath it.

She sensed the sigh trembling through him. He thrust his hands convulsively under the loose folds, stroking and caressing the warm silken sweep of her back, then invoking a violent shudder in her when he claimed her breast.

He moaned in his throat and his kiss was wild and intimate, the hard masculine contours of his body demanding the surrender of herself. Desire burned in Lissa like wild-fire and for just a moment of anguished ecstasy she tasted his mouth as never before and let her body mould into the hard passionate seeking of his before she cried out and tore herself from his arms.

'*No!* I'm sorry—I can't!' Tears smarted her eyes and choked her voice. 'Please don't make me! Please, Jarret, leave me alone!'

'Why?' he jerked explosively. 'Why are you pretending you don't want——'

'No, you don't understand! Please listen,' she begged desperately before her courage failed. 'I don't believe that sexual gratification will ever make me happy. In fact I think it would make me very unhappy.'

'You're wrong, Lissa.' He took a step forward. 'And I believe I can teach you how wrong. Won't you trust me?'

'It has nothing to do with trust.' She backed away, groping behind her for the edge of the door that led to the hall and escape. 'I can't, Jarret, and it has nothing to do with the respect and—and affection I have for you. It's something deeper than that. I want to be loved and be in love. And I want the man I love to teach me the ways of love, his way.' Her voice sank to a whisper. 'I want to be in love with a man who loves me as dearly as I love him.'

There was an intolerable silence. She stood framed in the doorway, her eyes haunted and dark with despair, her slender hands clutching at her dishevelled blouson. Why couldn't he understand? *Oh, why couldn't he love her?*

And then he moved.

'I see.' His features were a cold, bleak mask and he came towards the door without looking at her.

Cold to the heart, she moved to let him pass, and watched him mount the stairs with heavy, even footfalls, leaving her standing below in the lonely shadows of the hall.

She heard the sound of a closing door, then silence.

CHAPTER EIGHT

LISSA had never foreseen the day when she would welcome the end of a holiday as much as this one. The final week dragged by on leaden minutes that belied the glorious summer spell it brought. Jarret reverted to his most reserved self and spent four of the remaining days at Plymouth, completing the business matters he had mentioned before they set off. In her heart, Lissa was not sorry to see him go; the situation between them was unbearable, and his icy, formal attitude seemed to suggest that it was entirely of her making. At least back in London she could find tasks to occupy her mind and diversions to crowd her days and help drive out the unutterable sense of misery that hung like a grey pall over every waking moment.

The new term at Emma's school started three days after the return to London, and despite Lissa's unhappiness the days and the weeks began to slide away. Each evening darkened a few minutes earlier and a wet, misty autumn set in to depress even the most resilient of spirits. Soon it would be Christmas—as Emma informed anyone who would listen at every opportunity. She came running out of school one afternoon to the waiting Lissa and announced jubilantly that they had started rehearsing the Christmas play, and she was to play the part of Mary.

'There's going to be a meeting next week for all the mothers so that they can talk about the costumes.' Emma danced excitedly along. 'It's next Wednesday, at two o'clock. You won't forget, will you?'

'I won't forget,' Lissa promised, happy for Emma's signal honour.

'Oh, and Miss Brown says she hopes you won't decide to cut my hair before Christmas. You won't, will you, Lissa?'

'I hadn't even thought of it,' admitted Lissa. 'But you'll be wearing a robe that hides most of your hair, won't you?'

'Yes—for the play,' Emma hastened to explain, 'but there's sort of prologue before it. Singing carols—we haven't started to learn them yet—but there are going to be eight special singers—I'm one of them—and we've all got long hair. We have to wear long white dresses like angels.'

'An angels' chorus? Shades of Faust!' was Jarret's sardonic comment when his daughter proudly broke the news.

'What's Faust?' Emma asked.

'Faust was a man, not a what,' he informed her dryly. 'He sold his soul for eternal youth.'

Emma's face puckered. 'But how? Your soul's inside you, Daddy.'

'Is it?'

'Yes. Then when you die it goes to Heaven.'

'Presuming one has behaved oneself,' observed Jarret in an aside to Lissa.

'If you've tried to behave yourself and be good,' corrected Emma, who had remarkably sharp hearing. 'Ooh, won't Grannie be pleased that I'm in the play? Do you think she'll be able to come to see me on Christmas Eve. And Uncle Neil, of course.'

'I've no idea.' Jarret pushed his chair back and crumpled his dinner napkin. 'And now, if the theology session is closed I must ask you to excuse me.'

'You're excused, Daddy,' said Emma in a pert fashion that made Lissa want to check the child. But she restrained herself, knowing it was excitement and not impertinence.

When he had left the dining room Emma fiddled with her napkin, trying to fold it into the shape of a hat. Lissa took it from her, and Emma suddenly drooped.

'Why does Daddy always work at night in his study? He didn't used to.'

Her head bent, Lissa folded the napkin and put it through its ring. 'He has more work to do now,' she said with a little sigh.

'Like homework?' suggested Emma.

It was a useful cue and when Emma was settled with her books Lissa cleared the remains of the meal and washed up. The point at which Jarret had departed had underlined something that Lissa was vaguely concerned about already.

Ever since the return from the Cornish holiday Camilla and Neil had called at least once each week, and Emma's grandmother, while she was not so frequent a visitor, telephoned or wrote every weekend. Emma was already beginning to resent the duty replies she was obliged to pen to her doting grannie. Like most children she loathed letter writing. After thank you for whatever it was, and I hope you are well, inspiration ran out and she invariably needed several promptings to sit down and painfully compose those stilted sentences that people seemed to expect every time they wrote to her. But there seemed no doubt that the de Rys family was a possessive one. It worried Lissa somehow, although she could not pin down the reason why it should, and she felt reluctant to mention this to Jarret, especially in his present frame of mind regarding herself.

Yet it all appeared so innocent.

Camilla and Neil would breeze in, usually around half-past three or quarter to four, and Lissa would make afternoon tea. Camilla, with bored insouciance, would kick off her shoes and moan about the miles she'd tramped searching for the exact shade of something she required to match something else.

When Lissa apologised for having to leave them for a little while to go and meet Emma coming out of school Neil insisted on going himself, taking his car, which delighted Emma, and leaving Lissa with his fiancée. Lissa had to admit that Neil was difficult to resist, and it was easy to see why Emma readily returned his affection. He was fun, attentive and easy-going, and he usually brought some token for Lissa, perhaps a spray of flowers, or some chocolates, or a plant that had taken his fancy. Yet a suspicion came to her that he might not prove as thoughtful if some real difficulty or trouble were entailed. The affair of the musical box seemed to confirm this, although no one but Lissa seemed to notice.

Emma's musical box, an exquisitely hand-painted miniature spinet that tinkled out an eighteenth-century melody, was one of her most treasured possessions, and one of the last gifts from her Uncle Daniel before he died. One night she must have wound it too tightly—though she swore it had got hurt in the house removal!—and it gave a tortured ping, a dying wheeze, and went silent. Neil examined it, announced that it would be no trouble at all, just fit a new movement, and promised to buy one. Jarret had already attempted to repair the damage, without success, and offered to try to find another box as near as possible in design. But Emma was adamant; she wanted her own treasure, or nothing.

Three weeks went by, and each time Neil reported failure to locate the right type of fitting. On the third occasion Camilla giggled. 'Why not be honest, darling, and admit you forgot the moment you walked out of here? He has an appalling memory, I'm afraid,' she added to Lissa in a tone that seemed more admiring than deprecatory. Finally it was Jarret who located a craftsman clockmaker who fitted the particular type of Swiss movement to bring the little spinet back to tinkling life.

Emma was happy again!

She blurted out the good news next time Neil called, obviously showing no lessening of affection for him despite his failure to keep his promise.

It was about this time that Lissa noticed the pattern being established.

The visitors invariably timed their calls to coincide with Emma's emergence from school—and invariably took their departure before Jarret's return from his office. There was no question of any deliberate secrecy, of course; Emma would naturally announce the fact that they'd had company the moment her father got in the door. He responded to these announcements with a marked lack of enthusiasm, and although he never made any adverse comment Lissa gained a strong impression that the visits displeased him very much, even that he would prefer to sever the link completely.

But how could he object? she asked herself worriedly. There was a close blood tie involved, and they were devoted to the child. It was neither fair nor logical to expect the relationship to be ignored because Jarret had remarried. All the same, apart from the rather pointed way in which they avoided Jarret, there seemed to be undercurrents present which Lissa sensed strongly but could do little about. She tried to tell herself she was imagining things, that her inexplicable feeling of guilt was stupid. Jarret was so taciturn these days she hesitated to embark on discussions. And this was when the guilt nagged. His chill, distant manner dated from that night at the cottage—if only that night had never happened, she thought miserably. But for that she might have ventured her misgivings and talked over the unease she felt. But what could she do, except play the part to which he had relegated her? That of a façade in his life, a housekeeper, hostess and caretaker of his child—except for those moments on a sunlit Cornish beach when inadvertently she had roused him to sexual desire.

The crisis, when it erupted, came when she least expected.

Christmas lighted the fuse—in November.

The de Rys family wanted Emma for the whole festive season. Of course Lissa and Jarret were welcome for the actual holiday break, but when Jarret had to return to town after Boxing Day they wanted him to leave Emma with them until after the New Year.

Jarret said a cold and uncompromising 'No!'

In vain Mrs de Rys pleaded. Emma had been the heart of their Christmases for the past eight years; they couldn't imagine Christmas without her. And it would be such fun for her to meet all her former school friends again. She would see Jane, and there were all sorts of parties being planned in their circle, and there was the carol singing, and the Midnight Service, and the very important matter of Father Christmas's visit to Emma.

Jarret refused to reconsider his decision. He pointed out that Emma had made new friends at her new school and had received three invitations already to parties locally and had begged to be allowed to give one herself, and that at eight she could scarcely be expected to maintain permanent friendships with ex-schoolmates from whose paths her own had now diverged. As far as Jane was concerned the two children had already spent two holidays together and would doubtless spend others in the future. He added that Emma had informed Father Christmas of her new address, and that she was now committed

to Christmas at home because of the school's special performance on the Eve and her leading role in it. He then
quite gently reminded Mrs de Rys that Lissa's family
had to be considered and arrangements for a visit to them
to be fitted in. But there would be a visit to Rys House
some time during the holiday season.

Mrs de Rys was upset, very upset, and secretly Lissa
was aghast. While naturally she would have liked to see
her own family at Christmas she had been quite prepared to
find herself either in Kent or entertaining the de Rys
family in London. But the prospect of a quiet, intimate
Christmas at home with only herself and Emma and
Jarret was daunting. She tried to imagine it, the pretence
of loving togetherness for Emma's sake, the whole empty
bitter charade. Yet how different it might be, with love.
The miracle of Christmas; wasn't that what love was all
about? But what was the use of wishing?

The cold front descended rapidly. Rys House appeared
to be temporarily incommunicado and the afternoon visits
were suspended. Lissa felt concerned, even if helpless in
the face of Jarret's apparent complete dismissal of the
matter—however, she had plenty to occupy her mind, if
not her heart.

There were the two costumes to sew for Emma; her
white angel's dress with its flowing 'wing' sleeves and the
blue and white robes for her part as the Virgin. And if
Jarret meant what he said about Christmas at home she
would have to start preparing for it. Although she had
an extremely generous housekeeping allowance, and she
knew that Jarret would expect her merely to order whatever additional provisions would be required, some wistful little notion made her decide to make everything
possible herself. The cake, the pudding, the mince-pies, the
decorations; it was crazy, just stupid wishful thinking, but
she wanted to have this small satisfaction of pouring all
her love into this only way of expressing it.

Gradually the small heap of parcels in the high com-
partment of her wardrobe became larger as she added
to the store of surprises for Emma, and one day during the
last week of November Emma had an appointment with

the dentist, providing an opportunity to go Christmas shopping with the child when the somewhat unpopular business of the day was over.

Two fillings did not mar Emma's appetite; she announced that she was very hungry and for lunch she would like a hamburger with chilli con carne and french fries. She also knew exactly where to find her menu, leading Lissa firmly towards Knightsbridge.

Afterwards, it occurred to Lissa to wonder if there had been a pre-arrangement of which she had not been informed. But how could there? Certainly Emma's cry of surprise when Neil Hargill walked into the restaurant seemed entirely genuine.

He looked as charming and debonair as ever, asked if he might join them, and then entered into an earnest discussion of the merits of the various hamburger places in town.

'Of course, Emma is a connoisseur,' he informed Lissa gravely. 'But I expect you've already realised that.'

'No, not really. Of tomato ketchup, yes, and ice-cream, but not hamburgers.' Lissa smiled. Suddenly the meal had become fun and she felt a lightening of spirit she had not known for a long time. 'I think she's testing the efficiency of the dentist's handiwork.'

This prompted a blow-by-blow account of Emma's experience in the chair, received with suitable reverence by Neil, and his insistence that the hamburger celebration of the event must be his treat.

He had a superb sense of humour, Lissa had to admit, and even though she suspected that it was a kind of chain reaction that made Neil function—his humour and charm found an instant response from the feminine sex and this in turn made the humour and charm flow even more freely—she could not help responding herself when Neil chose to exert the full force of that attraction. But when Emma began to prattle on about Christmas Lissa felt a pang of remorse. Neil was so tactful, not making any mention of the slightly strained relations existing at present between Jarret and his first wife's family, that even at the risk of disloyalty Lissa felt it was unfair of Jarret to be so stubborn at this time of year. Christmas was the time of love, for forgetting, even if only temporarily, family differences and past enmities.

When Emma's appetite was appeased and she had decided that the fillings were quite permanently lodged Neil wandered out with them to browse happily among the shops. Christmas was getting into full swing, with the Santas, the glittering baubles, the holly and the tinsel and the fairy lights.

The afternoon sped by on enchanted wings, and Lissa as well as Emma was carried along by the irresistible air of gaiety that was rapidly enhanced by the early fall of dusk. Darkness made a perfect background to brilliantly lit shop windows filled with their special Christmas displays, and then there was the magic of Harrods.

Eventually they managed to extricate Emma from the pet department and emerged laden with gaily wrapped parcels. Neil insisted on treating them to tea, at a miraculously secluded little tea-shop which his mother had discovered during a shopping expedition one day.

'Sighs of relief all round!' Neil grinned. 'Kick your shoes off under the table, girls. Don't mind me!'

It was after seven when the taxi spilled out a tired but refusing-to-give-in Emma, a bemused Lissa, a load of shopping, and Neil looking as cool and unruffled as ever. He refused to come in for a drink, pleading an engagement with Camilla for which he dared not be one moment late, and after laughing farewells, kisses from Emma and salutes from Neil, Lissa put her key in the door at the same moment as the inner hall light flooded into life. Jarret stood there, and at the sight of his expression all the happiness of the afternoon ebbed from Lissa's face.

'So you're back,' he said acidly.

'Daddy, I had two fillings and we went to Harrods and Uncle Neil bought me a necklace and a new game you have to be very clever to play. He said it was really for Christmas but as I'd seen it I could have it now,' added Emma in the tone of one assured that Christmas would not fail to bring a proper surprise present from her favourite man—next to her father.

Jarret disengaged himself from his daughter's embrace. 'It's time you were in bed.'

'It's not time!' she wailed indignantly.

'It will be when all the preliminaries are done.'

Emma recognised the implacable note. She seized the carrier containing her own shopping and made for the stairs. Lissa stood with the familiar sick feeling gathering round her heart, then gathered up the packages that had to be put away upstairs for the time being. She went past him, aware of the simmering fury behind his icy control but knowing he would not voice it within Emma's hearing.

She followed the child, going through the nightly routine with mechanical practice. Clothes were hung up, the presents she'd chosen so lovingly were hidden away until she had time to gift-wrap them, and when Emma came out of the bath, scrubbed rosy and hair brushed and tied back ready for bed, Lissa went downstairs again with the little girl to make her bedtime snack.

Emma was not hungry now. She wanted only a drink and to steal the last ten minutes of one of her favourite television comedies. Jarret was in his study. The door was slightly ajar, revealing a long chink of light, and when Emma came reluctantly into the hall she glanced up at Lissa, her small face resigned.

'I suppose I'd better not interrupt Daddy. He's in a bad temper—again!'

So even poor Emma had noticed. Lissa shushed her and persuaded the thin, dressing-gowned little figure towards an unpopular bed. She tucked her in, whispered that her father would come in to say goodnight in a little while, and then descended the stairs on lagging feet. Suddenly Lissa was desperately weary, totally devoid of the essential inward strength she would need to face the storm that lay ahead. But it had to be faced, and she was not prepared to stand meekly under his censure because of his dislike of Neil Hargill. She tapped briefly on the door and thrust it open.

Jarret looked up, frowning, from the papers he had spread across his desk.

'Emma's waiting for you to say goodnight to her.' Lissa

stared at the bookshelves beyond his right shoulder, her mouth taut with strain.

'In a moment. Why wasn't I told about today's arrangement?'

'What arrangement?'

'You know perfectly well *what* arrangement.' He stood up, tall, with the menace of anger still simmering behind the suave, faultless tailoring. 'Do I have to spell out my opinion of Neil Hargill? Or are you devoid of any perception whatever?'

'It was an accidental meeting!' she retorted hotly, stung by the unfair taunt.

'I don't believe you!'

'Are you saying I'm a liar? Why should I try to make a secret arrangement, when I know that Emma is going to come home and tell you the instant she sets foot in the door? It doesn't make sense!' Lissa's hands clenched. 'I took Emma to the dentist, and then to have something to eat before we went Christmas shopping, and Neil walked in.'

'He walked in for the last time,' Jarret snapped. 'Emma is not to see him again. And neither are you.'

Lissa gasped. She stared at him, realising that he meant every word. With an effort she maintained her own control and said flatly: 'I don't know why you wish it so, therefore I'm not in a position to judge the right or the wrong of it. But isn't it impossible? In view of the relationships involved?'

'No. As for relationships, there's more than any blood tie involved. And I will not have Emma influenced.' He moved round the desk. 'I don't expect you to judge anything. I expect you to keep my daughter away from Neil Hargill.'

'But how can I?' she asked helplessly.

'You anticipate a problem?' His voice was withering. 'Or perhaps you too find the gentleman irresistible. Is that the truth of the matter?'

'That's unfair, unfounded, and an insult!' she flashed.

'Is it?' His mouth curled contemptuously. 'Then there should be no difficulty in avoiding Hargill's attentions. Listen,' he gritted, towering over her, 'you've already made it abundantly clear that you intend to stick to the last comma of our contract. So just in case you've forgotten, my dear wife by contract, let me remind you of your obligations. The principal one of these is to look after Emma, for which I'm sure you will agree I've paid you well, therefore I expect obedience and respect of my wishes regarding her upbringing. Is that quite clear?'

'Perfectly,' she said dully. 'But there is one point I would like to question.'

His mouth tightlipped, he inclined his head slightly.

'I can't promise to be responsible for what the outcome might be.'

'Meaning?'

'Meaning Mrs de Rys and her family.'

A strange, almost cruel expression narrowed his eyes. 'You may leave Mrs de Rys and her family to me.'

'And there's something else . . .'

'Well?'

'I think you'd better tell Emma yourself.'

'Why? Are you afraid of undermining the affection you've succeeded in inspiring in her?'

Lissa's mouth trembled with pain. 'No. That thought never entered my head until you voiced it. But I'll admit it's true.'

'It won't do you any good,' he said cruelly.

'I've already realised that.' She strove to prevent her voice breaking. 'I've also realised that where Emma is concerned you are the voice she recognises as authority. Therefore you must be the one to tell her.'

'You don't consider that Emma should be hurt, even if it's ultimately for her own good?'

'No—because there must be a gentler way. But then,' Lissa's head came up determinedly, 'that wouldn't occur to you.'

'You think it hasn't?' He jerked angrily towards her, as if he would seize her physically to enforce his statements. 'You believe I deliberately want to hurt Emma?'

'You make it difficult for me to believe otherwise.' Lissa was shaking now and fast losing control. 'How can I? When you would enter into such a heartless arrangement, bringing me into her life, risking her giving me her trust, knowing all the time that in five years' time it'll be over. Oh, I wish I'd never gone through with it! I must have been crazy—even to save my father. Not if I'd realised it would be at Emma's expense. But you! You have no concern over inflicting pain so long as it's necessary to enforce your own secret, twisted purpose!'

She had stunned him into silence. She saw the whiteness flare round his mouth, his frozen stance, as though he could not believe what he heard, then she burst into tears and ran out of the room.

*   *   *

Lissa did not see him again that evening.

Somehow she found herself in the kitchen, unaware that her limbs had carried her there, and for long moments she gripped the table edge while she struggled to regain control. At last she stirred to prepare a drink which she took upstairs to her room, despite the early hour of the evening.

She sat on the edge of her bed, fighting the need to break down into weeping that would only give her swollen eyes and a splitting headache to add to her heartbreak. He wasn't worth crying over, she tried to tell herself, but with lamentable failure. Despite his appalling suggestion that she was attracted to Neil Hargill, despite his cruel taunts and ruthless insistence on a course that could only lead to disaster for Emma's happiness Lissa knew she could never escape the power he held over her heart. Nor could she escape the questions that tormented her brain. Why did she hate Neil Hargill? Why was he so determined to remove Emma from all influence of the de Rys family?

The morning brought no answers, only a headache and a dull weight of misery. Emma seemed remarkably quiet, and oddly alert, although she made no mention of receiving any dictum from her father, and the bleak November chill outside was more than matched by the atmosphere within the house, a chill that no fire could dispel.

But heartbreak or no, living had to go on. Lissa put the finishing touches to Emma's angel dress and the following evening Emma tried it on. It fitted perfectly, and when she stood back critically Lissa felt the sting of tears in her eyes as she saw Emma's pale, anxious little face upturned to her. She blinked hastily, forcing a smile, and was about to slip it off the child when Jarret walked into the room.

'My! That's beautiful, angel girl', he said to Emma.

As usual, he avoided looking directly at Lissa, and his tone was not quite indulgent enough to be convincing. He walked round Emma, mock solemn, and said: 'How about an angel chorus? Do you know, Lissa'—still he did not look directly at her—'I haven't yet actually heard Emma sing.'

He waited, and Emma looked down at the floor. Then suddenly her face crumpled and she burst into tears. 'I don't want to sing! I won't! I don't want to be in the concert! I hate it!' Tripping and stumbling, she made for the door, her footsteps uneven on the stairs as she coped with the ankle-length dress.

After a moment of shocked indecision Lissa hurried after her, catching her up on the stairhead. She tried to halt the child's blind rush, and Emma flung herself into Lissa's arms.

'What's the matter, darling? Don't cry. You looked so lovely in the angel dress.'

'Daddy says Uncle Neil won't want to see me after Christmas, not any more,' Emma sobbed. 'He says he's going away. Uncle Neil never said that on Friday. He said——'

'Hush, darling.' Lissa cradled the trembling little girl tightly in her arms. 'I think you misunderstood what Daddy tried to tell you.'

'I didn't! He said that——'

'He meant that Uncle Neil will be marrying Aunt Camilla a few weeks after Christmas and going away to live with her. And perhaps they'll have a baby of their own, and naturally they'll love her best because she's their own special baby. Your father only wants to make sure you understand this, and don't feel as though they've forgotten you when this happens.'

Emma looked up, her lower lip quivering. 'Do you think so?'

'Yes, because it's quite true.' Jarret's tall shadow loomed over them, then he stooped down and lifted Emma up into his arms. 'Only I didn't explain it as clearly as Lissa.'

Lissa tensed, as though for a mental blow, and realised that irony was totally absent from his voice. She heard him whisper: 'I love you very much, my precious girl,' and glanced up to see him hugging Emma close and reaching down a hand towards herself where she still knelt on the stairhead.

As though she were in some strange dream, she took the hand stretched down to her and was gently drawn to her feet. Still linked together, the three of them returned downstairs 'Duck, Emma!' Jarret instructed before he walked through the doorway into the sitting room, and still held her high in his arms as he looked at Lissa.

'I'm sorry about the other night,' he said clearly. 'You were quite right.'

Still with that dreamlike feeling, she stared at the darkly handsome face so close to Emma's, with that same slight tilt of the head so characteristic of father and daughter. His eyes seemed to plead with her to accept the olive branch, and before she could speak Emma gave a great sigh.

'Are you going to be speaking to each other again now?'

'Yes—and I'm sorry too.' Lissa's voice was unsteady, and to disguise her emotion she added quickly, 'Come on, let's have that dress off before it gets hopelessly creased.'

'Yes, and I have to phone Mrs Bell and see if she'll babysit tonight,' exclaimed Jarret, letting Emma slide down out of his arms. 'I'm going to take Lissa out for a meal— if we can get a table somewhere decent.'

'But it's such short notice—for Mrs Bell,' protested Lissa, busily removing the dress and not knowing whether to laugh or cry in her relief that her personal cold war with Jarret had reached another truce.

'In that case we'll have to postpone our meal.' Jarret headed for the telephone while Lissa hung up the angel dress and started Emma's bedtime routine.

Perhaps the fates were feeling benign that evening, she thought when Jarret told her Mrs Bell wasn't doing anything special and he'd booked a table for nine o'clock. He departed a few minutes later to collect Mrs Bell, leaving Lissa to clear a few chores and then get ready, and by ten to nine they were stepping into the car.

Lissa wore a new white gown of georgette, with soft flowing lines which nevertheless clung lovingly to her slender curves, and a narrow belt of gold links encircling her slim waist. She had piled her hair into a sleek Edwardian style, wishing she had had time to wash it, to do full justice to the lovely dress she had intended to keep until Christmas before wearing it. She was aware of Jarret's hand possessively on her arm, and still could not quite believe that it was all happening.

It was an enchanted evening. They had a secluded table in a lamplit alcove, the food was superb, the wine unquestionable, the service impeccable, and Jarret seemed determined to be his most charming. Right at the beginning, when they sat down and the waiter brought the menu, Jarret looked at her. 'No inquests. Not tonight,' and she whispered, 'No, no inquests ...'

It was just after one when they reached home and took the faithful Mrs Bell back to her flat. Lissa waited for Jarret to return, not wanting to go up to her room and leave him to re-enter an empty hall. When she heard the sound of the car and the click of the garage door as he closed it as silently as possible she went and opened the front door.

There was something she had to say to him before the evening ended.

He closed the outer door, turning the mortice key and shooting the bolts. When he came into the hall she said tentatively, 'Jarret ...'

'Mm?'

'I—I just wanted to say thank you for tonight—and I'm sorry about all the dreadful things I said the other night.'

He came close to her, disturbingly, tantalisingly handsome in his dark evening clothes and snowy ruffled shirt. 'I thought we agreed no inquests? Want a drink before we call it a day?'

She shook her head. 'I think I've had enough already!'

'Me too—but isn't it fun to feel slightly sloshed now and again?'

'I—I don't know.' She knew the dangerous spell was

fast closing round her, but she did not want to break free, not yet. 'It's an unfamiliar experience for me.'

'Yes, I imagine it is.' Something unfathomable came into his eyes. 'Well, the traditional end to an evening . . .?'

She did not move, and he drew her against him, bending his head and hesitating for an unbearable moment before he touched her lips. She let her mouth cling, as though all the emotional bruising of the past months, ever since Cornwall, was flowing and melting away under the balm of his mouth. It was incredibly sweet, then quite suddenly he drew back, his features inscrutable.

'But I shouldn't do that. I forgot. It's hardly fair, is it?'

Lissa looked away, her mouth soft and quivering, and tried to laugh. 'Wine kisses . . .'

'And temptation,' he said softly. He stretched out his hand and stroked one finger down her cheek with a feather-light touch. 'I don't think you realise how sweet an invitation you are, standing there in your white dress—and Emma's innocence in your eyes.'

Suddenly tears ached behind her eyes. She caught at his wrist and pulled it away from her face. 'Don't—please!'

'Why not?' His other hand came up and closed over hers where it still grasped his wrist. 'I was just wondering why our life can't be like tonight all the time.' He drew her hand up, rubbing it against his own cheek, while his dark, unfathomable gaze probed down into her eyes.

'No——!' She pulled free, spurred by the sorrow of knowing that it was with the sweetness of wine he spoke, 'Please don't—I—I can't bear it when you're so nice to me.'

He looked astonished. 'But what do you want me to do? Swear at you? Beat you?' Humour played round his mouth. 'That might be fun!'

'No—none of those things!' Unable to bear his return to teasing good humour, to know he was actually laughing at her, she turned to escape. His voice arrested her in mid-flight half way up the stairs. She looked back, her hand gripping the banister rail, and saw all the humour had gone from his face.

'So it's true.' He advanced to the foot of the stairs, and she saw his mouth had gone hard. 'In spite of the fact we've known each other for almost a year you're still determined to keep to a cold, impersonal relationship.' He turned away, as though bored with it all now. 'Very well, if that's the way you want it ...'

The living room door closed with a slam, leaving her alone in the stairway shadows.

At three o'clock Lissa was still tossing restlessly, reliving the lovely evening and its miserable dénouement. Why did she always say the wrong thing? Why couldn't she have said a friendly goodnight the moment they got in? Instead of lingering there, wanting to extract the last moments of sweetness and only succeeding in ruining everything again. What a fool she was; no wonder he had made that strange little remark about the innocence of Emma in her eyes. But she wasn't so foolishly innocent not to realise that there would be times when her presence would be a sexual goad to Jarret. It was inevitable. Nor was she foolish enough to believe that it was purely her own attraction that proved the catalyst; wine, food, atmosphere and the right mood, and the warmth and scent of a feminine body was enough.

The wind was sighing through the trees, with the sharp cold note of winter, and somewhere the ancient timbers of the old house creaked protestingly. Lissa turned over yet again, dragging the duvet over her head and burrowing into her rumpled pillow. But it was no use; she had a raging thirst, and she was never going to sleep.

Making no sound, she got up, slipped into her dressing gown and crept downstairs. The familiar outlines of the kitchen seemed alien at this hour of the night, and the silent house seemed to be wakeful, watchful. How many sleepless owners and unhappy nocturnal wanderers had it known in two centuries? Seeking the solace of a warm drink as she did at this moment?

She measured out the milk, standing like a slim pale ghost in the nimbus of the single spot-lamp she had switched on over the hob. When the milk made its small warning hiss in the pan she poured it into a beaker and stood there for a moment staring at the blue and white tiles behind the hob, her eyes dark with unhappy shadows. The memory had forced its way back to that night in Cornwall when he had talked about their relationship, when he had told her to come to him if she needed him.

Lissa closed her eyes to shut out the memories. If only he knew just how much she needed him! Not just the helpless physical longing that in a moment of betrayal he had guessed at, the crying out of every nerve for his touch, but the supreme joy and satisfaction that came from knowing she was the one woman in the world he chose to give his love to. What if she did surrender to clamouring senses and the urgent desire he had awakened in her? How could she bear to contemplate the forfeiture of it all when the day of reckoning came? When Jarret gave her the freedom he had guaranteed her—and took his own? How could she know that he wouldn't meet some other woman and fall headlong in love with her? Fate could bring that to pass at any moment, long before the five years were past.

The very thought was a physical agony wrenching at her heart. Jarret in love with another woman . . .

She gulped blindly at the milk, scalding her mouth and bringing tears of pain to her eyes. Suddenly she did not want the milk; all she wanted was oblivion. She rinsed the beaker and upended it on the draining rack, then went on leaden feet back to her room. The soft rose light from her bedside lamp sent its shaft through the door she had left partly open, and she turned back, remembering to switch off the stairway wall bracket before she closed her door and stumbled wearily towards her tumbled, uninviting bed. Then she blinked, and gave a cry of shock. Jarret was standing in the shadows by the window.

He turned. 'I'm sorry, I didn't mean to alarm you. Are you all right, Lissa?'

'Yes—I couldn't sleep.' She drew her dressing gown closer with an unconscious gesture of defence. 'I went downstairs to heat some milk, to see if it would make me sleep. I'm sorry I disturbed you.'

'I wasn't asleep either. I heard your door, and when you didn't go to the bathroom I knew you'd gone downstairs.' He hesitated, his hands digging into the pockets of his robe. 'I was afraid you might be ill or something, and I was going to come down, then I thought I'd scare you if I walked in on you. I didn't realise it would have the same effect when you found me here.'

'It doesn't matter.' She picked up the bedside clock and looked at it, then set it down again. 'I hope I didn't wake Emma.'

'We'd have heard her if you had.'

'Yes, of course.' Her voice was unsteady. 'Would—would you like me to make you a warm drink?'

'No. Lissa, are you crying?'

She sensed his movement across the room. 'N-no,' she swallowed hard, 'of course I'm not crying.'

'No,' his voice was grave, 'of course you're not.'

His hands came to rest on her shoulders, gently turning her to face him. He looked down at her averted face, then put one hand under her chin, gently insisting until she had to look at him. 'You know why neither of us couldn't sleep, don't you?'

She was silent, too spent to resist any more, and there were no more words, only his arms opening drawing her within their circle and holding her against him.

For long moments he just held her, one hand tangling in her hair, curving in the warm hollow of her neck, breaking down the last frail barrier of resistance until he gentled her head back and kissed her with sweet, unhurried ease. When he began to caress her, when his mouth explored her temples, touched her eyelids, found the tender hollows under her ears and took the lobes between his lips, traced the long line of her throat, it was too late to resist. Love, longing too long denied, and the awakening fires of response kept her a willing prisoner.

He murmured something against her lips, but she did not know what, and she shivered violently as his questing hands slid under the silken folds of her wrap and homed to cup the warm frail curve of her breast. A ragged sigh shuddered through him and he groaned softly, murmuring her name, pressing her fiercely against him with a force that spoke of despair.

'Oh God, I need you so desperately ...' His mouth moved over hers, hard, seeking, feverish, as though it hungered for her sweetness, and the throb of her own pulses thundered in her head, obliterating everything except the crying needs of their bodies.

'*Let me have you, Lissa . . .*'

The whispered plea held all the passion of an invocation, and Lissa forgot everything except the need to know his love and give unstintingly of her own. She reached up and cradled his dark head, the yielding curve of her body against him communicating her answer, and for the first time in her life felt the surging of a man's body in passion.

She had no experience by which to judge a man's loving, she could only sense that he was striving to hold back, not to overwhelm her, and when the longed-for, aching moment of union came she surrendered herself ardently in utter trust. And then she cried out. There was pain. The lovely rapture was gone, and there was only cold, frightened sanity, and bitter disappointment. She moaned softly between bitten lips, eyes squeezed close, and then it was all over.

The room seemed cold, silent except for Jarret's quickened breathing, and the air icy against her burning body. Then he leaned over her, touching her face. 'Lissa . . .'

She gave a great sigh, seeking blindly to cover her nakedness, and a single tear escaped and trickled down on to his hand. He murmured sharply, and drew her head into the hollow of his shoulder. 'Don't cry, my beautiful. I know, it was the first time.' He reached down and pulled the quilt over her trembling body, murmuring soft incoherencies, until gradually her breathing steadied.

He stayed silent a long while, holding her and caressing her with featherdown strokes. Presently he said softly, 'Disappointed?'

She moved her face against his chest, and the mute response made his arms tighten. 'It won't be like this next time—I can begin to make love to you properly now,' he whispered.

'Begin?' It was a small, bitter, incredulous question, born of disillusion. 'No!' She pulled away from him and felt his arm barring the movement.

'Trust me, Lissa—for your own sake, please.'

She looked up into his shadowy features, and her eyes

were dark and haunted with failure, and the misery of unassuaged longing that made her want to clench her fists and weep out her despair.

'Aren't you satisfied yet?' she said bitterly.

'No—and neither are you.'

She felt cold and numb and sick. Although she knew in her heart that it was scarcely his fault that her body had betrayed its untutored readiness for the act of love she wanted to hit out at him, try to hurt him as much as she was hurt.

'I can't leave you like this,' he insisted. 'Won't you trust me, Lissa?'

'I think I've just proved that,' she said dully.

'Then why do you turn away?'

'If you don't know why you never will know.' She made her body into a dead, stone-like weight, refusing to move or look at him, knowing she was in danger of breaking down and betraying her innermost secret if she softened and yielded to the new tenderness she sensed in him. For she might be a stranger to the deepest and most intimate relationship between a man and a woman, but she was not naïve enough to fail to realise that a man could be a lover without feeling the depth of full loving commitment to the partner to his desire.

Almost too late she realised the danger. Were she to let him love her again, perhaps to bring her to ecstasy, how could she check the spilling of her love, the endearments that would leave him in no doubt of where her heart belonged? Those endearments so precious between true lovers that he had not once voiced tonight. Did not that alone prove how true the immortal words of Byron were? '*Love ... 'tis woman's whole existence.*' But a thing apart to a man, she thought bitterly.

She moved so quickly she took Jarret by surprise. He stared at her as she thrust her wrap around herself and made for the door. There she turned and said in a high, brittle voice: 'I'm sorry it wasn't more fun—leave my light on when you go, please.'

When she came back from the bathroom a short while later he was gone.

CHAPTER NINE

It was no use trying to pretend that nothing had changed.

The hours of the night had charged the whole house with their atmosphere. It subdued Emma, who after one glance at her father's face when he came down to breakfast mutely turned up her face for his morning kiss.

He greeted Lissa with an unsmiling 'Good morning,' drew out his chair and said, 'Please—nothing cooked this morning. I couldn't face it.'

So he too had a head, Lissa thought, and remained unsympathetically silent. She loaded the toaster, put the Lea and Perrins beside his tomato juice, and added an extra spoonful to his black coffee, then tried to force herself to eat half a slice of toast. When Emma had scraped out the last morsel of her egg, upended the shell in her egg cup and given it a satisfying bash with the bowl of her spoon, Lissa bade her hurry and clean her teeth, and get her things on ready for school.

Lissa stood up, swallowing the last mouthful of her tea before preparing to take Emma to school. Jarret put his hand on her wrist. 'I'll run Emma along to school this morning.'

She withdrew her hand from his touch, nodding, and his face darkened.

'Lissa! For God's sake don't look at me like that!'

Her mouth tightened. 'Like what? You don't expect rapture at this time of the morning, or do you?'

He closed his eyes despairingly. 'Lissa, I'm sorry about last night. But can't you understand? It happens that way sometimes. It—It's just one of those things.'

'Oh, yes,' she poured herself a second cup of tea, more to give herself something to do than because she wanted it, and refused to look at him. 'I do understand, more than you give me credit for, Jarret. I'm not totally ignorant. Now, I don't want to talk about it.'

A sigh of impatience escaped him. He glanced round

to make sure Emma was out of earshot. 'Lissa, believe me, I do have some idea of how you must be feeling—credit *me* with a little imagination.' His voice softened. 'It's a selfish man who takes his pleasure uncaring about the woman's.'

Her mouth trembled. She cradled her cup between her hands and stared unseeingly into the wavering circle of amber liquid that reflected herself.

'It isn't always easy for a man to give tenderness alone when it's needed, without natural chemistry taking control.' He stood up, and now there was bleakness in his tone. 'I'm well aware that all you want from me is the proverbial shoulder on your off-days. And I'm also aware that the four years ahead are never far from your mind. The time when you'll be free to marry the man of your choice, with all the old-fashioned marriage-in-innocence idea. I never meant to rob you of that.'

He fell silent, and she sensed his movement behind her chair. *Oh, God, don't let him touch me,* she prayed inwardly. *Don't let me make a fool of myself and start weeping ...*

'But you're crying for a dream, Lissa.'

She heard his footfall as he turned away, heard him call Emma, then Emma was running to the table to kiss Lissa goodbye, and the subdued look was still in her eyes. The door closed, and Lissa was left alone to face her day; life had to go on ...

The withdrawn mood lasted about three days, then the imperceptible effect of time began to take place. Lissa would not have believed that she could ever converse normally with Jarret again or that the resilience of common sense could remind her that she had to live with Jarret and no one could live continually either on an emotional peak or cast into emotional despair. And for Emma's sake they had to try to reconcile their differences and appear content.

Christmas made it easier; there was so much to do.

By the second week of December cards began arriving, and Lissa got down to the task of sending out her own quite considerable list. Jarret told her that his secretary had always attended to this for him and had mentioned it tentatively only the previous day. 'She'll let you have the list,' he said.

'Will she mind? I mean, if she's seen to them for several years.'

'Not at all. I'll get her to give you a ring. You'll find her very helpful.'

Lissa found he had not exaggerated. Mrs Bell had a comprehensive list of names that included Jarret's relatives and personal friends as well as business acquaintances, and the list was also coded by Jarret's efficient secretary with symbols against the names of those to whom formal cards were sent, those who received robins and Dickensian coaching inns in the snow, those who got trendy examples of exotic or abstract art, and the recipients of more personal cards. More important, Mrs Bell had all the addresses, reviving Lissa's memory of the frantic hunt at home for old address books, letters and the telephone directory.

The cards were a formidable heap when completed, with the addition of Lissa's own family and friends, plus Emma's little list. To Emma fell the job of sticking on all the stamps, and then came the glorious mess she made concocting decorations.

After several changes of mind the Christmas plans had been finalised at last. As Jarret had foreseen, Lissa's family were very anxious for a reunion and begged them to come 'home' for Christmas. Although the thought started pangs of nostalgia in Lissa the same, quite valid reasons made to Mrs de Rys had to be made again. Then Jarret suggested she invite her family to spend New Year with them.

'I'd love to—and I'm sure they would. Do you mean it?' Her eyes were bright.

'Why not? It's your home as well as mine,' he pointed out dryly, and went on to suggest that she might take Emma to see her parents the weekend before Christmas and spend it quietly. It would do Emma good to have a break, he thought, adding that she'd been looking a bit peaky lately.

So he had noticed it too. Lissa decided to follow his suggestion without further question. Jarret would drive them to Lingwood on the Friday afternoon and return for them on the Sunday evening. This arrangement would suit his plans too, because a business colleague would be in town and it would be an opportunity to further some preliminary talks for a new scheme mooted for the spring.

Lissa was packing a weekend case for Emma and herself on the Friday morning when the telephone rang. It was Mrs de Rys.

Lissa tightened her grip on the receiver, bracing herself for what might be to come, then relaxed as Mrs de Rys enquired graciously how were they all, and remarked how delighted she was to receive Emma's special card and little note.

She sounded sweet, and rather sad, as though she had accepted the inevitable, saying she quite understood that it must be difficult to fit everything in and that naturally Lissa would wish to see her own family at Christmas and the travelling distances involved, especially if the weather turned treacherous, would make it all very exhausting if they tried to include a journey to Kent as well. And of course there was Emma's little concert.

'You will reserve seats for us, won't you? We can't miss it,' said Mrs de Rys anxiously.

'Yes, of course—I've already put three tickets aside for you, in case you wanted to come,' said Lissa, who by this time was beginning to feel guilty about the whole business and sorry for the older woman.

'Bless you, my dear. Now,' Mrs de Rys paused, and a wry note entered her voice, 'if the mountain won't come to Mahomet ... I wonder, would it be convenient if I were to call on Christmas Eve, about four? But please don't hesitate to say if it isn't—I realise it's the worst possible time and you'll be terribly busy with the last-minute rush.'

'No—please do come,' Lissa said quickly, and hesitated for only a fraction of a second—after all, Jarret himself had reminded her that it was her home too! 'Have tea with us,' she invited, 'and then come along to the concert with us.'

'How kind of you, my dear. I'd love that. Then Camilla and Neil could meet us there. They've something special arranged that afternoon—I forget what.'

'Emma will be pleased,' said Lissa in the pause that followed. 'She'll be able to give you her present. She wouldn't trust it to the post—she was going to bring it when we visit you.'

'Jarret is intending to bring you both to stay with me?'

'I—I think so,' Lissa said cautiously.

There was a silence, then the older woman said slowly, 'You're still not very sure of him, are you, my dear?'

Lissa frowned. 'I—I'm not sure what you mean, Mrs de Rys.'

'Well, your marriage was something of a whirlwind affair, was it not?'

'Yes, I suppose so, but I don't see what——' Lissa's voice trailed away. What was Mrs de Rys getting at?

'Forgive me, my dear,' the calm, well modulated voice sounded conciliatory, 'it was something I couldn't help noticing. Naturally, I wouldn't have dreamed of asking you when we met, but now it seems quite easy over the phone. You see, Jarret never even mentioned you, let alone suggested bringing you to meet us. Even Emma was not told. He simply presented us with a *fait accompli*. It was quite a shock, and at first we were rather hurt, then I realised that Jarret was thinking of you. It would have been rather cruel to a young bride to bring her husband's first wife's family to her wedding. Don't you think so?'

'Well, it wasn't just that,' Lissa said awkwardly, 'my father had suffered a severe stroke, and our wedding was arranged in difficult times. I'm sure there was no intention of—of slighting you in any way, Mrs de Rys. We——'

'My dear, I know that! That's the last thing I meant,' Mrs de Rys assured her warmly. 'Please don't give it another thought. We're happy that Jarret has found such a charming girl to care for him—we certainly didn't expect him to renounce marriage for ever after my poor darling Claudine died. And as I've said before; I hope you'll look upon us and Rys House as your own family. Come and see us whenever you feel inclined—and don't let Emma grow away from us.'

'No, of course not.' Lissa was beginning to feel vaguely disturbed by the call, as though there were some other motive underlying it all, yet try as she might she could not pin down any valid reason for not accepting it on face value. Mrs de Rys was simply an elderly woman who had lost her daughter, doted on her grandchild, and was secretly terrified that the new wife might not wish to maintain the relationship, or that her son-in-law now seemed inclined to sever the once close contact. And there seemed more than vague suspicion that Jarret harboured quite definite intentions along those lines.

She was glad when Mrs de Rys rang off and for a while she forgot the call as she hurried to catch up on the preparations still to be made before she departed for the weekend. Check on the pie in the oven, and the piece of beef she was cooking so that Jarret would have something for sandwiches or snacks while she was away. He had told her not to worry, reminding her that he had lived alone for three years and coped without starving. But then the big luxury apartment could call on service, bringing a meal to the door if he chose to lift the phone.

He arrived very soon after Mrs de Rys's call, bringing Emma from school and a large Christmas tree. It took their concerted efforts to manoeuvre it out of the back of the car and into the house.

'How would you like to drive home with seven feet of Christmas tree sticking down the back of your neck?' he demanded of Emma when it was finally deposited in its tub in the living room.

Emma giggled. 'Christmas trees don't have any feet, Daddy!'

Jarret groaned. 'One more crack like that and I'll chop it down,' he threatened.

But it was difficult to win where Emma was concerned. After reminding him that the tree was already chopped down she added, 'Don't dare put the decorations on it before I come back, Daddy!'

'How would you like a decorated bottom?'

Emma laughed derisively but nevertheless put a safe distance between her threatened rear and her father's uplifted hand. Lissa called them to lunch, and sat down herself, a little breathlessly.

Something had niggled at the back of her mind ever

since she got up that morning, something she'd forgotten, but try as she might she could not pin down the elusive niggle. Now she was aware of a restlessness and little desire for the rich pie that had smelled so delicious while it was cooking. Suddenly she heard Jarret ask:

'Is something the matter, Lissa?'

'N-no, not really,' she frowned, and told him about the call from Mrs de Rys.

He did not make any comment, beyond acknowledgement, and because of Emma's presence she could not tell him of Mrs de Rys's remarks, and on second thoughts she deemed it just as well not to repeat the full content of the conversation. When she had cleared away, and completed the last round of small chores and Jarret was putting the case into the car she felt a strange sense of unease, a desperate need for reassurance, and it had to come from Jarret.

The odd restlessness persisted all through the two-hour drive, in spite of Emma's excited prattle and glee because she had gained a whole extra afternoon's holiday. When the familiar scenes began to pass and the car turned into the winding country road that had always meant home Lissa turned in her seat and looked at Jarret's intent profile.

'Jarret, I wish you were staying. I know you have to entertain this man, but it won't be for the whole weekend. Couldn't you drive back down tomorrow and have the rest of the weekend with us?'

'Oh, Lissa!' There was impatience in his tone. 'It'll be far easier if I don't. You know what it means, surely. How do we start explaining to your parents that we want separate bedrooms?'

She sighed back in her seat, deflated and saddened. It was perfectly true; how could she have forgotten? There was no chance of further argument, even if she'd had the spirit to persist. The car was turning up the drive and the front door was opening and her parents and Pippa were rushing out to greet them.

In the happy flurries of reunion Lissa forgot her misgivings and was even able to smile when Jarret was on the point of departure later that evening and mention was made

of his business engagement next day, whereupon Pippa
observed pertly, 'As long as it isn't a lady-friend!'

'I presume I'll have you to deal with if it is!' he said
dryly to Pippa as parental disapproval began to fall on
her head. 'Actually,' he added, 'my date's all of six feet
tall, with a polished pate, grey whiskers and a penchant
for large cigars. 'Bye Emma. 'Bye, darling.' He hugged
Emma and bent to kiss Lissa, and then the red tail lights
were disappearing down the road.

'Oh, I think he's gorgeous,' sighed Pippa. 'Why can't I
find somebody like that? Oh, and you'll never guess!
Martin's back. He's getting a divorce. That girl he went
off to marry left him and went to America with an Italian
film cameraman. His mother's furious! Everybody's saying
it serves him right for jilting you and he ought to have
married you in the first place.'

Martin. A faint smile touched Lissa's mouth. For a
moment she had had to stop and think who Martin was;
it seemed so long ago, and all so futile. How could she
have imagined that she ever loved Martin?

There was much village news—and gossip—to catch
up with, and she stayed up late that night, after Emma
had gone to bed, talking with her parents. Mr Vayle could
walk without sticks now, only occasionally having to
steady himself if he moved too abruptly. The business was
going ahead and the council had just accepted his tender
for the building of twenty-four new houses on Larkspur
Estate. Mr Brentlink was retiring in February, and Pippa
had decided she wanted to be a nurse.

The fire burned low, and Lissa stifled a yawn. Mr Vayle
looked at her flushed face and said, 'Time you were in bed,
lass,' much as he had said so often in bygone days, and
she went impulsively to kiss him before she made her
way up to the little room that had been her own haven
for so long.

It was both sweet and sad to feel the familiar contours
of her old bed enfold her as she settled down to sleep.
But the moment she switched off the lamp she was wide
awake and the strange nagging sense of something forgotten filled her mind. She checked mentally through everything she could think of, whom she might have forgotten

to buy a present for, something promised to Emma, something she should have ordered in the provision line, but the obstinate blank remained, a blank which surely should not invade her with this nagging sense of unease.

She told herself that when she got home she would have a thorough check through her lists and her kitchen diary, and tried to empty her mind that she might sleep. Soon she did drift into sleep, and the moment she awoke the first thing that fell into her mind was the missing piece of her enigma. At last she knew, and the knowledge froze her with sheer panic. It couldn't be!

Feverishly she scrambled out of bed and snatched her handbag from the chair by the dressing table. She rummaged through it and drew out her diary, to leaf through the pages with fingers that trembled so badly they crumpled the pages. November—oh no! She hadn't bothered to mark in her private monthly symbol, often she forgot, it didn't seem necessary ... Back to October; yes, there it was, the eighteenth.

A numbing sensation like an anaesthetic began to chill her body as she reckoned out the days and dragged her memory back to locate the date she sought. Then she remembered; it was the day she'd taken Emma to the Polish Dance Festival. She sank back on the bed, all remaining colour draining from her cheeks. She'd been due on the ninth and it was now the twenty-first. Nearly two weeks overdue.

Lissa put her hands to her face. It couldn't possibly be true! She couldn't believe it. But inner knowledge told her it was. She knew the normal rhythm of her body too well. Then anger and bitterness surged in her; surely it couldn't happen, not because of just one isolated act of love. *Love!* she whispered desolately. No, not that. Just physical need with a promise of ecstasy that turned to pain. Disillusion and pain without the joy of a love that could make pain exquisite.

And now she could be pregnant.

Lissa never knew how she got through that weekend without betraying her inward turmoil. For her parents' sake she tried to put on a happy face, but her mind waged continual conflict, telling her one moment she was worrying unnecessarily, there would be another explanation, and the next that there could be no other reason, reminding her that Jarret had taken no precautions and she certainly hadn't—it had all been too spontaneous. Then her tormented brain tried to imagine how she was going to tell him, what would be his reaction, how was it going to affect her future. But there was no doubt about that; it was a disaster.

Jarret looked tired when he came to pick them up on the Sunday afternoon, and perhaps because of this noticed no trace of the strain that gripped Lissa. Her parents refused to hear of him leaving straight away, there was the inevitable meal and a Christmas drink, and it was late in the evening when they eventually got home. When Jarret had left for the office and Emma was at school Monday suddenly became a lonely endless day. Lissa did every chore she could find, and several that were not necessary, trying to keep fear at bay. The afternoon found her hunting out every magazine she could find, seeking the answers she dreaded to find. But she had no other symptoms of pregnancy. No sickness, she didn't crave certain foods, she didn't feel any different, except for this strange restlessness that would not let her settle.

At last she stowed the magazines away, angry and impatient with herself. How could she tell in two weeks?

At four she donned her coat and went to collect Emma from her school party, and tried to lose her fears in Emma's excited chatter. That night they decorated the tree.

There was the inevitable hassle to get the lights working, and then Emma declared that there weren't enough baubles to make the tree look really dressed. Lissa promised to get a few more items and some miniature crackers the next day, and remarked, more to herself than Emma, that she mustn't forget her visitor.

Then Emma turned to her father. 'Daddy, you will take me in the car? I don't want to have my dresses packed in a case—they might get creased. Lissa said we could put them on hangers and just carry them in the car.'

'Yes.' Jarret sighed. 'The car will be at your disposal, madam.'

'Well, will you take me and Lissa first and then come back for Grannie? Or it'll be a squash. And I've got to be there an hour before it starts.'

Jarret nodded, and took refuge behind his evening paper.

'Lissa, do you think I could have some of your make-up tomorrow? Miss Jackson said we could wear a tiny bit of pink lipstick and some foundation, because the lights will be very bright, you know.'

'Yes, darling.' Lissa put her hand to her head. She could hardly bear Emma's incessant questions. 'Now it's time for supper and bed.'

Emma made a face. 'Daddy, Uncle Neil *will* be coming to see me in the play tomorrow? He's not going away with Aunt Camilla till after the New Year?'

'No, and I didn't mean that he'd be going away for ever—no farther than Sevenoaks, anyway,' Jarret responded sharply.

'Oh, I thought you did, Daddy.'

So did I, thought Lissa with a sigh.

Jarret looked at her above Emma's head. 'I should have left well alone,' he observed ruefully.

'Left what alone, Daddy?'

'That's enough! Now scarper!'

She moved reluctantly towards the door, pausing to study the rich dark green boughs of the tree. She looked back at her father. 'Is Grannie going to stay here tomorrow, for Christmas?'

'No. You know that Grannie hates to be away from home at Christmas. She likes everybody to go to her.'

'Daddy,' the child's head went to one side, 'won't we be going there any more at Christmas times? I mean now that Lissa's come to live with us.'

'I don't know, Emma.' He got up irritably. 'It all depends.'

Emma frowned, apparently uneasy, then looked at the fireside. 'That isn't as wide as the big one at Rys House. I hope Father Christmas can get down it.' With a mischievous giggle she ran from the room.

'Thank God,' Jarret muttered, raking weary fingers through his hair. He swung round, catching unawares Lissa's unguarded weariness. 'Are you all right?'

'Of course I'm all right!' she snapped, and was instantly sorry the moment the words were out.

His mouth tightened. 'I only asked. You've gone white.'

'I'm sorry—I-I'm just tired.' Before her control could break any more she made a mumbled excuse about seeing to Emma's supper and went from the room.

Dearly as she loved the little girl Lissa gave a sigh of thankfulness when Emma was settled and she made her own excuse of tiredness to have an early night. Jarret seemed quiet, withdrawn almost, once Emma's presence was gone, and Lissa had an impression that he was thoroughly weary of Christmas and all it entailed.

She slept badly that night and awakened with a headache that augured unfavourably for the busy day to be coped with. But it had to be faced. There was the last-minute shopping, bread and perishables to collect, she wanted to make the mince-pies and do as much as possible towards the feast tomorrow, Mrs de Rys was coming at four, and there were still a few presents waiting to be wrapped up. Thank goodness Emma was having her dinner at school today.

If only this shock had not assailed her, to cast its shadow across the festive season. And then the sad little voice of longing: if only it had been a true marriage, how joyous to be looking forward to her baby. Hers—and Jarret's.

Lissa closed her heart to dreams and swallowed two aspirins, then set off to complete her shopping. She had expected to do this in half an hour or so, but she found the shops were packed and the few odds and ends became two heavy shopping bags. She knew she was buying far too much, but the peculiar fever that grips most women at Christmas caught her and she could only think that she dared not risk running out of anything, not even the most unlikely items. Last of all she bought the decorations for Emma, stowed them carefully on top of the loaves, and turned her steps homewards, thinking longingly of a cup of coffee and a brief respite. It had turned bitterly cold, overcast by leaden skies, and wisps of mist hung over the Heath; typical British murk, she thought, not in the least like a Christmas card. Then she saw a car standing on the drive, and someone at the front door. The girl saw her and raised her hand, and with sinking heart Lissa recognised her visitor.

Camilla, soignée as ever, stamped her feet and waited impatiently for Lissa to find her keys.

'I was about to give you up. God! I'm frozen.'

'I'm sorry—the shops were jampacked. Have you been waiting long?'

'Long enough.' Camilla paused in the hall and clamped her gloved hands on the radiator. 'I was going to phone, but I had to come anyway. Mother's ill.'

'Oh, I'm sorry. Is it serious?'

'Well, not terribly.' Camilla followed Lissa into the sitting room and huddled down on the pouffe in front of the fire. 'She had a nasty little turn last night and the doctor says she must stay in bed today and take things very easy over Christmas. So I've brought the presents.' Camilla indicated the carrier bag leaning against the side of an armchair. 'Mother didn't want Emma to be disappointed.'

'I'm sure she'll be disappointed, not seeing her grandmother tonight.' Lissa bit her lip, unsure of what else she could say. 'Will you excuse me while I dump these in the kitchen and I'll make some coffee.'

When she returned a few minutes later with the tray Camilla had discarded her luxurious silvery fur coat and was reclining in an armchair. She refused biscuits, and there was something challenging in the sharp glance she raised to Lissa. After a moment she said flatly: 'I suppose you do realise that my mother is heartbroken over all this.'

'I'm sorry,' Lissa said with genuine sympathy, 'but no one can help illness.'

'Oh, for goodness' sake stop saying you're sorry,' the other girl said impatiently, 'and try to do something.'

Lissa stared. 'But what can I do? I wish I could help.'

'Then let's be candid.' Camilla raised that challenging

glance again. 'Can't you do something about this infernal boycott?'

'Boycott?' Lissa's eyes widened.

'Oh, come off it!' Camilla snapped. 'You know perfectly well what I mean. I mean that Jarret hasn't allowed Emma to make a single visit to my mother since the day you collected her nine months ago. But he was glad enough to leave her when he found a four-year-old was more than he could cope with. And we were very convenient for him last summer when he was hot after Lucy Paige and went off to Spain with her for a month. But dear Lucy didn't exactly fancy being a step-mum and providing Emma with baby brothers and sisters.'

Lissa recoiled. The spiteful little tale stabbed deeply, and the gleam in Camilla's eyes told her it was meant to. Suddenly an echo came from the past, from the day Jarret had taken her down to Rys House to collect Emma, and she had inadvertently eavesdropped on an angry exchange certainly not intended for her ears. She had thought of it once or twice, and then, as time passed, it had slipped from her memory. But now those scornful words returned. Accusations of revenge, and hate ... directed at Jarret.

'Well?' Camilla demanded. 'Do you think it's fair?'

Lissa shook her head helplessly. In the face of known facts it wasn't. Mrs de Rys had obviously cared devotedly for Emma for nearly three years, which was quite a long time. To be deprived of regular contact after that seemed cruel, to say the least. But there was something else that affected the issue, something Lissa did not know and could only sense, and love made her loyal, even if that loyalty might be misplaced.

She said at last, 'I'm sure you're mistaken. It's been a hectic summer, moving house, settling Emma at her new school, and you've all visited us many times here, and seen Emma.'

'Rubbish!' Camilla's lip curled. 'You know well enough we came on sufferance, when Jarret wasn't around to freeze us off the premises.' She pushed her coffee cup across the low onyx table and stared challengingly back at Lissa. 'Well, are you going to try to talk sense into Jarret about this Christmas business?'

'I—I'll do what I can. But ...' *I can't promise,* Lissa wanted to be honest and say.

Camilla finished the sentence for her, and sneered, 'The truth is, you've no influence at all where Jarret is concerned. My mother guessed it, and she's right. But then I don't suppose he's ever told you the truth.'

'The truth? What truth?' Lissa went cold as she met the other girl's cruel gaze.

Camilla smiled faintly. 'You mean you honestly don't know? You've never guessed?'

'I don't know what you're talking about.' Lissa's hands curled in her lap. She began to feel frightened.

'Emma isn't Jarret's child.'

There was a dreadful silence. Through it Lissa dimly heard the soft thud that sounded like another batch of cards landing on the mat. But her limbs felt paralysed and she made no move to get up and go to the door.

'I don't believe it!'

Camilla laughed scornfully. 'Why do you think I've been getting the cold shoulder treatment ever since I decided to marry Neil? Because Jarret is determined to keep Emma away from Neil. It's the only possible way in which he can take his revenge.'

Lissa's hand fluttered to her throat. She felt as though she'd stepped into a nightmare. 'No, it's not true,' she choked. 'It can't be!'

'Oh, but it is, I assure you.' Camilla's voice held the hard ring of assurance. 'Why do you think Neil's so fond of her? And she of him? There's a bond between them that the densest of blockheads could see. You've only to watch them together. Oh, no,' she laughed again, 'make no mistake about it, my dear Lissa. Neil is Emma's father. Jarret isn't.'

'The ... if it's true ...' Lissa felt sick and swallowed hard. 'It means that ...'

'Yes,' the unpleasant little smile played at the corners of the other girl's mouth, 'my dear sister was quite a girl. No man could resist her—Neil least of all. I was about fifteen at the time, when she got involved with Neil. He was crazy about her, but unfortunately he didn't have money then. His old aunty kept him on a very tight shoestring. Then Jarret landed on the scene, and Claudine married him exactly six weeks later. About three months after their wedding old Aunty Lil had the grace to snuff it and Neil got her pile at last—too late. So he went on the binge to end all binges, and one weekend while Jarret was abroad he persuaded Claudine to binge with him. She didn't take much persuading. They had a ball. And that was the start of our Emma.'

Camilla paused, her eyes reminiscent, apparently quite unmoved by the thought of the former infidelities of her husband-to-be and her sister. 'Of course Jarret found out. He has a built-in radar perception, and I think he'd begun to read Claudine long before that. There was a hell of a row, he walked out on her, Claudine panicked a bit, and then they made it up—for Jarret was quite berserk about her. But she told me she knew that Emma was Neil's, and I believe that Jarret was suspicious all along. Of course we never breathed a word of it to Mother. After that Neil decided he'd better vanish for a while. Aunty Lil's pile was getting smaller, and an old college friend had a holiday camp scheme under way in the Caribbean. Neil stayed out there nearly six years, then moved on to Spain, but the venture there flopped and he came home. Last year he decided to look me up and did a double-take when he discovered that skinny teenage sister Camilla had grown up very like Claudine. So we decided to get married.'

Camilla's revelations had left Lissa stunned. She still could not believe in what she had heard. And yet Camilla's tones carried the conviction of truth. Suddenly great anger possessed her.

'So you want Emma now!' she flared. 'How dare you? I never heard anything so abominably selfish! Not content with trying to ruin Jarret's life then you want to rob him of his child now.'

'Neil's child,' Camilla corrected. 'He wants her—he's very fond of children.'

'But you're not!'

'I didn't say that. I'm quite fond of her.' Camilla shrugged. 'But I'll be honest—the thought of childbearing fills me with horror. I just don't have the maternal instinct.'

There was a silence. Camilla smoothed her skirts over

her knees and smiled. 'I seem to have shocked you.'

'I'm appalled.' Lissa shook her head. 'I—I'd never have believed Neil could be so—so——'

'Such a rank old-fashioned bounder.' Camilla laughed. 'But he doesn't mean to—it's just he can't help his charm and loving the feminine sex.' She paused, and a curious look came into her eyes as she studied Lissa's pale, shocked face. 'You mean you honestly had no idea?'

'No.'

And my husband never told me anything about his life before we met, Lissa reflected sadly. *How could I have any idea?* Numbly she put the coffee things back on the tray, and Camilla glanced at her watch. She gave an exclamation.

'Heavens! I'm supposed to be meeting Neil at one and it's ten to already. And you know what it's like trying to park!'

She shrugged into the beautiful coat and wasted no time on a prolonged adieu. Lissa closed the front door and stood blankly in the hall. She felt completely shattered.

Emma was not Jarret's child!

But if it was true it explained so much that was puzzling, that rapport that Camilla called a bond between Emma and her 'Uncle' Neil. With these facts it was possible to date the start of the affectionate relationship back to the previous autumn. Not very long in which to forge so close a bond as undoubtedly existed between Emma and the man who could be her real father.

Lissa wandered unseeingly into the sitting room and shivered. Camilla's perfume still lingered on the air and Lissa had an urgent desire to spray air-freshener everywhere and open all the windows.

And then with blinding clarity the truth hit her like a tangible blow. The real reason behind the contract. The reason for Jarret's urgency in proposing their loveless marriage. The true motive for his extraordinary generosity to her father, to make his proposal impossible to refuse. What was it Camilla had said? That Jarret had a built-in radar perception? And he'd had no difficulty in reading Lissa like a book, playing on her devotion to her father.

Lissa closed her eyes against torment. He knew about Emma. The moment he heard of his sister-in-law's engagement to Neil Hargill he had acted, determined to remove Emma from their influence. It was his only chance of revenge—to make sure that Neil would never have the chance to claim his own child.

And I was the tool! Lissa moaned to herself. She had been used.

All the heartache of the past months, the disturbing discovery that she could be pregnant, and this latest shock fused into unbearable anguish. Tears came, slowly at first, and then with rending sobs that convulsed her whole body. She stumbled into the nearest chair and gave herself up to grief for lost illusions, vain hopes, and the agony of hurt.

At last she dragged herself up, unable to weep any more and feeling drained of life. Automatically she picked up the tray and slowly washed and dried the coffee cups. Life had to go on, even though she wished it wouldn't, and she supposed she should prepare herself some lunch, but the thought of food was enough to make her feel choked. She bathed her swollen face and reddened eyes, and wandered through the house like a zombie, unable to concentrate her will on anything. Wild thoughts of running away, going home, came into her mind, and she shunned them, knowing it wasn't the answer and not knowing how she would explain her action to her parents. When the telephone rang at two o'clock she was reluctant to answer it, afraid of breaking down again when she spoke, but she went into the hall and picked up the receiver.

'Is that Mrs Earle?'

'Speaking,' Lissa said dully.

'Janet Latimer here—Mandy's mum. I'm sorry to bother you, but I wonder if you could do me a favour?'

The words formed their meanings very slowly in Lissa's numbed brain. Mrs Latimer, Mandy ... she was one of Emma's classmates. They lived about five minutes' walk away. A pleasant, dark-haired young woman who wore beautiful classic clothes ...

'If I can,' said Lissa. 'Is something wrong?'

'No—but I'm in a hopeless fix. I'm getting surprise visitors flying in from Nairobi and I've just heard the

flight will be delayed. James has already left to collect his
mother—I'm going to have a real houseful!—and I have
to meet these friends at the airport. But it's Mandy. Could
you possibly take her for me? See that she doesn't leave
half her belongings in the dressing room and hang on to
her if I don't make it back before the end of the concert?'

Lissa had actually forgotten about the all-important concert. She struggled to pull herself back to normality and
said, 'Of course. What time would you like me to pick
her up?'

'They've to be back there by five-thirty, I believe—
Mandy!' There was an interchange at the other end, and
then the harassed young mother came back. 'Sorry, but
she's been under my feet since lunch and the moment I
want her she's gone. Just when you're on your way with
Emma. Bless you—I'll do the same for you some day!'

Something had clicked in Lissa's brain, jolting it out
of its apathy. 'Wait!' she cried. 'Did—did you say Mandy
was *home*?'

'Yes.' Mrs Latimer sounded puzzled and impatient.
'Didn't Emma tell you? All the children taking part in
the concert got away soon today—presumably to let the
mums bath and beautify the little darlings. She——'

'But Emma didn't come home!' Lissa fought down
alarm. 'She was having a school lunch today. Are you
sure?'

'Yes, that's strange. Just a minute ... *Mandy!*' Again
there was the interchange, and then the unmistakable
treble tones of a child. Mrs Latimer spoke again. 'Yes,
Mandy walked home with Emma. She says Carol was
with them, then Carol went straight on and Emma crossed
the road to go home.' There was a pause. 'Isn't she—didn't
she come home?'

'No—I thought—Oh, no!' Lissa saw the wall recede and
come back as though it would hit her. Hardly knowing
what she said she cried, 'I've got to find her—Goodbye—
Yes—I'll let you know!'

She stood with the receiver still clenched in her hand,
while her frightened heart thumped out its fear.

Emma was missing ... Emma was missing ... Emma ...

CHAPTER TEN

THE dreadful moments of panic subsided as Lissa mastered her weakness. She was still frightened, but cool, knowing she must waste no time. She drew the telephone diary towards her and began dialling.

Twenty minutes later she was still drawing blanks. She had telephoned Emma's form mistress, got the names of all of Emma's co-players, checked with all their parents in case Emma had gone to one of their homes, perhaps by invitation to lunch, perhaps with a childish idea of having an extra rehearsal. But even as she did this, Lissa knew that Emma was a sensible child who would not accept an invitation without letting Lissa know where she was going. Yet was Emma too logical? Had she remembered that Lissa expected her to be staying at school for lunch? And reckoned that Lissa would not worry?

But no one had seen Emma since she waved goodbye to Mandy at the Latimers' gate. Lissa's heart began to thud again. She tried to ring Jarret's number, but got no reply. He mustn't be back from lunch, and the faithful Mrs Bell did not seem to be answering phones either. Lissa knew there was only one thing she could do now: Emma had been missing for over two hours. She must phone the police.

Frantic as she was, she hesitated. It seemed like the final admission of all her worst fears, all the appalling, unthinkable things that happened to children. Obeying a wild, faint hope, she hurried through the house, looking into every room, just in case Emma had come home and perhaps gone straight to her bedroom. Perhaps she wanted to do some secretive wrapping of a surprise gift for her father. *Her father* ... A shiver ran through Lissa, but she pushed the thought away. At the moment it just didn't matter. All that mattered was to find Emma.

The house, except for herself, was quite empty. There was no trace of Emma's having returned, nothing in her

173

room was disturbed, it was exactly as Lissa had left it after making Emma's bed and tidying it that morning.

She ran downstairs, picked up the phone, and heard a key turn in the front door lock. She dropped the phone and rushed, dragging back the door, and almost fell into a bewildered Jarret's arms.

Unheeding of the gaily wrapped parcels and the carrier bag he shed at her onslaught, she cried incoherently the frightening news.

At first he did not seem to grasp what she was saying. He was staring at her, at her still swollen eyes, white face and the tell-tale blotches left by weeping, and alarm flared in his eyes. Then she almost shook him, and he jerked, 'My God! Emma!' and thrust her roughly aside.

'Have you called the police?' He had the receiver in his hand.

'I was just going to do that when you came.'

He was dialling rapidly, and suddenly he held out his free arm. It was a silent invitation she could not resist, drawing her into a circle of comfort, providing a strength she desperately needed.

It seemed to take so long, so many details, and it made Lissa's heart ache to listen to Jarret trying to build up a descriptive word picture of Emma. She could watch him now, his attention was so totally diverted that even though his arm still encircled her waist he was scarcely conscious of her presence. For the first time she saw the tiredness round his eyes, the faint shadows in the hollows, the drawn quality of the skin at his jawline. She wanted to comfort him, touch his face, smoothe away those faint lines that grooved his cheeks to the corners of his mouth. But she must not; it was not her comfort he wanted at this moment.

'I'm going along to the school,' he said abruptly. 'I must do *something*. Maybe one of the children can throw some light on where Emma is.'

Silent, thankful to be able to do something, Lissa went to get her coat, and looked piteously at him when he said she must stay at home.

'One of us has to stay—in case Emma turns up.'

The silence of the house closed round her when he had

gone, leaving her prey to a host of nebulous fears. She made a cup of tea, but was not conscious of hunger or that she had not eaten since that morning.

The leaden minutes dragged past. Lissa wandered from kitchen to hall, from hall to sitting room, from sitting room to kitchen, to the cup of chilling tea not drunk. It was turning to dusk outside. Soon it would be dark. Where was Emma? Where could they look?

When the phone shrilled she fled to it, and when the voice of the caller said, 'This is Marion Bell here ...' Lissa gabbled, 'Please—I'm sorry, but could you call back later—we're waiting for news—Emma's missing!'

'Yes, that's why I'm calling. Is Mr Earle there?'

'No—he's gone to the school to see if——'

'Mrs Earle, you'd better try to contact him—or give me the number. Emma's here.'

'What?' Lissa gasped with shock. 'Where? Why is she——?'

'I'll explain.' Mrs Bell's normally unflappable manner sounded a little shaken. 'I've just come from the hairdresser, to pick up some shopping I'd left at the office and to get a taxi home, and I found Emma in the lobby. She was just huddled there, refusing to move or listen to Jimmy the porter telling her that there was no one there, everyone had gone home because it was Christmas Eve. She said this was her father's office and she was waiting for him. No, she didn't want to——'

An icy flurry of wind gusted into the hall. The outer door slammed and the phone was snatched from Lissa's hand. Lissa heard the metallic sound of Mrs Bell's voice, and then Jarret said, 'We're on our way.'

Lissa threw on her coat and grabbed her bag, running to keep up with Jarret's hurried strides out to the car. He did not speak, concentrating all his attention on getting to the City in the fastest possible time. Traffic was heavier than ever, the air was full of winter murk, and Jarret broke every driving rule in his frantic rush. Once, chafing impatiently at the lights, he said, 'She walked! She *walked*!'

Light streamed from the ground floor of the tall office block as Jarret slammed the car to a halt. The burly form of Jimmy hovered anxiously outside the broad glass doors.

Jarret took the eight steps three at a time, and Lissa
rushed up after him, stumbling in her haste. The doors
swung wildly, and Lissa glimpsed the small figure huddled
at the far side of the lobby. Then the blue of Emma's
coat blurred and a tall plant in a black and white pot
teetered and fell. Emma hurled herself into her father's
arms, clinging frantically to him and sobbing her heart out.

Jarret's words were as incoherent as the child's. Mrs
Bell looked at Lissa, then at the distraught child, and they
were both silent. And then the incoherencies became
broken little utterances.

'—and I don't want Uncle Neil to be my father. I want
you to be my daddy! Please—don't let them take me to
live with them again! I want to stay with you! I won't
go back there again. I won't! I won't!' she cried frantically,
uttering great rending sobs that hurt Lissa physically just
to hear the child.

She took a step forward, her hand going out in a mute
little gesture to try to still the child's weeping. Emma
raised a tragic face and her mouth convulsed. She cried
against her father's shoulder, 'Why are you sending Lissa
away? Why can't she stay for ever—not just five years?
Don't you want her to stay? Like——'

'*Emma!*' Jarret drew the child's head hard against the
side of his face. 'Where on earth did you get that idea?
I never said—who told you all this?'

'You did! You told Lissa it was a contract. I heard you!
And Lissa said it was wrong. And I asked Miss Jackson to
tell me what a contract is, and she told me it was when
business people made an agreement for a job, or to sell
things, and it was for so long, or so many things. She asked
why I wanted to know, but I said it wasn't anything special,
and I thought I'd got it wrong and you'd been talking about
something else. But you sounded as though you were cross
with each other. And then today Aunt Camilla said you
weren't my father and Uncle Neil was my real father, and
I had to come and find you and ask you.'

Emma paused to take unsteady breaths, and knuckled
one hand into her eyes. Jarret looked at Lissa and his face
was a mask of anguish. Mrs Bell sniffed a little and
groped for a tissue. 'Little pitchers,' she said on a sigh.

'Emma,' said Jarret, 'it isn't true! And when we get home I think I can prove it to you. You *are* my own little girl, no one else's.'

Emma was not crying now. She looked at him, not convinced. 'Listen,' he went on, 'I wouldn't have you to live with me if you weren't my own special daughter and very dear to me. And I'm not going to send you away anywhere.'

She heaved a great sigh. 'Promise?'

'I promise, and when you're a bit older and able to understand adult relationships I'll try to explain why people who seem quite nice can still say and do very unkind things.'

'But why did Aunt Camilla say that?'

'Well, it's quite a long story, but the main thing was because of Uncle Daniel's money.'

'Oh.' Emma evinced no interest whatsoever in Uncle Daniel's money. She looked imploringly at her father. 'You won't send Lissa away?'

'*I* won't send Lissa away.'

Over the child's head his eyes beseeched Lissa not to deny the lie. She stayed silent, and Emma seemed at last to accept the reassurance. She wriggled suddenly, and Jarret set her down. He brushed his hand across his brow, and at that moment a policeman walked into the lobby. He glanced at the group of distraught people, coughed, and said:

'Excuse me, sir, but is that your car outside?'

Jarret exclaimed, but before he could speak Emma ran forward. 'Yes, if it's a Lancia 2-litre silvery blue with——'

'It is.' The policeman looked down at her.

'It's my fault if Daddy's left it on double yellow lines.'

'Oh.' The policeman's mouth twitched. 'Then I'd better give the ticket to you, young lady.'

'Yes,' said Emma, her small, tear-stained face deadly serious. 'I'm sorry.'

'Well, seeing as it's Christmas Eve ... But no more parking on yellow lines, young lady.'

'No—I promise. Merry Christmas.'

The interruption had broken the almost unbearable tension. Jarret hurried them outside, said goodnight to Jimmy, and insisted on taking Mrs Bell home. Then Emma remembered the play, and the drive home became panic stations. All Lissa's protests that Emma must be far too tired after her marathon walk into the City, after her frantic dash from the house without any money in her pocket, met with indignant rebuttals. She wanted her tea, quickly, and they would have to hurry because she was in the first item ...

There was scarcely time for a hurried snack, which Emma insisted on eating standing up. Her small face was pinched and wan, and her eyes were huge and over-brilliant against the smudgy shadows of fatigue. But a fierce determination seemed to be burning within the child and for once neither Lissa nor Jarret made any further attempts to subdue her, realising how great a crisis she had faced this day, a crisis not yet over, Lissa knew, and they must let her cope with it her own way this one time.

They reached the school theatre with little time to spare. Lissa left Jarret to make explanations as best he deemed while she quickly got Emma ready for the first item. 'Good luck, precious,' she whispered, and felt the child's thin body cling fiercely to her for a second before the children were hurried into the opening grouping by an anxious Miss Jackson. The lights darkened in the auditorium as Lissa slipped back to her seat.

It was her first respite in one of the most harrowing days in her life, to be likened to the dreadful day almost a year ago when her father was stricken. She kept her gaze fixed on the stage, not daring to look at Jarret and praying he would not make any movement or say anything. If he did she knew she would break down. Gradually her tightly clenched hands slackened a little, and then the first half of the programme was over and it was time to hurry backstage and make sure Emma was managing to don her blue robe, and the circlet halo Lissa had made so carefully was safely in the charge of the older child who was to help Emma to fix it on her head for the last part of the Nativity play.

When the curtains parted to reveal the inn and the weary little family seeking shelter it was all very obviously a simple, cut-out profile of scenery to suggest an inn, and the characters played by children who were at times patently nervous less they forgot their well-rehearsed lines. One of the shepherds got a little confused at one point, and another stumbled over the hem of a slightly too long garment. Once, Joseph's lantern did not respond to nervous small fingers and light when it should have done, and once Lissa was sure that Emma looked frantically out across the auditorium in search of her father's face. And then at some indefinable point the magic took over.

The Three Kings brought the gifts and spices of the Orient, the wonder was in the eyes of the beholders, and when Emma cradled the doll in her arms her small intense features conveyed total belief in her role. She was Mary. The doll in her arms was the Holy Babe.

A lump came in Lissa's throat. The soft singing began in the background and the lights dimmed to one circle centred on the Holy Family. Tears began to trickle down Lissa's cheeks, and she groped blindly in her bag for a tissue. Then she felt a cool soft handkerchief pushed into her hands. She dabbed at her eyes, then Jarret's hand reached across and curled round her fingers.

'Not you as well!' he whispered, and she shook her head wordlessly.

The wry tenderness made her heart ache, and she almost wrenched her hand out of his clasp when the play ended a few moments later and the hall echoed with enthusiastic applause. Personal emotions had to be subdued again. Emma's costumes had to be packed, Mandy collected and dropped off on the way home as her mother had not yet returned from the airport, and then a desperately weary Emma to be tucked into bed.

Reaction was setting in now, when the excitement of the show's success began to subside. But she was still reluctant to give in, sitting stubbornly in her dressing gown in front of the fire, hands curled round the comforting warmth of a beaker of hot milky chocolate and waiting for the carol singers. The soft little treble voices sounded at last. Silent Night ... Holy Night ... and Emma went to the door to drop her contribution in the tin.

'I'm going carol singing next year,' she announced, shivering as she hurried back into the warm room.

Jarret was taking a packet out of the bureau, and he held out his hand to Emma.

'I'm going to ask Lissa to look at two pictures,' he said in casual tones, 'and tell us what she thinks. Then you can look at them.' He drew two postcard-sized prints out of the thick envelope and passed them to Lissa, his free hand going round Emma's shoulders.

Wonderingly, Lissa held them apart, studying the older, slightly faded photograph of a boy aged about eight, his hair ruffled over his brow, his expression determined as he stood guard at an improvised wicket on a sunlit stretch of beach. It was undoubtedly Jarret, and the other picture of Emma was the one Lissa had already seen on that day in Egypt that seemed so long ago. The resemblance was quite remarkable, and a quick mental flash of Neil Hargill's sturdy build, bantering mouth and breezy charm faded as quickly as it had come, to be dismissed for ever. Lissa gave a sigh and handed the photos to the anxiously waiting Emma.

'Well?' said Jarret.

'If I didn't know that this boy was grown up I'd think he was your twin brother,' Lissa said flatly, looking at Emma. 'Don't you think you look alike?'

'Yes, quite a bit.' Emma frowned, obviously wanting to be completely convinced but unable to forget the cruel words of her aunt. She looked up her father. 'I don't know why Aunt Camilla said such stupid things, Daddy.'

'Neither do we. Now let's forget it and think about nice things—like Christmas!' Jarret swept Emma high into his arms, oblivious of her shrieks, and carried her into her room where he dropped her in a tangle of dressing gown and falling slippers on her bed. 'Five minutes, young lady,' he admonished, 'and if you're not asleep I board up the chimney!'

But the forced gaiety had left his face when he returned to the living room. He crossed to the drinks tray, glancing at Lissa with the unspoken query, and when she shook her head he fixed himself a drink and slumped wearily into a chair.

It was nearly nine-thirty and the mundane essentials of homekeeping had to be done, no matter how much the

turmoil of life battered the emotions. She said, 'I'm sorry
—there should have been a roast ham supper tonight, but
with everything that happened I didn't get it cooked.'

'I'm not hungry.' He did not look at her. 'Anything will
do.'

'I'll do some pâté on toast.'

When she returned with the simple snack on the trolley
Jarret was still sitting there, his drink scarcely touched,
and the two photos on the side table by his chair. 'Did
you mean that?' he asked, as though she had not been out
of the room.

She knew what he meant, and said steadily, 'Yes. I'm
surprised that there should be any doubt once one has
seen you and Emma together.'

'God! The times I've looked at those pictures and tried
to convince myself.' His mouth compressed and his eyes
were bleak. 'Knowing that Claudine and Hargill ...'

'But even if that was true,' Lissa said desperately, hating
to see him torturing himself with doubts, 'Emma is still
yours. You've got to believe that, for her sake as well as
your own.'

'Yes—purely by chance!' he exclaimed bitterly.

He lapsed into moody silence, and Lissa made no
attempt to encourage any further confidence; she had had
as much as she could take for one day. Suddenly she was
cold and shivery despite the warmth of the room and it was
an effort to make her body obey commands as though it
belonged to her still. But only two tasks remained, then
at last she would be free to escape to the sanctuary of
her room and seek the blessing of oblivion

After they had eaten she rinsed the dishes quickly and
went to sort out the hidden carrier bag containing the
things to fill Emma's Christmas stocking.

Jarret helped her to stuff the small gifts into the two
long white socks Emma had hopefully left draped over the
end of her bed. He seemed weary and dejected, and Lissa
could not even summon up a sad nostalgia for her own
childhood Christmases of yesteryear. Jarret was silent until
the job was completed, then he said sadly, 'Next year she'll
be too old for the Santa lark—if she doesn't know already
and keeps us believing in it all.' He sighed. 'Life takes away

the magic so quickly in a child's world today.'

He watched Lissa gather up the bulging socks. 'Shall I take them?'

She shook her head and turned away. 'I'm going up now. Goodnight, Jarret.'

She knew that reaction to the day's turmoil was setting in as she walked unsteadily up the stairs and tiptoed into Emma's room. There was no sound or movement from the child and the darkness increased the sense of disorientation as she tried to place Santa's offering across the foot of the bed without disturbing Emma. When she reached the door again a wave of dizziness made her head swim.

She held on to the door, fighting to shake off the light-headed feeling, and saw Jarret coming up the stairs. He looked at her gravely.

'All right?'

She nodded, closing the door softly behind her, and waited for Jarret to pass before she moved towards her own room. But he stopped, his eyes searching her white strained face.

'Lissa, I'm sorry. I never intended you to take the brunt of Camilla's troublemaking. You've had an appalling day.'

'It doesn't matter,' she murmured wearily. Suddenly she felt sick with bitterness. What did it matter how she felt? This was what she was paid for, wasn't it? Now even Emma knew that it was all a sham; a sham rapidly turning into disaster for herself. She moved past him, insensate to the detaining hand he put out, dimly hearing him exclaim in a low, intense voice: 'But it does matter! I want to——'

His voice seemed to fade. Another sick cold wave washed over her again and everything started to slide away. She reached out blindly for the edge of the little table that stood in a niche near the head of the stairs, desperately seeking support as she tried to fight free of the rushing darkness. But the table didn't seem to be there. Her hand was clutching at empty air, and her stumbling step forward seemed to sink down into nothingness. Then the hissing, roaring blackness was waiting to engulf her as she crumpled into a heap on the carpet at Jarret's feet.

The next thing Lissa knew was cold hard glass being

forced between her lips. She moaned softly, trying to turn her head away, and his voice said sharply: 'Lissa—try to drink!'

She opened her eyes, not remembering or knowing where she was, and the familiar outlines of her own room began to come into focus. She was lying on her bed, propped against several pillows, and Jarret sat on the edge, supporting her in one arm and holding the glass to her lips.

'Come on, Lissa,' he urged again. 'This will help.'

She was remembering now, and all the misery was rushing back like cruel winged darts. She didn't want the brandy she could smell in the glass, but her body seemed totally devoid of strength to argue. She took a sip, then a second one, then turned her head away. 'Just some water, please, and I'll be all right.'

'You look anything but all right,' he said grimly, going to the handbasin and refilling the glass with cold water. 'You went out like a light. Did you hurt yourself?' he asked anxiously as he came back to the bedside.

'I—I don't know,' she said stupidly. 'I—I don't think so.' He was sitting down again, gathering her close, and the tenderness of it brought a lump in her throat. She clutched the glass, drinking thirstily and trying to hide her tears, but the tremors of her body gave her away.

'Oh, don't—please.' He drew her face to his shoulder. 'Don't be upset—it's all over now, and I'll take damn good care that neither you nor Emma are ever hurt again.'

She took a tremulous breath, fighting for control, and he said softly, 'I'm sorry, Lissa. I realise now how unfair it was to involve you in all this without any warning that repercussions might result.' His voice hardened. 'But I never dreamt Camilla would go to these lengths.'

'I couldn't believe it,' Lissa choked. 'I didn't know why.'

His eyes had gone bleak. 'The same old answer. The de Rys family never really liked me— I didn't come out of a quite high enough drawer for Mrs de Rys. As for Camilla ... She tried her wiles on me when she was still a schoolgirl, and has never forgiven me because I was still gauche and young enough to laugh at her. But most of all, I forgot that money corrupts even the people we believe we can trust. I should have realised that Daniel de Rys's will couldn't fail to cause trouble.'

'Emma's uncle?'

'Her mother's uncle. He doted on Claudine, and when her father died he took over the family. He was a bachelor, lonely, who could make money from everything he touched but had no luck with women, so it seemed natural he should make his permanent home at Rys House. His brother was a gentle man without much business acumen, and Mrs de Rys was only too thankful to have Daniel take over the responsibilities. It was sad in a way; Daniel had that one blind spot in that he never learned the futility of trying to buy love or loyalty.'

Jarret paused, and his mouth was bitter. 'Daniel had no time for Neil Hargill, said he was a charming fortune-hunter and threatened to change his will if Claudine insisted on marrying Hargill. And Claudine knew very well where her best prospects lay. But none of us could have predicted that Daniel would survive Claudine by three years, or that suddenly, just before his death, he would decide to change his will in favour of Emma.'

Lissa felt Jarret sigh against her before he went on: 'The old man was very fond of her, and she of him. I expect she's told you all about him already.'

'A little,' Lissa murmured. 'She showed me the lovely things he gave her at one time and another.'

'Yes, he was very kind to her, but I'd rather he'd left his wealth to the de Ryses, instead of to Emma, with Mrs de Rys as trustee. Oh, I can understand it to a certain extent. My personal life was bleak at the time, Claudine had destroyed any illusions I might once have had, I hadn't the remotest intention of marrying again, and so it seemed taken for granted I would eventually hand Emma over to them completely. Even though I realised that with the ample provision I was already making for her care and Daniel's money Emma was a very profitable asset for Mrs de Rys. She and Camilla are extremely extravagant, for which I could forgive them, but when I found Hargill was back on the scene and Camilla announced that they were planning to marry I saw red. I was determined to get Emma away from them all, and fast.'

He stopped, and Lissa stirred uneasily. She knew what

must follow and she did not want to hear it. But a chill, almost masochistic compulsion kept her silent.

'It had to be marriage,' he said flatly. 'Mrs de Rys would have soon disposed of a housekeeper the moment my back was turned—she'd already proved this during the first few months after Claudine's death and I tried to struggle on with Emma.'

Lissa nodded. She could well imagine how it was done. The hints and insinuations to the unfortunate housekeeper, the touches of arrogance and the occasional patronising approval, until the inevitable blow-up and the indignant exit of a housekeeper who could take no more. Until Jarret was forced to place his child into her grandmother's possessive charge.

'But a wife would be a different matter.' Jarret sighed, and a strange note entered his voice, almost like puzzlement. 'The idea came like one of those mad impulses that carry all reason before them. I remembered you from that November day, Sam had just broken the news about your father, and somehow it all fell into place. I went to see you that same night, and when I found how you were coping,' he gestured, 'I just knew I'd found the girl I wanted. The circumstances meant I was able to strike a bargain, and something told me you were the kind of girl who would put her own happiness last. But I never intended you should be a victim of Camilla's spite.'

'Why didn't you tell me?' she asked.

'Because I didn't think you'd believe me. You were so honest and sincere yourself you wouldn't credit it. Also, I didn't want to risk your sympathies being won over to the de Ryses—as they almost were! Nor did I want you to meet Emma in case your conscience got the better of you and you refused to go through with the wedding, despite the desperate straits your family was in at the time.'

'I very nearly did,' she said in a low voice.

'I know. It was an incredibly cold-blooded scheme.' His voice was heavy. 'I married you as a form of revenge. But try to understand. For eight years I've lived with the torment of wondering if Emma is really mine. When Hargill came back I could think of nothing else but taking Emma away from them all. The fact that they were going through

Emma's inheritance was of secondary consideration. Taking Emma back was the only way I could assuage the hurt they'd caused me.'

He looked down at her wan face. 'I'm sorry, Lissa,' he repeated. 'I never intended that you should be hurt.'

Suddenly his lips touched her brow, and the tenderness of the gesture brought an ache bursting in her chest. For the first time she felt as though he was truly concerned about her, but it was only the tenderness of a man who had discovered unsuspected pangs of conscience, and whose emotions had been tested today as severely as her own. Except for one thing ...

It cost her a tremendous effort to steel herself against turning into his arms, pressing her face into his shoulder, and pouring out all her love. Instead she sat upright and put her feet to the floor, toes seeking her slippers and giving up the search. She stood up.

'Lissa, are you all right?'

'Yes.' At least that was true, she thought thankfully as the room stayed steady and on its usual bearings. She kept her back to him. 'Except—there's something I'd better tell you. Jarret, I think I might be going to have a baby.'

'What?'

'I'm not sure, except that ...' Trying to keep her voice matter-of-fact, she counted out dates and her conviction, and then her shoulders were grasped and her words broken as he wrenched her round to face him.

'It can't be! Not that one night!'

'I'll go to the doctor as soon as the holidays are over,' she said feverishly, frightened by the dark intensity in the eyes boring down into hers as though they would wrest the truth from them. 'It might not be true—I shouldn't have told you until I had it confirmed. But we should know soon, in case ...' she broke off, biting her lip.

'In case *what*?' The intensity deepened in his eyes. 'Lissa! Just what have you got in mind? You don't in-tend—not to have the baby?'

'But what else can I do?' Her voice trembled. 'How can I? We never meant—it'll ruin everything.'

'No! Never!' His fingers hurt her when they tightened

fiercely. 'It'll end that infernal contract once and for all. I'm glad!' he almost shouted. 'I hope it's true! I hope we *are* going to have a baby!'

'W-what?' she quavered, wondering if he had taken leave of his senses. 'Jarret, what do you mean? You——'

'Oh, Lissa—darling! Don't look so terrified. I can't bear to see you frightened.' With a muffled exclamation he pulled her into his arms, holding her tightly, fiercely, possessively.

'It's no use,' he said against her hair, 'I want you, and I'm going to keep you. I think I've wanted you since the first time I saw you. Oh, Lissa, can't you try to love me? I need you so desperately.'

Her face was held so close to his chest she could scarcely breathe. Her senses were spinning again and she thought wildly that she must be imagining the things he was saying. Then his hand was under her hair, convulsive in its movement to make her look up at him, and she saw the torment in his eyes.

She whispered unbelievingly, 'You—you want me? Because you——?'

'I want you because I love you so desperately I dare not imagine my life without you. Lissa! For God's sake, don't look at me like that! Don't weep!'

'I can't help it.' For the first time in her life she knew what it meant to be laughing and crying at the same time. 'Oh, I can't believe it. Tell me again, Jarret! Tell me I'm not dreaming!'

For a moment he looked like a man out of his mind with torment, and then she put her hands round his head and pulled him down till his mouth was within reach of her own. All the longing and despair of the past months and all of her pent-up love went into her kiss. He stayed still, letting her drain the last dregs of the sweetness of that kiss, then he lifted her high in his arms, swung her round and gazed down into her starry eyes as though he was still not quite convinced the miracle had happened.

'You were always so cool,' he exclaimed. 'Always so determined to keep our relationship static. Frozen, the way it was the night I asked you to marry me.'

He touched his lips to her brow, then each eye, then her soft, wondering mouth. 'Why didn't you tell me?'

'I couldn't!' she protested. 'Why didn't you tell *me*?'

'I couldn't—for the same reason. Oh, what idiots we've been,' he groaned. 'I knew you were becoming aware of me, I dared to believe you were even a bit attracted, but I discounted any reaching out of love. I had to keep reminding myself of my previous experiences of women and that the old traditional ways don't mean so much to a lot of girls today. The old inhibitions that stopped a woman exerting her right to sex have gone, and with them a lot of the old mock modesty. I wished with all my heart that you'd give me some indication of how you felt, but I felt bound to respect your wishes—after all, I'd laid down the terms.'

'If only I'd known!' she sighed.

'No intuition?'

'None at all. I was convinced I was literally a chattel for five years—one whom you were prepared to be kind to—and one you wouldn't be averse to making love to now and again. But that was all.'

'Oh, my darling! I nearly told you that night in Cornwall. Then you let me know so clearly that you wanted to be in love, totally, with the man you married.' His mouth curved ruefully. 'What else could I infer from that? Other than that you had no love for me? That to you our relationship was still a sterile contract with a definite time limit?'

'Oh, Jarret!' Her eyes darkened with distress. 'How could I tell you that you were that man? That I loved you so much I couldn't bear to think about the end of the five years? That it was torment every moment I was near to you, not being able to love you and have your love?' She clung to him, pushing her fingers through his dark hair, pressing close to him, trying to convey how much she longed for his love.

He did not speak. His eyes searched her face, and in them she read everything she had always desired. Then he carried her across the room to the bed, there to become the lover she had so often dreamed of in her innermost heart. And now there was no barrier to the joy of uninhibited surrender of heart, spirit and body.

At last he was her beloved, taking her with him on a surging tide to the shores of ecstasy, where there were no more doubts, no bitterness, only the supreme fulfilment of giving and taking of one another.

'Love me?' he whispered on a sigh.

'Don't tell me you're still in doubt?' she exclaimed softly against his mouth.

'No—but I want to hear you say it.'

She lay in his arms, his skin clinging to hers, and the warm male scent of him sweet in her nostrils. At last she was utterly slaked, totally happy. They lay quietly for a while, still lost in the wonder of discovery, and his head was a warm, beloved weight on her breast. Her arm curved across him, firm with the intense protectiveness of love. He had vanquished all the pain and uncertainty of the past months, and she in her turn knew now how much he had suffered, could divine the depth of disillusions and unhappiness the unfaithful Claudine had given him— even to the ugly doubt that his adored Emma might not be his. At that moment Lissa made a fervent vow that all her love would go into making a new happiness for him. And yet she could not find it in her heart to spare no pity for Mrs de Rys.

'Jarret . . .' she whispered.

'Mm——?' His mouth made small sweet kisses where it lay.

'You won't keep Emma away altogether from her grandmother, will you? I mean,' she added hurriedly as the delicious little tokens suddenly stopped, 'I think she genuinely loves Emma, and I don't believe she deliberately——'

'You mean she could see no wrong in her two daughters, and closed her eyes to anything she didn't want to see.' Jarret turned and lay on his back, staring up at the ceiling. 'No, it would be cruel to deny her access to Emma—even though I find it difficult to feel any great affection for my former in-laws. But then——'

She never knew what he was about to say. Somewhere in the distance the chimes of midnight rang out on the air. Jarret turned to her.

'It's Christmas, my darling.'

'Happy Christmas,' she whispered.

'And to you—and our Christmas baby.' He sought her willing lips again, and then through the kiss she heard the sound of voices, of happy revellers returning home. A young voice began to sing 'While Shepherds Watched,' and other voices took up the old loved carol.

Jarret reached for her wrap, folding it round her slender body, and his eyes were dark with tenderness as he watched her run on bare feet to the window and draw back the curtain like an excited child. He came to stand behind her, his arms holding her close as they looked out on the first hour of their first Christmas.

There was white frosting over roofs and gardens, and fat snowflakes were just beginning to pattern the midnight dark with their soft white drift.

'It snowed on our wedding day—remember?' she whispered.

'And now it's snowing on our wedding night,' he returned softly.

Snow had never looked quite so beautiful.

The Mills & Boon Rose is the Rose of Romance

Every month there are ten new titles to choose from — ten new stories about people falling in love, people you want to read about, people in exciting, far away places. Choose Mills & Boon. It's your way of relaxing.

February's titles are:

SUMMER OF THE WEEPING RAIN *by Yvonne Whittal*
Lisa had gone to the African veld for peace and quiet, but that seemed impossible with the tough and ruthless Adam Vandeleur around!

EDGE OF SPRING *by Helen Bianchin*
How could Karen convince Matt Lucas that she didn't want to have anything to do with him, when he refused to take no for an answer?

THE DEVIL DRIVES *by Jane Arbor*
Una was in despair when she learned that Zante Diomed had married her for one reason: revenge. How could she prove to him how wrong he was?

THE GIRL FROM THE SEA *by Anne Weale*
Armorel's trustee, the millionaire Sholto Ransome, was hardly a knight on a white horse — in fact as time went on she realised he was a cynical, cold-hearted rake . . .

SOMETHING LESS THAN LOVE *by Daphne Clair*
Vanessa's husband Thad had been badly injured in a car smash. But he was recovering now, so why was he so bitter and cruel in his attitude towards her?

THE DIVIDING LINE *by Kay Thorpe*
When the family business was left equally between Kerry and her stepbrother Ross, the answer seemed to be for them to marry — but how could they, when they didn't even like each other?

AUTUMN SONG *by Margaret Pargeter*
To help her journalist brother, Tara had gone to a tiny Greek island to get a story. But there she fell foul of the owner of the island — the millionaire Damon Voulgaris . . .

SNOW BRIDE *by Margery Hilton*
It appeared that Jarret Earle had had reasons of his own for wanting Lissa as his wife — but alas, love was the very least of them . . .

SENSATION *by Charlotte Lamb*
Helen's husband Drew had kept studiously out of her way for six years, but suddenly he was always there, disturbing, overbearing, and — what?

WEST OF THE WAMINDA *by Kerry Allyne*
Ashley Beaumont was resigned to selling the family sheep station — but if only it hadn't had to be sold to that infuriating, bullying Dane Carmichael!

If you have difficulty in obtaining any of these books from your local paperback retailer, write to:

Mills & Boon Reader Service
P.O. Box 236, Thornton Road, Croydon, Surrey CR9 3RU